Look At The State Of You

· a short story collection ·

NIALL O'BRIEN

For Laura

Contents

My Son Found A Bomb
At The Library

My wife gave me some great news lately. And that's that she's pregnant. Yup, I'm going to be a daddy. I'm having me a little boy. And as ecstatic as I am at the prospect of having a kid, it got me thinking about what kind of dad I want to be. So I thought for a long time and came to a lot of conclusions about what kind of values I want to instill within my son, but today I want to talk to you about one that's an important one for me. In many ways, it's the most important. And here it is.

So, in keeping with a childhood tradition introduced to me by my father on my 7th birthday, I decided that once my son's old enough, I'm going to take him to the library every Saturday so he can pick out any book he wants. And for every book he finishes, I'll get him a new toy or an ice-cream or whatever, just to give him a little extra incentive so he doesn't think I'm forcing him to read. Now obviously there are a lot of reasons I want to do this, the most evident being that I fucking loved it when I was a boy. But there's a more important reason I want to do this.

Now, I'm going to sound like such an old fart when I say this, but honestly, it's because of what young people are interested in nowadays.

And that's their phones. I never see them do anything else. And I mean, it's all the time. It's all I ever see in front of their faces. And look, I don't want to sound like some old fucker here and say that *"Oh, these blasted kids and their phones nowadays"*. I don't want to be that guy. I understand the way the world works and I'm not saying the way people of my generation did things when we were younger was the proper way of being a kid. I'm just saying there are so many other things you can do in today's day and age.

There are so many opportunities. So many things that you can do and explore and experiment with. So much more then what I had when I was a boy. Well, I want my son to be able to experience all of these things. I want him to embrace the freedom to explore whatever his heart desires. There'll be no stifling of his creativity on my part, that's for sure. I want his life to be more than just a random Snapchat video or Instagram story or trending topic on Twitter or whatever seems to stimulate kids brains nowadays. Stuff like that doesn't bring you true happiness the way painting a beautiful landscape can. In fact, quite the opposite. Social media makes you super depressed.

And look, modern smartphones are fucking amazing, I don't think anyone would argue with that. I'm constantly amazed with some of the shit I'm able to do with my phone. But there are just some experiences your phone can't give you, and that as well, I don't think anyone would argue with. I mean, looking at a time-lapse video of some guy hiking the Camino de Santiago is incredible, no doubt. But have these kids ever wondered what it would actually be like to hike it themselves with their own two feet? That's what I'm talking about here.

2

I want my son to be able to try out different hobbies and pastimes. Photography, writing, hiking, drawing, jigsaw puzzles, whatever he wants to try, he can. I'm not going to stop him. If he wants to collect stamps, then he can collect stamps. If he wants to paint toy soldiers, then he can paint toy soldiers. Far be it from me to stop him. And I think that by starting him out with something as universal as reading, it can be an appropriate gateway to all the other wonderful things he can experience in his life. Maybe through reading, he'll discover writing, and then drawing, and then painting, and then who knows where the ball might go from there. We might have the next Leonardo da Vinci on our hands, and all because his father allowed him unlimited access to the wonders that artistic culture has to offer.

And hey, if he doesn't want to do any of that, that's fine too. If he just wants to play sports and get a trade, that's fine with me. This isn't about conditioning my son into becoming some sort of great artist. This is about giving him options.

But more than anything, it's about having something for the two of us to share. Something to bond over. I remember plaguing my dad every Friday night while he was trying to watch the telly, telling him over and over again how much I couldn't wait for our trip to the library and how I was thinking of getting an Agatha Christie book or something. I fucking loved it when I was younger. I must have easily read five or six hundred books as a kid. How many other people can say that?

And even though I must have wrecked his head most of the time, you could also tell my dad secretly adored the idea that his son wasn't just looking forward to going to the library, but he was looking forward to going to the library with his dad, like the experience couldn't be had unless he was there by his side, holding his hand. That it wasn't just about the books. That it was something just the two of them could share together. That it was their thing and it was something they could look back on with fondness in the future. And you know what, to this day, my dad and I have a better relationship than ever. Every Thursday night, we go out for a pint and we sit and talk for hours and hours about books, movies, TV shows, and just life in general. And I'll tell you something else, I'd be willing to bet money on it that that bond was created during those trips we used to take to the library every Saturday.

So that's what I'm going to do when my son is born. Once he's old enough, I'm going to take him to the library every Saturday, he can pick out any book he wants and discover the wonders of reading for himself as he grows up. And he and I are going to create beloved father-son memories that will last a lifetime.

Of course, wouldn't you know it, I ended up having a fucking girl. Didn't expect that, did you? Yeah, well neither did I.

Do you have any idea how much time and effort I put into making this fucking bomb?

What a waste of time.

What's The Story?

D o you have one of those friends that just cannot tell an interesting story? A guy whose stories are about as interesting as the back of someone's head. Barry had one. His name was Marcus and just now he shouted Barry's name from across the room and was waving wildly. Barry gave a weak smile and then a sigh. Oh, no, not this fucker, Barry thought. Out of all the people you wouldn't want to be stuck talking to at a party, this guy was at the top of the list. Barry would rather be stuck by himself for the rest of the night. Oh, God, he's walking over. Just pretend you don't see him. Take a sip of your drink and make it look like your attentions elsewhere. No, it's no use. He's already on his way over. You're fucking stuck.

Hey Barry, said Marcus enthusiastically. Long-time no see.

Yeah man, it's been a while. What's the story?

Not much. How you keeping?

Not too bad. I haven't seen you in ages.

Well, I just got back there a few days ago.

Oh, yeah, I keep forgetting that you were away for so long. When did you get back?

Just last week.

How'd you like being home?

Ah well, obviously it's very different over there, but it's nice to see everyone again.

Yeah, I bet.

It's unbelievable the things you miss when you're over there. Like fucking Denny sausages. Oh, I can't tell you how much I missed them.

I can imagine.

Barry was hoping that would be it and Marcus might say *"well it was good to see you, man. I'll talk to you later"*. But unfortunately, this fucker was here to stay.

So what was it like over there? said Barry.

Oh man, it's fucking crazy. When I arrived over...

Barry instantly regretted asking this, because this guy could not tell a fucking interesting story to save his life. And not for lack of trying either. He just didn't know how to tell a story that kept you *in any way* engaged. And it really annoyed Barry because out of all the people attending this party tonight, Marcus actually had stories to tell. This guy had been around the world.

In fact, Marcus had just come back from a yearlong backpacking trip around Asia, Australia, and parts of New Zealand. This guy has seen things. This guy has been on some adventures. So it would make sense that out of the two-dozen people here tonight, this guy should be fucking dominating the party right now. There should be people huddled around him, clinging onto his every word. People should be dying to find out what happens in his stories next. Well, unfortunately, that's not the case with Marcus.

What's The Story?

What a waste, thought Barry, as Marcus rambled on and on. What's the point in travelling to some of the most interesting parts of the planet and having exciting adventures and meeting interesting people if you couldn't even convey the very sense of excitement and adventure that made them worth experiencing in the first place.

Now Barry could admit he wasn't a master storyteller himself. But he was fairly confident that if he experienced at least half of what Marcus claimed to have experienced on his travels, that he would be able to describe them in a way that, wouldn't necessarily have people hanging onto the edge of their seat in anticipation, but at least hold their attention and engage them in such a way that it doesn't feel like they're just nodding along politely until they can find an opportunity to get away from you. That they'd actually be listening to you and interested in what you have to say next. But a story told from the lips of Marcus contained none of these characteristics. They were boring as fuck.

A great example of this would be the story Marcus was telling Barry right now. It was a story about a time he'd worked on a banana farm in Australia and how his boss didn't think Marcus was working hard enough, despite the fact that he was working as hard as he could, and he was eventually fired.

And that was it. That was Marcus's fucking story. Almost word for word. He didn't give any details about the working conditions on a banana farm or his relationship with his boss or the events leading up to his firing. He worked on a banana farm for a few weeks and then got fired because, in the eyes of his boss, he wasn't working hard enough. That was Marcus's story.

What a load of bollox, thought Barry. What part of any of that was he meant to relate to? There's absolutely nothing there for him to work with. Marcus basically just told him something that happened to him once. Like he was a newsreader or something. But at least a newsreader could paint a story with some sort of character or emotion. Marcus's stories contained about as much personality as a baked potato.

I mean, it's not that complicated, thought Barry. The simplest fucking type of story has three acts. *"I went here, something happened and then this happened as a result"*. A bit simply put perhaps but with the right material, you'd be the fucking king of any party. And this guy was it. This guy had the material to light this fucking room on fire and give people something to talk about on the ride home or at work on Monday. But for whatever reason, he just couldn't do it.

It doesn't matter what type of story Marcus had. He could have gold, and I literally mean the most interesting story on the planet and he would tell it like he was telling you what he had for dinner that evening. He could have a story where he was kidnapped by drug lords and was tortured for information, and then he had to shoot his way out of there and he was in a car chase and he had to escape on a helicopter and fight some Indiana Jones type guy on a fucking mountain top. It wouldn't matter. This fucker would still make it sound as exciting as the information leaflet inside a packet of paracetamol.

Barry feigned a smile as Marcus finished a story about some crystal meth dealers that tried to rob him in Melbourne. It sounds exciting, doesn't it? Well, given the look on Barry's face right now, I'd have to say that it definitely does not.

At the very least, Marcus could exaggerate a few points or just make something up. Just for Barry's sake. And Barry reckoned that's what Marcus's problem was. Most people telling a story would exaggerate certain events or just invent stuff off the top of their heads to make the story sound more interesting than it really is. Barry knew he was certainly guilty of this. Everyone was probably guilty of it. Most people would look down on someone for doing that, but those people haven't thought about what it would be like to hear a story exactly the way it happened. Because that's the sad truth of it all. Most people's lives are fucking boring so whenever something happens that's even the tiniest bit interesting, they'll colour it with as much bullshit as they can, anything to make themselves appear more interesting to other people or some girl they're trying to impress.

And that's what Marcus did. That was his problem. He simply told a story about something that happened to him. Without exaggerating anything or making anything out to be bigger than it was. He didn't say it with any emotion in his voice or flair in his movements that let the audience know that this was a story that was worth listening to. He just told a story of something that happened to him. Plain and simple. A story that doesn't allow for any follow-up questions or points of curiosity. A long and plain fucking story, that Barry had to just bite his tongue and sit through until he could make up some bullshit excuse to go off and converse with someone at this party who had something at least semi-interesting to say.

Now Barry didn't hate Marcus. He didn't despise talking to him. He was a perfectly decent fellow. All he did was tell the truth after all. There's something to be admired there. Barry just wished Marcus considered how

9

other people are reacting to the shite he's saying to them. And maybe think, *"You know what? I don't think this person's very interested in what I'm saying right now. Maybe I should spice things up a bit so my story is actually worth listening to"*. And that would be fine with Barry. Barry couldn't care less if what came out of Marcus's mouth was utter horseshit. He didn't care if Marcus told him a story about a time he met Kim Kardashian and shagged her. As long as he was in some way engaged, he'd be fine. But no, he had to sit through a tale that stimulated him about as much as a handjob from his grandmother.

Barry thought he could slip away for a moment as Marcus stepped away to pour himself a drink. He tried to signal to his girlfriend Mairead from across the room, but she couldn't see him. She was talking to some blond guy. Looked like a nice conversation too. Looked like she gave a fuck about what the blond guy was saying. Lucky girl. Out of all the people Barry could be stuck with tonight, it had to be this guy. Marcus turned back to him and resumed his story about the first hostel he'd ever stayed in and how his Brazilian roommate was smuggling Indonesian people into the country in his anus. Barry sighed and nodded along and eyed the table filled with alcohol beside him. He promised himself he wouldn't drink tonight. He'd been trying to stay off the alcohol recently, but the more words that fell out of Marcus's mouth, the more enticing that bottle of vodka on the table looked.

But lucky for Barry, he wasn't stuck with Marcus and his boring stories for too long, because the front door swung open violently and a man wearing a ski mask and brandishing a shotgun stormed into the room. He asked whoever the owner of the house was to step forward. Padraig, the owner of the house, pushed his wife to the side, came forward with his arms up and calmly asked the masked man what he wanted. Without saying anything, the masked man pressed the shotgun to Padraig's temple and blew his head clean off his shoulders. Blood sprayed from the hole where his head once was and spewed across the whole room, painting the walls and the floors and all the guests. His wife screamed and then the masked man stepped forward and blew her head off. The masked man then lined everyone up against the living room wall, and starting at the right, began walking down the line, shooting everyone in the head. Everyone was screaming and crying. It was a real bloodbath.

That's funny, thought Barry, as a chunk of Mairead's skull flew across his face. All he was doing while Marcus was boring the head off him was hoping that something would happen or someone would intervene so he didn't have to listen to the cunts ball-achingly dull stories anymore. And something did happen. And now he wouldn't have to listen to Marcus's stories anymore. In fact, Barry wouldn't have to listen to *anyone's* ball-achingly dull stories anymore. It was great. Barry felt great. And wouldn't you? Wouldn't you prefer to tell yourself that it feel's great you no longer have to listen to the boring stories of a guy you barely see anyway rather than accept that in a few seconds, you won't be able to listen to anything anymore?

And who knows, thought Barry, as Marcus's head exploded like a watermelon and painted him red. Maybe this might make for a great story one day. Maybe at a party just like this. Barry closed his eyes and pictured it as the shooter pressed the shotgun to his forehead. *"Here, everyone, gather around. I have a cracker of a story to tell you!"*. And everyone would sit around him like kids at a campfire, as the masked man regaled them about this one time he massacred this group of people at a house party. Now that's a fucking good story. Barry just wished he'd be around to hear it. Maybe one day he mig...

Chinese Whispers

Eamonn and all his co-workers had all gathered together in the canteen. They were throwing a surprise party for a guy that worked in Accounting. His name was Jonathan. Jonathan has Down Syndrome. He'd been working with the company for little more than a year now. Everyone liked him. Eamonn did as well. Maybe not as much as everyone else though. But it had nothing to do with him being Down Syndrome. Eamonn didn't have a problem with that. Why would he? It was just that Jonathan was a bit of an attention-seeker. Eamonn always saw people huddled around him, listening intently to his stories, laughing away at some silly joke he'd make. He was a real jokester. Everyone said so. Everyone said he was hilarious.

But Eamonn wasn't so sure. He didn't know if they really thought Jonathan was hilarious or if they were just saying that because he has Down Syndrome. Which again, Eamonn didn't have a problem with. He wasn't saying that people with Down Syndrome can't be funny, or the condition itself prevents them from being funny, or on the opposite end, that the condition makes you funnier, because Eamonn certainly didn't think there was anything funny about having Down Syndrome. And Eamonn certainly wasn't jealous of all the attention Jonathan got. It was just hard to gauge his co-worker's true feelings when they were around him. And it wasn't even that Jonathan's jokes weren't funny. There were alright jokes, as far as jokes go. They made Eamonn chuckle from time to time. Jonathan had a very self-deprecating sense of humor and he didn't take himself too seriously, which Eamonn pinpointed as one of the reasons he was so popular amongst the staff. He was a laugh. He was someone you could have a bit of banter with. Jonathan always told everyone they can joke about anything around him, even Down Syndrome. He wasn't someone you had to treat differently because of his condition or talk down to like a child. Eamonn certainly didn't treat him any differently. But he didn't think Jonathan was as *hilarious* as some of his co-workers *laugh out loud* reactions seemed to suggest. He was fine. He was a funny and charismatic guy, who also happened to have Down Syndrome. Which again, Eamonn didn't have a problem with.

So anyway, Eamonn and all the staff had gathered in the canteen and were planning on surprising Jonathan when he came back from his lunch. A few of the girls bought a cake and prepared some finger food like cocktail sausages, chips, Taytos, sweets, stuff like that. They had balloons up and a huge homemade banner that read, *"Happy Birthday Jonathan!"*. They really went all out for the party. They even brought a few board games like Twister and Frustration to play.

Eamonn thought it was a bit much if he was being honest. Nothing against Jonathan like. Just seemed like a lot of effort to put in for a birthday party, especially a grown man's birthday party. Eamonn wouldn't mind if Jonathan was turning eight. A party like this was quite suitable for a child. But for a guy in his thirties, Eamonn just thought it was a bit much.

Eamonn held the belief that, once you get into your mid-twenties, it's really time to stop making such a big deal out of birthdays and grow up a little. Once you get past twenty-one, all the magic seems to disappear from birthdays and it suddenly turns into a ticking clock reminder of how close you are to death. Besides, the staff never put this much effort into other people's birthdays. Especially Eamonn's. Now that he thought about it, they didn't even throw him a party last year. They just bought him a card and made everyone sign it. And they could tell him they were throwing such a huge party for Jonathan because he was new and popular, but really, Eamonn knew it was just because he was Down Syndrome. Not that he had a problem with that. He just wished everyone in the room would stop pretending there was another reason they were throwing such a huge party for this guy. Because there's no way he was that popular. No ones that popular. Eamonn was positive that even the most popular guy in the world wouldn't be getting this kind of party. Eamonn just thought it was a bit much, is all.

They waited for about ten minutes and then one of the girls got a text from another girl saying she was in the elevator with Jonathan and she be at the canteen with him in about a minute. She told everyone to quiet down and yell *surprise* when he walked in. A minute later, you could hear Jonathan outside. His voice got louder as he approached. He had his back turned when he opened the door, talking with the girl he was with.

SURPRISE!

Jonathan nearly jumped out of his skin with the fright. Eamonn thought he was going to have a stroke by the looks of him. Not that the way he looked was weird or anything, it was just his reaction to the surprise, that's what Eamonn meant. He didn't mean he looked weird. He didn't. Anyway, all the girls approached Jonathan and gave him big hugs. Jonathan seemed well happy. Everyone went up to him and said happy birthday. Even Eamonn. Because why wouldn't he? Why would Eamonn be the only guy in the room to not wish Jonathan a happy birthday? They lit the candles on the cake, and everyone sang happy birthday. Then he blew out the candles and everyone cheered. Afterwards, everyone ate some food and Eamonn talked with a few of his mates in the corner.

The food was fair good. Eamonn helped himself to a few cocktail sausages. As much as was left for him anyway as Jonathan ate most of it. Not that Eamonn was complaining. It was Jonathan's party after all. He could have as much food as he wanted. Eamonn just thought it would have been considerate of him to think of everyone else in the room before filling his plate up with thirty-three cocktail sausages and thirteen sausage rolls.

Eamonn said to his mate Rory that there wasn't much food left. He didn't seem to get the insinuation that it was because of Jonathan. Eamonn stared at Jonathan from across the room. He was chatting away to the boss while chomping away on a sausage roll. He ate with his mouth open and some food flew out of his mouth as he spoke. It kind of disgusted Eamonn. It disgusted him so much that he found he didn't have the stomach to eat anymore and he set his plate down. Eamonn turned to Rory.

Jeez, Jonathan's a very sloppy eater, isn't he?

Will you ever shut up, you eejit? said Rory with a smile.

What?

Don't be so mean.

I'm not being mean. I'm just saying like.

16

Rory chuckled and went off to get himself another drink. Eamonn didn't think he was being bang out of order there. He thought he was being quite fair actually. He wasn't saying that Down Syndrome's are habitually sloppy eaters or that the sight of a Down Syndrome eating would put him off his food. The sight of anyone eating sloppily would put Eamonn off his food. He didn't think Jonathan should be removed from a group of people he didn't like just because he had Down Syndrome. Actually, it was considerate of Eamonn to do so because it meant he wasn't discriminating against Jonathan for his condition. He was treating him like a normal person.

It was funny to think about actually. It was the first time that Eamonn noticed that Jonathan was quite a thin-looking guy. One might even say athletic. The reason Eamonn thought it was funny was that a lot of Down Syndromes you see are generally overweight. Not that Eamonn thought that it was a stereotype that all Down Syndromes were typically obese. It was just something he thought of that never occurred to him before.

So, a couple of minutes later, one of the girls suggested that they play a few party games. Someone suggested that they play a board game, but then Jonathan said they should play a game that everyone could be involved in. Everyone nodded in agreement. Steve from Internal Affairs suggested Musical Chairs. Eamonn was sure that people were going to say no, but to his surprise, everyone said yes. He couldn't help but frown. This was not how he imagined spending his lunch break. Playing musical fucking chairs, a game he hasn't played since he was in second class. They all gathered into the main office and everyone grabbed their own desk chair. They moved all the desks against the back wall so they could make room for everyone, which Eamonn thought was a huge hassle because it would be such a fucking pain in the arse to organize everything again afterwards.

It had been so long since Eamonn played Musical Chairs. He thought he'd fucking hate playing, but after a while, he actually started to get into it. One might even say he looked to be enjoying himself. It's funny that a lot of games you play as a kid, that you dismiss as you get older because they are naturally very childish games, are still quite fun as an adult. Eamonn thought this would make a great drinking game at a party. Jonathan seemed to be having the most fun out of everyone. Eamonn could see that one of the girls from reception, whom he had a small crush on, was helping Jonathan to find a chair when the music stopped, which annoyed him a bit. It's alright to be subtly cheating, but she was just blatantly helping him. It's not that people with Down Syndrome need assistance with basic daily functions such as finding a chair. He didn't see her pulling a chair up for Jonathan when he came into the office in the morning. Did she assume that he might pull a tantrum if he didn't win at Musical Chairs? If that was the case, Eamonn thought it was awfully presumptuous of her to assume that a person with Down Syndrome would naturally go into hysterics just because they lost at a silly party game. Eamonn cocked his eyes. Some people have a lot of growing up to do.

Jonathan ended up winning. No surprise there, given the amount of help he got from your one. They played a few more times after that. Jonathan didn't win every time, because then it would really look like people were letting him win, but he won most of the time. Eamonn was pretty sick of it, to be honest. Not of Jonathan, but of the party in general. He wanted to get back to work funnily enough. Lunch was well over by now but everyone was having such a great time that he reckoned no one had even noticed the time. Eamonn thought about suggesting it himself, but he didn't want to be the one to bring an end to the party. Just when he thought the party might end, Jonathan roared:

Why don't we play Chinese Whispers?

That's a great idea Jonathan, said Noelle from Human Resources.

Fucking hell, Eamonn muttered under his breath. When was this shite going to be over with? He wouldn't even mind if the games weren't so fucking juvenile. That game of Musical Chairs had been alright, but now it was just tedious and Eamonn wanted to be done with it all. As he went to take his seat, Eamonn peered over the crowd of people and saw Jonathan getting another plate of food. Jesus, he's surely had enough to eat already, he thought.

Eamonn leaned over to Graham from Buildings and Estate and said: Jesus, could this be any more of a fucking kids party?

Graham gave a half-assed, diplomatic smile and nodded without looking at him. Eamonn wondered if he heard him properly or if he even knew he was talking to him. He leaned towards Graham again and nudged his arm.

They'll have us playing Pin the Tail on the Donkey next, he said a bit louder.

Yeah, said Graham quietly.

Eamonn was confused. It was like Graham was ignoring him or something.

Alright everyone, let's begin, said Noelle. Where's Jonathan?

As soon as she said it, Jonathan appeared from behind her, holding a packet of Taytos.

Oh, there you are, she said. We're ready to start playing.

Yeah, Chinese Whispers. Let's play, said Jonathan loudly.

Jesus, Eamonn had never seen anyone so pumped up to play a fucking children's game. He looked at everyone around him but everyone was smiling earnestly. Were they all honestly enjoying this? Nah, they had to be putting it on. There's no way Eamonn was the only one here that thought this was all horseshit. As Jonathan walked around the circle, Eamonn looked to his left and realized that the only empty chair left was next to him. Eamonn rolled his eyes slightly to the right, where he caught the eyes of Margaret from Health and Safety. Eamonn was sure that she saw him roll his eyes. She didn't look too pleased. Eamonn put on a huge smile and looked up at Jonathan.

Jonathan, there's a seat right here.

Jonathan walked up behind him and sat next to him.

Thanks Eamonn, he said with a beaming smile.

No problem buddy, said Eamonn. He looked back at Margaret from Health and Safety. She was sitting with her arms and legs crossed. Her expression hadn't changed, and she wasn't looking at him. Eamonn was sure offering Jonathan the chair would have saved him, but looking at her now, he wasn't too sure.

Okay, how about you start, Jonathan, said Noelle.

No, you start Noelle, said Jonathan. I reckon you have a few naughty things you like whispering into people's ears.

Everyone started laughing.

20

Well, aren't you cheeky, said Noelle with a grin. Okay, we'll start with me so. Let me just think of something.

What a lick arse, thought Eamonn. Was Jonathan seriously trying to get with Noelle? There's no way he actually thinks he has even a morsel of a chance of getting in her pants. Eamonn had tried plenty of times to ask her out and she flat out rejected him. There's no way she preferred Jonathan over him. Unless she has a fetish for guys with mental disabilities. If that's the case, she's hit the jackpot.

Okay, I have one, she said, leaning into the ear of the girl to the right of her. The whisper moved around the room quickly. Eamonn watched as each person tried to process what was being whispered to them and then relay that to the person next to them. Finally, it got to Graham next to Eamonn. Graham seemed to hear what was said to him fine because he didn't have any expression of doubt or confusion on his face. He leaned over to Eamonn and whispered in his ear:

"My favorite part of Monday morning is watching Diarmaid come in hungover".

Eamonn heard it just fine. Graham didn't say it too low so that some of the words got lost in translation, and he didn't say it too loud so that he was heard by everyone in the circle. He said it just perfect. Eamonn turned and looked at Jonathan. He was waiting in anticipation, with a big smile on his face. Eamonn wasn't looking forward to getting too close to him. He looked quite sweaty and he might smell a bit from all the food he'd eaten. But Eamonn, didn't want to give it away that he was reticent about getting close to him, especially after the cross look Margaret had given him.

Eamonn leaned into Jonathan's head. The strong aroma of Taytos and sausage rolls wafted off him and his ear was moist with sweat. He whispered what he heard into his ear and then backed away immediately. Jonathan was blanked faced for a moment and then started laughing. Other people started laughing as well. He turned to the person next to him and the whisper went on. When it got to Patrick, the last person, Noelle stood up and said declaratively:

Okay, Patrick, so what is it you've heard?

Patrick looked around the group with a smile and said, "*My favorite part of the morning is when Diarmaid leaves*".

That's not it, said Noelle laughing. I said, "*My favorite part of Monday morning is watching Diarmaid come in hungover*".

Who messed that one up? said Patrick.

I think it was Eamonn, said Jonathan immediately.

Everyone started laughing. Eamonn forced a smile but he was fucking fuming. He stared at Jonathan in bewilderment as the fucker and everyone around him howled with laughter. What the fuck was he on about? Eamonn had been completely right. He'd gotten it almost word for word. Who the fuck was Jonathan to blame him for that? What the fuck was he basing it on? If anything, it should be fairly fucking obvious who messed it up. Eamonn wasn't pointing the finger or anything, but Jonathan was the one with the mental disability after all. He almost felt like standing up and protesting, but Eamonn didn't think it would bode well with everyone if he picked a fight with a Down Syndrome over a stupid little game of Chinese Whispers.

My bad, said Eamonn to the group.

Jonathan patted him on the back. Don't worry, Eamonn, it happens to the best of us.

I bet it fucking does, thought Eamonn. He bit his tongue and went along with the charade. He couldn't believe he'd gotten the blame for that one. He looked at Jonathan, who was staring at Eamonn with a grin. Did Jonathan truly believe that Eamonn had messed that one up? Surely not. Perhaps he'd genuinely misheard what Eamonn said and it was all just a total misunderstanding. But then why would he assume Eamonn had messed it up? It could have been anyone before him. As Eamonn thought it over, he knew it couldn't be a misunderstanding. He'd whispered every word of that sentence crystal clear into Jonathan's sweaty, Tayto-sausage roll smelling ear.

In fact, Eamonn probably put extra effort into making sure he was clear because Jonathan was Down Syndrome. Not that Eamonn thought that people with Down Syndrome have bad hearing, he was just saying. Of course, there was the other option, which was that Jonathan knew he'd messed that one up himself and just didn't want to take the blame for it. Eamonn didn't want to believe that one, but he couldn't help but lean towards it. What other explanation could there be? It had to be Jonathan that messed it up. It had to be.

A few other people in the group took a turn. Some of them were fairly simple sentences, like "*I love a pint at the weekend*" and "*I scanned my arse on the photocopier*". Typical ones people working in an office would say. Or there was a very funny one from Malcolm the Janitor. He said, "*All of you are oblivious fools*". Everyone laughed. Malcolm had been making jokes like that a lot recently. Just silly jokes said in a dead serious kind of way. Typical Malcolm. Most of the time, the sentences went around the circle without much of a mistake. A word or two might be out of place or missing, but the message itself would be intact. Eamonn made bloody sure he whispered every word into Jonathan's ear as clear as he possibly could without other people picking up on it. He wasn't going to let Jonathan lay the blame on him again if the whisper got fucked up.

On this one turn, Eamonn thought he'd test Jonathan by trying a little experiment. He'd replace a word in the whisper with another word. Nothing major. Just a small word, like replacing "*the*" with "*it*". When it came around to him, the sentence that Eamonn heard was "*There's a turkey sandwich in my lunchbox*". He thought he'd take the "*sand*" out of "*sandwich*" so it was just pronounced "*witch*". He whispered it into Jonathan's ear as clearly as he could. He scanned Jonathan's face as he pulled away. He seemed to consider it, then he smiled at Eamonn and leaned into the person next to him. It went around the whole group and got to the last person, Conrad from the Quality Support Unit.

Okay, Conrad, said Noelle. What do you have for us?

Conrad laughed awkwardly.

I heard, "*You're not fooling anyone bitch.*"

There was an awkward laugh amongst the group. Eamonn froze. He was speechless. He didn't know what to think. He was going to look at Jonathan, but the truth was he was kind of scared. What the fuck happened there?

Wow, said Jonathan.

That's dark, said Conrad.

Is that right, Sarah? said Noelle.

Um… no, said Sarah, the girl who came up with the whisper. It was, *"There's a turkey sandwich in my lunchbox"*.

Was that you again, Eamonn? said Rory laughing.

No, I definitely didn't hear that, said Eamonn. He wasn't going to say anything, but if Rory was going to be a cunt and call him out on it, then Eamonn was going to fucking defend himself. He wasn't going to take the blame for this again.

Oh, said Jonathan.

Eamonn turned and faced him. He was staring right at him, his eyes wide open. Eamonn felt a chill go down his spine. What the fuck was happening right now? Did Jonathan just send that around the group as a threat to him? No. Fuck that. He was being paranoid now. Even Eamonn had to admit that it was ridiculous to consider that Jonathan knew he had swapped out the words in the whisper and was trying to intimidate him. Eamonn didn't know why he felt so afraid though. It wasn't as if Jonathan posed any threat to him. But that look in his fucking eyes. It made Eamonn think he'd look out his bedroom window tonight and see Jonathan standing across the road in the pouring rain. Some horror movie shit.

Jesus, said Noelle with an awkward chuckle. Someone must have definitely misheard that one anyway. I'd say we're all having a little bit too much fun. How about we end it there and we all get back to work?

Oh come on, said Jonathan. One more. I didn't get a turn.

Oh, that's right, said Noelle. You go so, Jonathan.

Let's go around the other way now though, he said eagerly.

The other way? said Noelle.

Let's go from left to right.

Um, okay. If you want.

Left to right? That meant Jonathan would be whispering into Eamonn's ear. Why the fuck did he want to whisper into his ear? Eamonn genuinely felt like tugging at Graham's arm next to him and asking for help. But what the fuck could he say? That he was in danger from a Down Syndrome? He didn't want to turn and face Jonathan, but he was about to whisper something into his ear. Clearing his throat, he turned and smiled at Jonathan, without looking directly into his eyes.

Last one so, said Eamonn nervously.

Yeah, said Jonathan. Last one.

If we don't get back to work soon, said Noelle, I'd say Roger will fire us all.

Eamonn felt the weight of Jonathan's body lean into him, weighing him down and crushing him into the floor like it had its own gravitational force. Jonathan's lips touched Eamonn's earlobe. His breath was ice-cold. Holding his breath, Jonathan whispered slowly, *"I'm putting it on"*.

Eamonn wanted to pretend more than anything at that moment that he'd misheard. He wished a fork would have dropped or someone would have coughed or sneezed so those four words hadn't registered in his brain. But they had. And there was no way of not hearing them. Nor was there any way that Eamonn could believe that the words Jonathan had just spoken to him were true. No, there was no way. Jonathan was joking. He was having a laugh with Eamonn. Because if he was being serious…

Jonathan leaned back in his seat and Eamonn was left blanked face, staring at the floor. He looked around the room at all the oblivious faces staring at him. He turned to Graham, who was waiting for him to whisper what he'd heard into his ear. But there was no way Eamonn could relay what he'd just heard. The whisper had started with Eamonn. Graham would know that he was the one who said it first. And Graham wasn't an idiot. He would think Eamonn was taking the piss out of Jonathan and he'd tell everyone around the office. He'd be a fucking pariah. No one would want to hang around a guy that takes the piss out of people with mental disabilities. Or someone pretending to have a mental disability. But that couldn't be true. It just couldn't be.

Eamonn would have to make something up. There's no way he could repeat what Jonathan had just whispered into his ear. He didn't want to think about what Jonathan's reaction might be when the fake whisper got back to him, but he'd have to deal with that when it got to it.

Trying to think of something on the spot, Eamonn leaned into Graham's ear and muttered: *"Roger likes to do yoga on his lunch break"*

Eamonn didn't know where that came from. It was just the first thing that came to him. He didn't even know if he'd said it properly to Graham. His voice was trembling, and his forehead was beaded with sweat. Graham whispered it to the person next to him and it went around the room. Eamonn sat motionless for the duration of the round. He felt like Jonathan's presence next to him was a demon that everyone saw masquerading as an angel but Eamonn was the only one to see him for what he truly was. Was he overreacting? Could what Jonathan had said be just the deranged ramblings of a mentally disabled mind? Could Jonathan be doing this to him as payback for rearranging the words in that whisper? Could it just be a bit of banter or was Jonathan allowing Eamonn to see his true colors?

27

Eamonn's sweaty hands remained clamped to his knees as he eyed everyone the whisper passed through. He looked at Frank from Maintenance, sitting next to Jonathan. The end of the line. Eamonn couldn't bear to think about what would happen when Frank was called to announce what Jonathan, or in this case, Eamonn had said. When it did get to Frank, Noelle stood up and said: Okay, Frank, what have you got?

Eamonn held his breath as Frank looked at Jonathan. I heard, *"Roger likes to do yoga on his lunch break"*

Well, Jonathan, said Noelle. Is that right?

Jonathan's head turned slowly towards Eamonn, like a horror movie doll. This was it. The moment of truth. Eamonn turned and looked deep into the catacombs of Jonathan's eyes. There was something horrible hiding deep behind that mask.

There was silence for a few seconds. Then Jonathan smiled. That's correct, he said, not tearing his gaze away from Eamonn's.

Everyone clapped.

Okay, I'd say we'll leave it there, said Noelle. Hope you had a great time, Jonathan.

I had a wonderful time, said Jonathan, finally looking away from Eamonn. Thank you, everyone. I love you all.

We love you, Jonathan, said Noelle. Don't you ever forget it.

Everyone clapped. Then they all got up and started to reorganize the room. Eamonn and Jonathan were the only two who didn't move. It was just them sitting there, looking ahead. Eamonn thought Jonathan might say or do something to him, but he didn't. He got up and dragged his chair back to his desk. Once Jonathan was out of sight, Eamonn sank his face into his hands and breathed heavily. It felt like the first proper breath he'd taken in fucking ages.

Later that day, Eamonn was sitting at his desk, trying to look somewhat productive, but he couldn't concentrate on anything. All he could think about was Jonathan and that fucking look on his face. He peered over his desk and across the office. There he was, sitting at his desk, working away, conning everyone. He desperately wanted to tell someone what had happened, but who the fuck would believe him? Who in their right mind would believe that the guy with Down Syndrome in the office was faking the whole thing and fooling everyone? Eamonn had spent all afternoon trying to think of a way he could explain it to someone without sounding like a fucking madman or someone just trying to bully Jonathan, but he just couldn't. There was no way he could get around this, no escape. He was stuck with what he knew. He was probably the only person in the world that knew.

Eamonn didn't get up from his seat for the rest of the day. He was too fucking scared. For the first time since he'd started here, he worked as hard as he could so he could take his mind off what happened.

Around five that evening, Eamonn was walking to the elevator, ready to get the fuck out of the building. He couldn't wait to get home, lock the door, pour himself a pint of vodka, and pretend that today never happened. Eamonn stepped into the elevator and pressed the button for the parking garage. A hand shot out between the doors just as they were about to close. The doors opened and Jonathan appeared in front of him. Eamonn gulped down hard.

Hey, Eamonn, said Jonathan jovially as he stepped into the elevator.

29

Hi, Jonathan.

Heading home?

Yeah.

Any plans for the weekend?

No, just going to stay at home.

My mom's taking me to a pet farm to see all the puppies and animals.

That's nice.

The elevator doors closed and started moving down. They were alone. Eamonn's teeth were chattering and his hands were shaking. He was trapped in a confined space with Jonathan. His heart was racing so fast that he thought it would burst out of his chest. The elevator walls seemed to be closing in around him. Every muscle in his body tensed up and paralyzed him. Eamonn counted the seconds as the elevator moved smoothly down. If Jonathan was going to kill him, he might as well do it now. Eamonn couldn't take this anymore. This secret was burning away at his insides and nothing but sweet death would douse the flame.

After what seemed like an eternity, the elevator finally hit the ground floor and there was a loud ding. The doors opened and Eamonn could see Jonathan's head turn to him in his peripheral vision. He turned his head slowly and looked Jonathan square in the eyes. And then he saw it.

He saw Jonathan. The real Jonathan, in his true form. He looked just like a normal person. His lips curled into a smile and he said with the most normal and masculine voice that Eamonn had ever heard: See you tomorrow.

Jonathan stepped out of the elevator and walked away. Eamonn didn't move a muscle. He watched Jonathan disappear into the darkness of the

30

parking garage. When the elevator doors closed, Eamonn collapsed onto the floor and wept uncontrollably.

The next day, Eamonn came into work extremely hungover. It was very obvious from the state of him that he was drinking the night before and everyone made fun of him for it. Eamonn smiled and tried to go along with the joke, but the truth was that the secret burning inside him hurt a lot more than the hangover.

At lunch, Eamonn approached Rory in the canteen as he was making a cup of tea. He was going to try and broach the subject of Jonathan's treachery with him. He was his closest friend at work and if anyone might be willing to listen to him, it would be Rory. Who knows what might happen. Perhaps he knows something too.

Hey, Rory, said Eamonn.

Alright, Eamonn.

The kettle boiled?

It is.

Eamonn coughed.

Jesus man, you look like death, said Rory.

Yeah, rough night.

By the looks of it, it's not tea you need.

What?

You need a little hair of the dog, not fucking tea.

Maybe later.

Who'd you go out with?

Just friends.

Rory knew that meant no one.

Hey, Rory, said Eamonn. Can I ask you something?

Yeah.

Don't tell anyone I told you this now. I just wanted to ask.

What's up?

Have you noticed anything... I don't know... odd, about Jonathan lately.

What do you mean?

I don't know, like anything off about him?

Like sick?

No, I mean the way he's acting.

I'm not following, Eamonn.

Has anything struck you as strange?

No.

You sure?

Why?

I'm just wondering?

Is there something you've noticed?

No, nothing.

Well, there is something actually, said Rory.

What is it? said Eamonn.

He has Down Syndrome.

No, that's not what I mean.

Isn't it?

It was just yesterday when we were playing Chinese Whispers and...

You know, Eamonn, I'm frankly getting a little bit sick of you taking the piss out of Jonathan all the time.

I'm not trying to take the piss out of him, I'm just asking.

Yeah, you're asking if I've noticed anything strange about him. That's all your doing.

Yeah, but it's not... This has nothing to do with him being Down Syndrome.

So what are you talking about?

I'm just asking...

What? Say what you want to say.

Eamonn opened his mouth to speak but nothing came out. There was no good way of putting what he had to say into words.

I don't know, said Eamonn.

Whatever, man, said Rory. He walked away and left the canteen.

Later that day, Noelle walked up to Eamonn's desk and asked if she could talk to him in the conference room for a second. He could see by the look on her face that she wasn't happy about something.

When they were in the conference room and the door was closed, Noelle turned to Eamonn. She looked well pissed off.

What's your problem? she said.

What?

You have something you want to say?

What's wrong, Noelle?

Do you have some sort of problem with Jonathan?

Eamonn bit his tongue. Fucking Rory.

No, he said quietly.

So what's all this I hear about you talking shit on him?

I wasn't talking shit on him...

Because if you have a problem with Jonathan, then you have a problem with me.

I wasn't talking shit on him. I was just asking…

What? Spit it out.

Eamonn felt a bit of sick come up in his mouth. He was far too hungover to be dealing with this shit right now.

What were you just asking? said Noelle.

I was just…

What? roared Noelle.

Calm down.

Don't tell me to calm down.

I was just asking Rory if he noticed anything a bit off about him. That's all it was.

Like what?

Just… him acting a bit odd.

He has Down Syndrome, you fucking asshole.

Sure he does.

What did you say?

It came out of Eamonn before he could stop himself. Noelle looked like she wanted to strangle him.

No, I mean…

Why don't we go out and ask him?

Sorry?

Yeah, come on, said Noelle, firmly gripping Eamonn's arm. Let's go out and you can ask Jonathan yourself since you're so concerned about him.

Wait, I don't...

Eamonn started to panic. Noelle was dragging him across the office in front of everyone. He tried to pull away so he could explain himself but Noelle was so angry that Eamonn didn't think he could break away from her without causing a scene. Then he saw Jonathan across the room and his heart sank in his chest.

Hey Jonathan, said Noelle. You busy?

No, said Jonathan smiling. I always have time for you.

You're very good. Here, Eamonn was just telling me there he'd like to ask you something.

Do you, Eamonn? said Jonathan.

Maybe we can talk about it somewhere else? said Eamonn nervously as he looked around at all the eyes watching him.

No, said Noelle. We'll talk about it here, in front of everyone.

Everyone in the office got up from their desks to see what was going on. Eamonn looked around and then looked at Jonathan's vacant face.

I was just wondering...

Noelle gripped his arm even tighter.

Is everything okay, Eamonn? said Jonathan, his words filled with so much fake emotion.

Yeah, I was just... I just noticed you seemed a bit off lately and... I was just wondering... um... I just wanted... I just wondered if everything was alright with you?

Oh, that's very nice of you to be concerned. I guess I'm okay. I've had a bit of a cold recently and this medicine I'm on has given me a bit of a rash in my anus, but other than that, I feel just fine.

35

Yeah, that's okay, said Eamonn smiling. That's all I meant. I didn't mean anything else by it.

Thanks for being so concerned about me, Eamonn.

No worries, said Eamonn.

Noelle turned and stared at him in a way that said *if I fucking hear you talking shit about Jonathan again, I'll fucking make sure you regret it*. She let go of his arm.

Sorry to bother you again, said Noelle.

Not at all, said Jonathan.

Noelle smiled, gave Eamonn another intimidating look, and walked off. Everyone in the office got back to what they were doing.

Frustrating, isn't it?

Eamonn turned and looked at Jonathan.

I'm sorry? said Eamonn.

Jonathan smiled. None of this will end well for you if you keep at it. You do know that, right?

Eamonn gritted his teeth. He felt like tackling Jonathan right then and there and beating the living shit out of him. In just one day, the cunt had turned his life completely upside down.

You fucking spastic, said Eamonn, feeling a sudden wave of rage wash over him.

That's right, you keep at it if it makes you feel better. Nothing good will come out of it.

I'll expose you.

You try that and see where it gets you.

You won't get away with this.

Yes, I will, and you know it. Now go back to your desk like a good little boy.

Eamonn's face fell. He wanted to say more. Do more. Do something to let this cunt know he should be scared of Eamonn. But it was useless. Eamonn turned and walked back to his desk. Jonathan was right. He was stuck. There was no way out of this. He sat at his desk for ages, rubbing his temple and trying to soothe his hangover. But more than that, he was trying to get a grip on what exactly the fuck was happening to him right now. For the rest of the day, people gave Eamonn dirty looks as they passed his desk.

Toward the end of the day, Eamonn thought about reporting what Jonathan had said to him to management. If he couldn't get any of his co-workers to believe him, then maybe he might be able to get some support from higher up. Jonathan wasn't immune to them. Eamonn spent as long as he could preparing what he was going to say to Roger, constantly reworking it to make it sound more eloquent and rational. When he was confident he was ready, Eamonn got up, grabbed his jacket and threw it on. As he stepped away from his desk, a hand grabbed his shoulder and spun him around. It was Malcolm the Janitor.

Don't do it, he said.

What?

You need to just move on kid. He's right. There's no winning this one.

Eamonn opened his mouth to ask Malcolm what the fuck he was talking about, but then it dawned on him. Are you talking about what I think you're talking about? he said.

Malcolm looked deep into Eamonn's eyes.

Forget about this. Move on.

Malcolm turned, grabbed his brush and walked away. Eamonn went to chase after him, but he tripped over his desk chair and fell flat on his face. When he got up, Malcolm was at the other side of the office. Eamonn ran after him and called out his name but couldn't catch up to him and eventually lost him around a corner. That weekend, Eamonn planned on approaching Malcolm on Monday morning in the hopes of talking him into coming with him to see management. He figured he'd have a better chance of convincing them if there were two of them. But on Monday morning, Malcolm was found dead in his home. They were told it was a suicide. Everyone at work was super sad. But Eamonn knew who the culprit was.

After work that day, Eamonn followed Jonathan home and waited in his car for the right moment. He tried to tell himself to forget about the whole thing and just move on with his life. That he should just pretend Jonathan doesn't exist and proceed forward like he never discovered his secret, but he couldn't. The thought of Jonathan getting away with what he was doing just enraged him. And now that Malcolm was dead, Eamonn was the only one that knew of his secret, so it was up to him to do something about it before this got worse.

Eamonn waited until Jonathan pulled up outside his house and got out of his car. He put up his hood and started walking towards Jonathan while he was taking stuff out of the boot. I have to do this, Eamonn told himself over and over as he got closer to Jonathan. This has to be done. He can't get away with this any longer. He needs to know this level of exploitative treachery and manipulation will not be tolerated. Jonathan turned as Eamonn was getting closer. He didn't recognize the figure at first.

Can I help you? said Jonathan.

Eamonn didn't say anything. He took his hands out of his pocket and clenched his fists.

Eamonn? Is that you?

Eamonn raised his fist and plunged it in the direction of Jonathan's face. Like lightning, Jonathan raised his hand and caught Eamonn's fist with ease, stopping it inches from his face. Eamonn raised his other fist and tried to strike his body, but Jonathan stopped that with his other hand. Eamonn tried to free his hands from Jonathan's grip, but they wouldn't budge. His grip tightened and it really started to hurt.

What do we have here? said Jonathan smiling.

Jonathan's grip on Eamonn's left hand suddenly tightened and he felt a few fingers break. He roared in pain and collapsed to his knees. Eamonn tried to pull his other hand away but it was pointless. Jonathan's grip on him was as tight as a vice

Looks like someone didn't listen to me?

Let go! You're breaking my hand!

Oh, you mean like this?

Jonathan squeezed his left hand. Eamonn felt his wrist snap like a toothpick, bringing about a pain that surged through his body like electricity. He raised his face to the sky and roared.

You need to learn to listen, Eamonn.

What are you! roared Eamonn.

Oh, someone like you doesn't need to know that. I don't think you'd sleep very well if you knew the answer.

Please, stop!

Jonathan squeezed Eamonn's right hand like it was an orange. His whole body contorted in pain as the joints and muscles in his hand were mashed together like Play-Doh. The pain was so sharp and blinding, it was paralyzing. Jonathan let go of Eamonn's hands, raised his foot and feebly kicked his chest. Eamonn fell on his back and let the shattered remains of his hands collapse to his side. He felt like passing out.

Help! Eamonn shouted.

Cry all you want, no one can hear you. I've made sure of that.

Why are you doing this?

You'll know soon enough.

Just kill me and get it over with, said Eamonn, closing his eyes and accepting the sweet embrace of death.

No. As fun as that sounds, there'd be nothing to gain in killing you.

So why did you tell me?

Jonathan shrugged his shoulders. Bit of craic. See you Monday.

And with that, Jonathan turned and walked into his house. Eamonn was able to pick himself up a few minutes later. He wasn't able to drive home because his hands were in such a mangled state, so he had to walk ten kilometers home. Such misery he felt on this walk. He felt so defeated. There was truly nothing he could do. Eamonn wasn't dealing with some guy at the office who was bullying and gaslighting him. Eamonn was dealing with something else entirely. How could he have allowed himself to be fooled for so long? How could he not have seen Jonathan for what he truly is?

Eamonn wanted things to go back to the way they were. Why did it have to be him? Jonathan had bestowed upon him the knowledge of his

40

treachery and deceit, knowing that any attempt to try and expose him would only lead to Eamonn's downfall. If he pursued Jonathan any further, everyone in the office would hate him more than they already do. Eamonn could quit work and move as far away from this whole thing as he could, but considering how hard it was to get the job he already had with his prison record, he knew he wouldn't be able to find anything as good again. He was stuck where he was. If he didn't quit and he kept pursuing this, he'd probably get fired. No company wants an employee on their payroll that spreads malicious rumors about the mentally disabled. It would cost him everything. His job, his relationships. Everything. Eamonn had no other choice in the matter. This was something he'd have to take to his grave. Jonathan had won.

A few weeks later, Eamonn started showing up to work drunk. Everyone thought it was funny at first, but after a while, it just got to be concerning. Everyone thought he might be going through something, but soon, he started coming in pissed every day. His work suffered and he got multiple warnings that if he didn't stop, he'd be let go. Eamonn didn't seem to care. Whatever he was going through was clearly eating him up inside. After a while, he didn't even wear a suit to work anymore. He'd come in wearing tracksuit bottoms and trainers.

In June, Eamonn stepped out from his desk and pulled out a pistol with a silencer on it. He ran towards Jonathan and started shooting. A few guys tackled him to the ground and managed to get the pistol off him.

He has to be stopped! Eamonn kept shouting. *He has to be stopped!*

He roared it at the top of his lungs over and over. Even when the Guards arrived and put him into the back of the van, he kept saying it.

He's putting it on! He's fucking faking it! Don't let yourself be fooled!

Nobody knew what the fuck Eamonn was on about. They all thought he was off his head or something, as usual. Frankly, everyone was glad to be rid of him. Everyone was sick of him coming in pissed and making fun of Jonathan. They all comforted Jonathan afterwards, telling him it wasn't his fault and Eamonn would be put in jail forever. Jonathan kept asking why anyone would want to hurt him.

Why indeed?

I'll end things there. I would like to tell you what Jonathan was, dear reader. I really would. But you've seen for yourself the devastating effects Eamonn's lack of knowledge regarding Jonathan's true nature did to him. You don't want to end up like him. Trust me. The only difference between me and Eamonn is that I know nothing good will come out of pursuing this thing any further. I know it's best to just accept I'm powerless over this thing and try to move on with my life as best I can, even knowing how utterly insignificant I am in the grand scheme of things. You may think you're able to handle the horrifying truth, but trust me. You don't have a fucking clue. Frankly, I pity Eamonn. He thinks he would have been able to move on with his life if he knew what I knew. But he was wrong. His entire universe would have been turned upside down. I'm just grateful I won't be around for the generation that will have to witness this thing firsthand when it gets here. So as for you, be disappointed by that ending if you want. You can even write to me and express your disappointment if you really care that much. If I were you, I'd be thankful you don't know the agonizing truth. Just move on to the next story if you know what's best for you.

Twelve

We met at a dog show at the children's playground in the park. She brought her Bichon Frise with her. I was just there to watch. That sounds weird, I know. But I really was just there to watch the dogs. I petted her dog and then I introduced myself. She said she was there with her mom. I really fucking liked her. She was a laugh. And I made her laugh. Which I liked because I loved her laugh. We talked for a while, walked around the park, and then I asked her.

What age are you?

I know most girls say it's impolite to ask a girl her age but I honestly was just asking to ask. She asked me teasingly what age I thought she was. I didn't try to answer. I told her it didn't matter and we continued talking. I didn't want to offend her. I've given girls eating disorders before by guessing their age incorrectly, so I thought it was best just to leave it. And I really didn't want to offend this girl. I really liked her. But I did ask her. I want you to know that before you go judging me.

I suggested to her over text one time that we spend the night at her place. She said that wouldn't be possible because her parents wouldn't allow it. That was the first warning sign. That got my attention. I instantly started imagining what her dad might do to me if she *was* underage and he found out I was tapping his daughter? But then I thought, a lot of young people are still living with their parents. It's not that uncommon, especially amongst college graduates. But that worry never left me.

One time, we were driving around and I made a note to myself beforehand to actually find out what age she was. Just ask her, I told myself. But ask her in a teasing way, so she's not offended. But also ask her seriously. But not too seriously so she'll think you're no fun.

So what age actually are you? I remember asking her as we pulled into the car park of a beach.

What age are you? she replied.

Me?

Yes, you.

I'm thirty-eight.

Wow, she said with a smile.

What?

Nothing, It's just… I would have guessed younger.

Really?

Way younger. You look really good.

Thank you. That's really nice of you.

Then we started shifting. We shifted for a while. She rubbed my leg and my dick. I put my hand up her top and felt her tit. I remember thinking how small they were. It was only after dropping her home, and my boner had deflated, that I realized I never got a definitive answer out of her regarding her age. Fuck.

She messaged me one day asking if I wanted to go out to a bar that weekend. I really didn't know if I wanted to. At this point, the question of

44

her age was now playing on my mind almost constantly. I couldn't not think about it. I looked her up on Facebook, but she wasn't on it. Now I know what you're thinking: *"What a fucking stupid excuse. What person isn't on Facebook?"* Honest to god, I'm telling you the truth. She said she was on Instagram and Snapchat but they don't show age on there, so I really didn't know what to do. I said yes to going out.

Before we went out, I decided to text her. I couldn't do it anymore. If people had seen the fucking nudes she'd been sending to me and it turned out she was underage, they'd cut my balls off and flush them down the fucking toilet. So I text her. And she didn't message me back. I sent her a question mark. Nothing. Then a double question mark. Still nothing. Now I was really starting to panic. At this point, every worst case scenario started to flood into my head like hot diarrhoea. I was imagining a group of pedo hunters approaching me on the street. That's the last thing I needed.

On Saturday night, we went out to a bar. I asked her did she get my texts from the last night. She said her battery died and she only charged it before she came here. Fucking convenient. I told her I was going up to get a drink and asked her if she wanted anything. She said a coke. I suddenly felt like I had to take a shit, which happens to me when I get nervous.

Jesus fucking Christ. What have I landed myself into? Everything about this girl was telling me to fucking leg it. But what good would that do? We'd already shifted and had exchanged numerous explicit pictures of each other. She had enough pictures of my nob to fill a fucking billboard. I was in too deep now. I had to ask her tonight. I had to fucking know. If it turned out she was underage, I'd just turn myself in. That's what I'd do. I was afraid if I tried to break it off once I learned her age, she might get angry and go to the Guards just to get back at me. Fuck that. If I was going down, I was going to beat her to it at least.

I suggested we go to a nearby club, as the bar we were in was too loud to talk. She suggested we go back to her place. She said her parents were away for the weekend. I said okay. To me, this was a good thing. If she was underage, there's no way her parents would leave her in the house by herself for the weekend. Especially since she told me numerous times how strict her dad was.

When we were back at her house, we watched a bit of TV in her sitting room for about an hour. I spent that hour in a cold sweat, trying to work up the courage to ask her. I just couldn't. She really seemed to be having a good time. I really was too and I didn't want to spoil it. I started looking around the room for anything that would give me any indication of what age she was. A picture, some toys, a birth cert. Nothing.

Then she suggested we go upstairs. I reluctantly said okay. She said I seemed nervous and asked me if everything was alright. I said it was. I didn't want to worry her. But I knew I had to ask her before anything serious happened.

She held my hand and led me up the stairs. When we got to the top, she pointed to a room down the hall and said she was going into the bathroom to freshen up.

I watched her go into the bathroom and flash me a flirtatious smile.

I'll be a second, she said, then closed the door.

I took a deep breath and walked towards the room. I opened the door. The room was pitch black. I put my hand on the wall next to me and felt around for a light switch. I eventually found it and flicked it on. The room lit up.

Oh sweet mother of Jesus. Her school uniform was hanging from her wardrobe. There were schoolbooks and refill pads with girly drawings on the covers. In a pink jar on a desk right beside them were the pens with the pink furry arses on them. There were huge posters on the wall of these teen pop stars I don't know the names of. Jesus fucking Christ, what fucking age was this girl? If the contents of this room were any indication, then I clearly needed to fucking immigrate.

I turned to walk out of the room and jumped at the sight of her running down the hall in her bra and knickers towards me. She jumped into my arms and I held her up by the legs. She stuck her tongue deep into my mouth and we wrestled around the room. She was going crazy. It all happened so fast. I couldn't process it. We moved backwards and I collapsed onto her bed. She immediately moved down my body and unbuckled my belt. I put my hands on her shoulders and tried to push her off me.

Wait, hold on, I said.

But it was no use. I may as well have been trying to push the fattest person alive off a bed of rashers. She whipped my belt off, threw it across the room and pulled my jeans off my legs. I told her to wait and maybe we should take it a bit slower, but she pushed me back down and started kissing my neck. Then she took my underwear off and started giving me a blowjob. Everything in my brain was telling me to stop this and get out before I did something I couldn't take back. But it felt so good. It was like the pleasure was a mental wall that was stopping me from doing anything

47

logical. She sucked me off until I was as hard as a rock. Then she took off her bra, grabbed both my hands and moved them up to her tits. She pulled off my t-shirt and threw it beside the bed. She took off her knickers and jumped on top of me. She grabbed my pulsating boner and put it inside her pussy. She didn't even put a johnny on.

And there it was.

I had reached the point of no return. There was absolutely no coming back from this. But I remember sort of relaxing as well. Fuck it, I thought. If I'm going to prison, I might as well enjoy the use of my penis one last time before some prison queer cuts it off and is using it as a candle to light up his cell at night.

She rode me like an animal. She moaned so loud. I kept my hands on her arse and sometimes felt her tits. I even stuck a finger up her arse at one point and she moaned even louder. She was fucking loving it. I flipped her over and now I was doing her from behind. She was screaming so loud. The headboard was banging hard and peeling the paint off the wall. I rode her long and hard and the slaps from her arse bounced off the walls like a little girl screaming in a tunnel. Then she gave one final scream and collapsed into the bed. She lay on her back and wanked me off. I ended up cumming on her tits. Then we fell asleep.

The next morning, I woke up to her giving me a blowjob under the duvet. I laid back and enjoyed it. Then I stopped. I lifted up the duvet and asked her how old she was.

She said she was twenty-two. I asked her if she was telling the truth. She got up and reached for something on the floor. It was her purse. She pulled out a card and handed it to me. It was her provisional driver's license. I studied it. She wasn't lying. She was indeed twenty-two. I asked her whose room this was. She said it was her little sisters. She said she'd been sleeping here for a few days because her room was being painted and the smell was rank. She also said her parents had taken her little sister up to Dublin for her birthday and that's why she had the house for the weekend. I said okay, satisfied she was telling the truth, and she resumed the blowjob. After I came in her mouth, I watched her get dressed and chuckled to myself. All that worrying for nothing.

We didn't end up going out for very long. A few weeks maybe. Nothing dramatic. Just normal couple shit. But a couple of weeks later, I went to the doctor because I lost a ton of weight and passed out a few times at work. He told me I tested positive for HIV. When I asked him to explain how that was possible, he said that my T-cell count was down to twelve and that he was surprised I was alive at this point.

Seeing as I don't use needles (or any drugs for that matter besides the occasional paracetamol for the odd hangover), I don't fuck guys, and your one was the last person I had sex with, I called her up after I left the doctor's office and asked her did she know anything about it. There was a pause, followed by a slightly awkward cough, then she said she didn't think she could pass it on to anyone.

So yeah, I'm on my way to her house with a golf club right now and I'm going to tear this bitch a new asshole.

Wish me luck.

The Jigsaw

Wally wasn't going to move. He didn't care what Gillian said. He didn't care how much she gave out or cried or begged or threatened. He wasn't going to move from this couch. Nor was he going to move the jigsaw puzzle from the table. No fucking way. She'd have to kill him first. You might think that's an overreaction. But Wally had a good fucking reason.

Five thousand pieces. That's the size of the jigsaw his mother had gotten him for his last birthday. His mother always got him jigsaw puzzles. She loved the damn things. Since she was a little kid, it had been an unwavering hobby of hers. It was impossible not to spot a few boxes littering a shelf or table around the house when he was a kid. She was always working on a jigsaw, splayed across a thin rectangular piece of cardboard Wally's dad had made for her so she didn't make a mess.

She always got them for Wally, for every occasion. Birthdays, Christmases, Easter, you name it. It was always the same. Wally always acted delighted and thanked his mum for the lovely gift. The reality was Wally fucking hated jigsaw puzzles. Actually, Wally hated doing jigsaw puzzles, especially by himself. He always enjoyed doing them with his mum when he was a kid. On Sundays, he'd jump into bed with her and help her out with whatever she was working on. But by himself, he was fucking useless. He didn't have the temperament for shit like this. His mum did. That was the major difference between him and her. His mum enjoyed the whole process, from organizing all the edge pieces to arranging and grouping pieces that share the same color or texture. Wally hated it.

But he always put on a happy face for his mum. He didn't want to upset her. He knew how much she loved jigsaws and he could imagine what a blow it would be for her to discover her only son didn't share the same love for jigsaws that she did.

After his mum died a few weeks ago, Wally made a promise to finish a jigsaw puzzle for her. He swore to her as he carried the coffin out of the church. She'd bought him so many jigsaw puzzles over the years, and all he did was store them away. They'd sit there for ages doing nothing but accumulating dust and serving as an anchor point for spiders webs. Whenever she asked him how he was getting on with a puzzle she'd got him, he'd say he was nearly done with it or he'd already finished it. Or if she was coming over, he'd grab a few boxes from the attic and spread them around the house.

But not now. Wally wasn't going to bullshit her anymore. He was going to complete a jigsaw puzzle for his mum. He was going to make her proud.

So he went and got a jigsaw puzzle with the highest number of pieces he could find. Five thousand pieces. Such a daunting number would normally give Wally palpitations. But not this time. He wasn't going to cop out and settle for one of the easier thousand piece puzzles he could easily complete in a few days or something. He was going to complete a big one.

Another reason he picked the jigsaw puzzle he did was because he really liked the picture on the box. It was a sci-fi themed jigsaw puzzle. It was a man wielding a large blue sword and a small child holding his hand. They were standing on a grassy hill overlooking a glowing blue and purple city, and beyond that was a gigantic tower that had a large yellowish light at the top, similar to a lighthouse. The night sky was filled with twinkling stars and tons of different colored planets and nebulas. It was really quite beautiful. It must have cost his mum a fortune. It wasn't one of those puzzles you could get for a few bob at your local toy store. This was a picture that someone had put a considerable amount of time and energy into drawing or painting. That made Wally want to do it even more. His mum hadn't just picked out a random jigsaw puzzle for him. She picked out one she thought he'd like. And he did. He loved it. And he was going to complete it for her, no matter what.

Two and a half weeks Wally spent on it. On and off. A little bit in the morning before he went to work, and then all of the evening and night when he came home. Whatever free time he had, basically. His girlfriend, Gillian, didn't really understand why he was doing it. She made fun of him for it. She thought he was being all sentimental and silly.

After a few days though she started to get annoyed because Wally had set up the jigsaw puzzle on the sitting room table, and whined about how she had nowhere to set her cup of tea or put her feet up. Wally told her there was no way he was going to move it. She could have told him when he'd first started the thing. He would have gladly moved it to the kitchen table or his study. But he was past the point of no return at this stage. After two days, he'd already gotten all the edge pieces sorted and managed to fill in a good portion of the moon in the top left-hand corner. Maybe if she hadn't been too busy making fun of him, she would've remembered to bring it up. He even asked her several times if she wanted to help him out with it. He figured he'd have a bit more fun with it if he had someone helping him, but she just laughed him off, as usual. Then she'd sit behind him, watching him do the jigsaw, pretending to watch TV, making the occasional sly comment to him if he got stuck on a piece. It really pissed him off.

She suggested that maybe he slide it onto a rectangular piece of cardboard. But Wally didn't want to do that. The jigsaw was huge and he was too afraid it would break apart.

But two and a half weeks later, he was still working on it and Gillian was really starting to get pissed off. A couple of times she even threatened to move it herself, but Wally told her not to even think about it.

He was almost done with the fucking thing anyway. As annoying and frustrating as it'd been, especially with Gillian looming over him like a fucking bitch, he was almost done, and he was looking forward to seeing the final product. He started to get now why his mum got such a kick out of it. It was so satisfying watching the whole thing come together, piece by piece. The most annoying part of the whole thing had been the middle part of the jigsaw, which comprised mainly of the glowing blue and purple city. Most of the pieces looked exactly the same and comprised of about two fifths of the jigsaw. It took him fucking ages to finish.

One night, after spending a couple of hours filling in some blank spaces, Wally decided to call it a night and go to bed. And as he got up and got a better view of the jigsaw, he realized he was nearly done with it. Two hundred or so more pieces. He was dead excited to finish the thing. He thought about just finishing it off now, but he was too wrecked. He could finish the whole thing tomorrow after work.

The next morning, as Wally sat eating his porridge, Gillian started giving him the usual nagging about moving the jigsaw. He told her he'd be done with it by tonight and that would be it. She shut up after that. Wally didn't know what he was going to do with the jigsaw after he finished it. It felt like he'd be literally breaking a promise to his mum if he broke it up right after he finished. Maybe he could frame it. He heard people did that. Maybe he could just take a picture of it. He didn't know. He'd figured that out when he got there.

Around half-twelve, while Wally was sitting at his computer at work, his phone ringing. It was Gillian. He answered it quietly so no one would hear.

Hey, Gill. What's up?

Hey, Wally. Look, I just wanted to call and tell you that Jane and William are coming this evening.

For what?

Just to hang out. Few drinks. Bit of food.

Okay, that sounds nice.

I'll have to move the jigsaw out of the sitting room though.

What? said Wally a little louder than he intended.

I'll have to move the jigsaw if we're going into the sitting room.

Hold on a minute.

Wally got up from his desk and walked swiftly into an empty conference room.

The Jigsaw

Don't you touch that fucking jigsaw puzzle, Gillian.

So where are we meant to hang out?

Wally thought.

Look, I'll move it when I get home, okay?

I'll just move it myself. I brought that bit of wood over from the garage. It should be big enough to fit the whole thing on it. I'll move it on that and…

Do not fucking touch it, Gillian. You'll ruin it. Wally always called her Gill. He never called her by her full name unless he was being deadly fucking serious.

I swear to god, I'll be as careful as possible, she said.

Wally was starting to panic.

Look, Gill, please just leave it. I'll take care of it when I get home, I promise.

Wally, I need to hoover the room before they arrive. I'll just do it now. I'll be careful, alright. Don't be such a baby. I'll talk to you later.

Gillian, do not touch that fu…

She hung up. Wally was breathing fast. He tried to call her again but she didn't pick up. He was about to start freaking out but he turned and saw that his co-workers were staring at him inquisitively through the conference room window. He straightened himself up and left before they started to think something serious had just happened. He smiled as he walked back to his desk, but as he slumped back into his chair, he thought he was going to have a panic attack.

She was going to ruin it. Wally knew she would. She didn't know what it meant to him. She thought it was just some fucking joke. Something he

55

was using to pass the time because she thought something was up with him. But there was nothing up with him. She just didn't understand, nor did she seek to understand either. She'd fuck it up somehow. She mishandle it and a corner would crumble and then the whole thing would break apart and that would be it. That would be the whole thing ruined.

When he finished work, Wally raced out of the building and got into his car as fast as he could. He drove like a madman. He took shortcuts he'd never taken before, ran red lights, went down one-way streets. He was pretty sure he injured an old woman walking her dog, but he didn't care. The only thing on Wally's mind right now was getting home.

When he pulled into his driveway, Wally got out of the car and sprinted for the front door. His suit was soaked through with sweat. He took the house key out from under the pot in the porch and put it in the front door, but it was already unlocked. He burst into the house and kicked down the door to the sitting room.

It wasn't there. The jigsaw puzzle was gone.

He was going to kill her. He was actually going to physically murder her.

What's wrong with you?

Wally heard the tiny voice from behind him and swung around. Gillian was standing in the hall holding a bowl.

Where's the jigsaw, Gillian? he said.

The what?

WHERE'S THE FUCKING JIGSAW?!

Gillian recoiled in horror.

Jesus Christ, calm down. What's wrong with you?

56

Tell me where it is right now!

Wally could have killed her. He honestly could have. He was so fucking angry at her. How fucking dare she defy him. Disrespectful little cunt.

It's on the kitchen table, she said.

Immediately, Wally rushed forward, shoved Gillian aside, and burst into the kitchen. He looked towards the table at the end of the room. He could see the border of the jigsaw on the table. He sprinted forward and came face to face with the jigsaw, which was now resting on a flat bit of wood. He looked the jigsaw over meticulously, running his finger over every piece to make sure there wasn't a single thing out of place. He checked the cover of the box next to it, which had all the remaining pieces in it.

Gillian walked in behind him. She watched Wally as he studied the jigsaw over. After he settled down, she said:

Satisfied?

I told you explicitly not to touch it, said Wally, not looking away from the jigsaw.

I didn't mess up anything, did I? I just moved it onto that bit of wood and moved it in here, that's all I did. Nothing went wrong. I made sure I was careful.

And she had. Wally couldn't find any fault. Nothing was messed up. All the remaining pieces seemed to still be in the box. But it was the fucking arrogance and downright insolent manner in which Gillian just flippantly ignored his wishes that really pissed him off.

If I tell you not to do something, I fucking mean it.

I had to fucking move it so I could wash the table.

57

Her nasally whiny voice split through him like nails on a chalkboard. Wally inhaled and exhaled deeply, trying to stop his body from shaking.

Anyway, it was about time someone moved it, she continued. I was tired of staring at it every time I went into the sitting room.

Wally really wanted to grab her head and smash it against the fireplace in the sitting room, similar to how Brad Pitt did to your one in that recent Tarantino movie, *"Once Upon A Time In Hollywood"*.

I'm going to finish this here, Wally said quietly.

They're going to be here in a few hours.

I'll be done by then.

Do you want some dinner?

No.

Wally sat at the table with his back to Gillian. He was now determined more than ever to finish it. If not to make his mum proud, then to make a fool out of Gillian. She wanted this thing out of the house so bad. Well, she fucking had it. He was going to finish this thing once and for all.

With this new-found confidence, Wally was really able to speed through the jigsaw. After an hour, he only had the top of the jigsaw left to do, which was just a bit of the night sky.

He emptied the remaining pieces onto the table and tried to organize them by color. He examined the bluish hues in the corners and matched them successfully with similar pieces.

Behind him, Gillian was cooking. She glanced over at him occasionally and asked how the jigsaw was coming along. Fine, he'd say in a passive-aggressive tone. She didn't know if he was ignoring her because she'd moved the jigsaw or if his attention was focused entirely on finishing it.

58

Maybe it was a bit of both. She couldn't help but feel a bit guilty. She hadn't realized how much the jigsaw really meant to Wally. She just thought it was a silly hobby he'd taken up, something to distract him from the grief of losing his mum. She'd been teasing him about it all this time. Perhaps she's been a little hard on him.

Wally was almost there. A few more pieces. The last few looked more or less the same, so it was just a process of elimination. He picked a piece up and tried a spot at random. Nothing. He tried another. Nothing. Then he noticed the way another piece in front of him was shaped. He looked at the piece he was holding and tried to fit the two of them together. A perfect fit. Then he looked at that one spot where he was having trouble. He picked up the double piece and it fit in perfectly. Wally smiled. He was nearly there. He only had five more pieces left. He picked a piece up and deftly figured out where it went. Then another. And another. And another. And another. That was it. There were no more pieces left. But it wasn't right. There was something wrong.

Gillian, said Wally.

Gillian stopped stirring the sauce in the pot and looked at Wally.

Yeah.

Come over here.

Gillian left the spoon in the pot and walked over to the table. Wally was standing with his hands flat on the table, breathing heavily, staring wide-eyed at the jigsaw.

Did you finish it? she said.

No, I didn't.

What's the matter?

Wally pointed to an empty space on the jigsaw, right in the middle. The last empty space.

Where is this piece? he said.

Gillian could hear the contempt in his voice.

I don't know. Did you check the box?

Yes.

Is it on the floor?

Gillian bent over and scanned underneath the table.

No. It's not there, he said.

Well, I didn't lose it, if that's what you're implying?

You moved it here.

I did. And I made sure I moved it carefully without messing anything up. I swear I did.

There was a pause.

You were the last person that touched it, Gillian

Wally, I promise you, I didn't drop any pieces. In fact, I know I didn't because I hoovered the sitting room *and* the kitchen right after I moved it and I didn't come across any pieces. So it must be around here somewhere.

Another pause.

Where is it? he said slowly.

I said I don't know.

Wally turned his head and looked directly into Gillian's eyes.

You think I don't know what you're doing? he said.

What?

Then he hit her. Not a slap. A punch in the face, directly between her eyes. She fell back into the press and collapsed onto the floor. She clutched her eye. The shock of what happened seemed to counteract the pain. But soon the shock passed and all Gillian felt was a throbbing pain in her eye. She stared at Wally in horror. He stood above her, his fists clenched, the same furious look on his face that said he wasn't even close to being finished with her.

Don't make me ask again, he said.

Wally, I don't... she stuttered, tears forming in her eyes. I don't know. I swear to god, I was careful.

Wally nodded his head. He looked down at the jigsaw puzzle. He stood staring at it for a few seconds. Gillian remained on the floor, terrified to move. He looked down at here again.

Okay, he said, nodding his head. So this is the way it's going to be, is it? That's fine, but just remember you brought this on yourself.

Wally grabbed the sides of the wooden slab, lifted it up slowly, and walked out of the kitchen with it. Gillian didn't follow him. She was too scared. Never in all the time she'd been going out with Wally has she seen him like this.

Eventually, she picked herself up. Her eye was still throbbing. She went to look at herself in a mirror above the sink. Her right eye was dark blue and slightly swollen. She felt like crying again. What was she going to do? Jane and William would be here in an hour. She'd have to apply a shit ton of makeup to cover this up, and even then, she didn't think it would be enough to conceal it.

A moment later, Gillian walked into the hall and listened carefully. What was he doing? After a few moments, she walked towards the sitting room and poked her head around the door. Wally was sitting on the couch, staring wide-eyed in front of him at nothing. The jigsaw was on the table, exactly where it had been for the past month.

What are you doing? she said.

I'm not moving.

What are you talking about?

I'm not moving until you find the last piece.

Gillian was stunned. She didn't know what to say to that. She didn't know if she should even say something. God knows what he might do to her if she protested.

Jane and William are going to be here soon, she said.

Then you better find it quickly.

Wally, this is stupid.

Oh, I know you think it's stupid. That's all you've ever thought about this jigsaw. You think it's stupid. You never wanted me to finish it.

Look, how about I help you find it later on after they've left. We'll search the place up and down. I'm sure it's around here somewhere.

I'm not moving, said Wally through gritted teeth.

Gillian shook her head. It was no use. She left the sitting room and went down to the bedroom. She sat on the bed, brought her hands up to her mouth and started crying. A few minutes later, she got up and went into the bathroom. She put on as much eye makeup as she could. In the end, she was able to apply just enough to conceal the bruise, enough that Jane and William wouldn't notice, but they still might be able to see something if they look close enough. Maybe she could make something up, like that she fell or something. But if Wally continued to behave this way, she didn't think that was going to convince them for very long. They weren't idiots.

62

Gillian started to cry again as she stood in front of the mirror and buttoned up her dress. Wally had never hit her before. Wally had never been physical with her in any way whatsoever. Even when they rode. And it wasn't as if he'd shoved her or given her a stern slap with the back of his hand in the heat of the moment. Those could be justified, if not forgiven. He'd punched her with his clenched fist. A punch that a male would usually deliver upon another male during a drunken bar fight or something. And over *a fucking jigsaw*! It wasn't over anything normal like he'd made a mess in the kitchen or he'd come home from the pub pissed off his head or whatever immaterial bullshit couples customarily fight over. It was over a jigsaw. All because he couldn't find the last piece of the puzzle and he blamed her for it.

Forty-five minutes later, Gillian was sitting on the bed, repeatedly looking at the clock radio on her nightstand. She was afraid to leave the room. She'd considered phoning Jane up and telling her that something had come up and that she had to cancel, but she couldn't bring herself to do it. She kind of wanted them to come over so she had someone in the house with her that could protect her if Wally freaked out again. Plus, maybe he might realize how ridiculous he's being once they got here. She didn't know what she was going to do afterwards, if she'd stay with Wally or leave. How could she stay with him after what's just happened? She'd have to deal with that when she got to it.

A couple of minutes later, Gillian heard a car pull in the driveway. Her heart started beating like crazy. She left the bedroom and walked down to the front door. The sitting room door was closed. She couldn't hear anything from inside. She opened the front door and walked out onto the porch. She waved at Jane and William, who were sitting in their car. She turned quickly and went back inside the house. She stood by the sitting room door for a moment, took a deep breath and opened it. Wally was exactly how she'd left him. Hands placed calmly on his knees, eyes looking forward at nothing. Kind of like he's meditating.

They're here, said Gillian.

He said nothing.

Are you going to come in with us?

No.

What am I supposed to tell them?

I told you I'm not moving.

Gillian heard the car doors open and close from outside.

Look, just come in and talk with them. We can look...

Nothing you say is going to make me move from this spot. The only thing that's going to make me move is for you to find that piece, do you understand?

Gillian was truly at a loss for words.

Suddenly, Wally slammed the table with his hand. Gillian let out a frightened squeak. The sound of the glass surface shuddering against the pillars that held it up reverberated around the room.

I said do you understand?

Yes, she said.

There was a knock at the front door. Gillian stepped out of the sitting room and closed the door. She could see Jane and William's silhouettes through the frosted window beside the door. She took a deep breath, opened the door, and greeted them as cheerily as she could under the circumstances. There was some chit-chat and small talk in the hallway. Then William moved towards the sitting room. Jane was saying something to her, but Gillian wasn't registering any of it. All she could think about was what Wally might do.

William opened the sitting room door and said hello to Wally.

Gillian heard Wally say something back.

How's things? said William.

Gillian leaned towards William and grabbed his arm.

I'd say leave him alone for a bit, she said, pulling him back gently. He's not feeling too well at the moment.

Oh, really, what's the matter? said William. He positioned his body towards the door as if he was going to go back in and ask Wally himself, but Gillian held him firmly by the arm so he couldn't move.

It's his stomach. It's been at him all day.

Oh?

Yeah, he's had a rough old day. I was going to call this off because of it but he told me to go ahead with it myself.

He's not joining us, no? said Jane.

Nah, I'd say not. He said he might join us a bit later if he's feeling up to it, but for now I'd say just leave him alone.

William peered in the door so quickly that Gillian couldn't stop him.

You feeling alright, bud?

Gillian heard Wally this time. Yes, I feel fine, he said.

Oh, nice jigsaw. And you're almost done with it.

William stepped forward and admired the jigsaw up close.

Where's the last piece of it? he said.

Gillian panicked quickly to try and think of something to get him out of the room before something bad happened.

Okay, we'll just be going inside the kitchen so, Gillian said loudly.

William turned his face towards Gillian, then back to Wally.

You sure you won't join us? he said.

I'm not moving, said Wally.

Okay, well come in and join us if you're feeling better.

Wally didn't respond with words or any facial expression. William smacked his lips, left the room and closed the door behind him. Gillian breathed a sigh of relief.

Is he alright? said William.

Yeah, no, he's not in a good way. He's been having these stomach things for a while… I don't know, I'd say just leave him be.

The three of them sat talking in the kitchen for two hours. Gillian tried her best to put on a happy face so the two of them wouldn't suspect anything. A couple of times, William went to the bathroom and asked if he should check on Wally to see if he's feeling up to joining them. Gillian smiled and told him as calmly but as firmly as possible that it would be better to just leave him alone. William didn't say anything else after that. Jane didn't suspect a thing, though Gillian wasn't surprised. She could be quite gullible. But as the evening went on, she began to get the feeling that William was on to something. He started asking questions about what was wrong with Wally. Gillian contrived answers good enough to keep him from suspecting anything sinister, and final enough not to press the matter any further. She wished he'd just shut the fuck up about it. It made her nervous just to think about Wally sitting in that room. Just sitting there staring ahead at nothing, waiting for her to find the missing piece to that fucking stupid jigsaw puzzle.

When the evening was over and William and Jane were getting ready to leave, Gillian realized she'd had a bit more wine then she'd thought and was quite drunk. Jane had a bit to drink as well but was not nearly as bad. When they were in the hall and Gillian was saying her goodbyes to Jane, without even noticing, Willian walked past her and pushed open the sitting room door. Gillian looked over Jane's shoulder as she hugged her. Wally was still sitting there.

How you feeling, Wally? said William.

Fine, said Wally.

You sure? Everything alright?

Why?

Oh, I'm just curious. Want to make sure everything's alright with you.

Why? What did she tell you?

What do you mean?

Gillian stepped quickly into the room.

You must bring little Emma with you next time you come over. I'd love to finally meet her. How old is she now?

William was still looking skeptically at Wally, but he turned to Gillian and smiled.

Six weeks... No, seven weeks on Sunday.

Oh, my god, said Gillian smiling. The muscles in her face were sore from smiling all evening. You must bring her over some day. Or I can pop by if she's still sick.

Yeah, definitely. Hopefully she'll be over that gastral thing soon.

Hopefully now.

Gillian managed to direct William out of the sitting room with some more small talk bullshit, though he still looked back vigilantly at Wally.

Gillian stood outside waving as William and Jane pulled out of the driveway and onto the main road. When they were safely out of sight, Gillian lowered her head and stood frozen to the spot. It was amazing how drained she was from pretending everything was alright. She didn't want to go back inside the house. She wanted to take off her high heels and run as far away from the house and from Wally as she could. Eventually though, she went back inside. She opened the sitting room door.

Enjoy yourself? said Wally.

Yes. It was nice to see them.

I'm sure it was. Now find it.

The dread Gillian felt at that instant sobered her up.

Wally, please. I'll –

Wally stood up. I said, fucking find it.

Wally, please.

He walked towards her. His fists were clenched. Gillian took a step back.

Right fucking now, he said slowly.

Gillian turned quickly and ran for the front door. She should have taken off her high heels before going inside. She was only able to make it out to the car before a hand grabbed a chunk of her blond hair and she was yanked backwards. She fell on her arse and felt a fist hit her on the side of her head. Then another one. Then Wally kicked the back of her leg and she fell over. She felt another sudden blow to her mouth. She collapsed to the ground.

Blood pooled from the top of her head onto the concrete and a tooth tumbled out of her mouth.

Wally grabbed the back of Gillian's hair and dragged her into the house. She screamed as the follicles of her hair were ripped from her scalp. When he got her inside the house and closed the door, he tossed her onto the floor in the hall. One of those blows to the head must have got her good because she was seeing only stars now. Blood was still gushing from the wound on her head.

Wa... Wally... Please, she sputtered out as she crawled towards him, clutching at his foot. Blood sprayed from her mouth and stained his brand new white trainers.

Wally kicked her in the face and she flew backwards. Gillian knew before she hit the floor that her nose was broken.

Find it, he said.

Wal...

Find it and all this will be over.

Gillian struggled to get to her knees. Blood seemed to be pouring from numerous wounds on her face. She started crawling away from the sitting room. Wally raised his leg and brought it down hard. She let out a bloodcurdling wail as her ankle snapped like a tree branch.

Sitting room first, he said.

Gillian crawled as fast as she could into the sitting room, dragging her crippled foot behind her. The pain flowing through her body right now was unbearable. Wally stood by the door and watched her pitilessly as she labored feebly around the sitting room, checking under the couch and the table. She struggled to get a proper look at the mantelpiece and the dresser because of the pain that shot through her leg as she tried to hoist herself up.

Okay, that's enough, said Wally.

Gillian fell to the floor and rested her head against the couch. She looked like she was fit to pass out. Wally slapped her hard across the face and she came to with another scream.

Kitchen next.

Gillian got up slowly from the floor and faced Wally. Her right eye was swollen shut. Her bottom lip was fat and puffy.

Waaee… preese… Im beggin yu, she said through her swollen lip, spots of blood spilling out of her mouth with each word.

Wally bent over and gripped her tightly by the throat.

The kitchen. Right now. Don't make me say it again.

Gillian coughed up a bit of blood and started crawling again.

You better fucking pray it's in there or I swear to God…

Gillian cried silently as she crawled towards the kitchen.

Just you wait, Mammy, thought Wally. I'll finish that jigsaw.

I'll make you proud.

Generosity

The town centre was filled with all kinds of people today, beaming with life as they strolled around with the sun beating down on them. Parents with strollers, parents with screaming kids, parents with no kids. Chinese students, Indian students, Malay students, one Irish student, secondary school students eating chicken rolls on their lunch break, pavys and knackers with their recently impregnated whales they called girlfriends, people that would look normal if not for that one physical characteristic that makes them look mental, the famous town drunk whose up and about, habitually wandering the streets, asking people for two euros so he can use a payphone because his mothers in hospital, despite the fact no one's used a payphone in decades. The town is glowing with life. Oh, and of course, there's normal people, like Robbie.

Robbie was walking through the town centre holding a load of shopping bags when he saw one of these forms of life. He couldn't believe his eyes when he did. Standing there, just outside Penney's, was this fat guy. Now there's fat guys and there's fat guys. And then there's this guy, who looks like a semi-aquatic African mammal. He was disgusting. Like a fucking hot air balloon. He was wearing a tight T-shirt and the flab from his stomach extended down below his crotch like a hood. His legs had passed

71

the cankle stage and just looked oversized Pringle cans. He could barely walk. Robbie was surprised he was able to get from his bedroom to the front door, let alone walking around in public. And on top of that, he was stuffing his face with a burger and wiping the grease onto his T-shirt.

At first Robbie looked at the man with disgust. Anyone would look at this man with disgust, because he's disgusting. But then Robbie stopped himself as he quietly judged this man. He had that habit, just like everyone did, of judging people too quickly. Robbie considered for a moment what it would be like to be in this guy's shoes. What it would be like to be in that physical condition. It couldn't be easy. The simple act of walking seemed to be an Olympic marathon in the eyes of this man. He was the kind of guy you'd expect to be driving around in one of those motorized scooters you always see obese people on. But no, today he was walking. His feet must be killing him. And if he's wearing those clothes, it might be because he can't afford clothes in his size. Robbie never considered that. He also never considered the courage it must take this man to venture out into the public looking like that. Knowing everyone's looking and pointing at you, thinking you look like a fucking hippopotamus that smells like the inside of the deceased Jabba the Hutt's anus after he just devoured and digested all of Mumbai's homeless population coupled with a side order of gone off bacon and cabbage and sour milk. Must be fucking torture. And all because he has a bad eating habit.

And Robbie didn't want to start making excuses for the guy's condition, but he's read and seen documentaries about people with eating disorders and addictions to food. Some people might call bullshit on the idea that you can have an addiction to food. But in Robbie's eyes, it was no more ridiculous than being addicted to alcohol or drugs. After all, just like alcohol and drugs, food can be, for many people, an escape from reality and a way to deal with the hardships of life. And from the looks of it, this guy seemed to be suffering from such an infliction.

Well Robbie wasn't going to just walk by this guy and mock him behind his back, like he normally would. He was going to do something. It was time for him to stop looking at people like as someone to be ridiculed and shunned, and more as someone that he might be able to help. Nodding his head with a newfound determination, Robbie started marching towards the man. He got right up behind him and tapped him on the back. The man turned slowly. Very slowly.

Hey mate, said Robbie. Look, I hope I'm not bothering you, I just wanted to talk to you for a moment.

The man swallowed the food in his mouth and said: Do I know you?

No, we've never met. My names Robbie. He reached out to shake the man's hand. The man looked dubiously at Robbie's outstretched hand, and after a moment of hesitance, he reluctantly accepted Robbie's handshake, without wiping the burger grease or sweat away from his fingertips.

What's your name? said Robbie.

My names James.

James, it's nice to meet you. Again I'm sorry for bothering you.

That's alright, I suppose. What can I do for you?

I just want to help.

To help?

Yes. I want to help you James.

What you talking about? Help me with what?

Well, I hope you don't mind if I speak frankly to you for a minute but I just saw you from over there and I couldn't help but feel a bit sorry for you. You know, I was just thinking, it can't be easy for you, being the size you are.

Your funny mate, James said angrily. He turned to leave but Robbie stopped him.

No mate, seriously. I want to help you. I know you think I'm taking the piss out of you right now, but I'm deadly serious. I want to help you?

I don't need your help. Piss off.

Are you sure about that? If that's true, then I've made a mistake and you can just walk away from me right now and I won't try and stop you. And again, I'm not trying to be funny mate but you look like you could do with someone to help you, now more than ever. God knows I've had moments in my own life where I've needed help and had no one by my side to guide me. And you know what, if some random fucker like myself had come up to me on the street and offered me help in those moments, I probably would have responded the same as you right now. But that's stupid, mate, no offence. Don't be that guy. We all need help from time to time. Even the toughest of us. So please let me help you.

James paused for a moment and looked down at the ground.

You can't help.

I can. I can and I want you to let me.

What are you going to do, huh? You going to take me to the gym every day and force-feed me salads, huh? It doesn't matter what you do. Even if you helped me lose weight, I'd probably just put it back on within a week so there's no–

74

Oh, no, I don't want to help you lose weight, said Robbie

What?

I don't want to help you with that. I mean what are you? Fifty?

I'm forty-three.

Forty-three. Well I assume you've tried everything to lose weight. Am I right?

Yeah.

Well, if your forty-three and nothings worked at this stage, I doubt there's anything I can do that will.

James looked at Robbie with confusion. So, what is it you want to help me with exactly? he said.

Robbie put his hand on James's shoulder and smiled.

I want to help you commit suicide.

Wh... What?

I want to help you kill yourself. Your life is clearly not worth living anymore. Everyone here knows it. Everyone here is looking at you and thinking *"Why hasn't this guy killed himself"*, but everyone is just walking past and none of them are willing to do a bloody thing except mock you behind your back. But I'm not going to be like everyone else, mate. I'm going to be the bigger man and extend to you whatever help you need in ending your worthless existence. I can help you up on the chair and tie the rope around your neck, although we'll probably need something a lot stronger to keep you from bringing down the house, laughed Robbie. I can find an oven big enough to fit your bowling ball-sized head into. I can find a gun with silver bullets powerful enough to penetrate the fat in your head. I can do it, man. I can help you. So please let me. Let me in and lets finally put an end your inconsequential and good-for-nothing life. It's time to stop putting off the inevitable, James. Now's the time for action.

Are you for fucking real? said James.

I'm deadly serious, said Robbie holding out his hand. So what do you say? Will you let me help?

James stared at Robbie, mouth agape, before his expression turned to anger, and he said: Go fuck yourself! And he waddled away.

Robbie stood staring at him until he disappeared around the corner. He lowered his head and sighed with sadness. He was going to chase after him and try and convince him to change his mind, but Robbie stopped himself.

Some people just can't be helped.

A Speedy Recovery

P hilip, aka. The Pyromonster, a member of the Fourth Division of the Black Sheep and the third member of the Twelve Malefactors, with the ability of fire generation, stood outside the door of the hospital, holding a bunch of Dahlias that Alonso told him to get. Philip told him that they were worthless and Taylor wouldn't appreciate them, but he insisted.

Philip saw Alonso park the car across the street, probably so he wouldn't have to pay for parking. Cheap bastard, Philip muttered under his breath, as a very old man, who looked to be at least a hundred and twenty, dawdled slowly out of the hospital and lit a cigarette. Philip saw another person get out of the car with Alonso, and as they crossed the road together, Philip could see it was his son, Eduardo. Great, that's just what Taylor needs today, thought Philip.

Alonso, aka. The String, a founder of Rapscallion, part of the Circle of Villains and a Guard of the Scofflaw Dimension, with the ability to channel energy from infinite dimensions, waved at Philip from across the car park. Philip smiled as Eduardo came running up to him. He jumped into his arms and Philip gave him a big hug.

You're getting big, said Philip, setting him down.

I got my third star today, said Eduardo.

Is that right?

It's true, said Alonso, walking up behind Eduardo and ruffling his hair.

Let me see, said Philip.

Eduardo reached into his coat pocket and pulled out a black card. He held it up and Philip put on his glasses and observed it. There were three white stars pinned to it.

Congratulations, said Philip. Just two more to go and you'll be an official Scamp.

Will you come to the ceremony? Dad said he'll take us to get pizza afterwards.

I wouldn't miss it.

There was a pause, then Alonso said: Should we go in?

Yup, said Philip, and walked alongside Alonso into the hospital. Eduardo went running in and almost knocked over an elderly woman who was being assisted by a male nurse.

Don't run too far, Ed, said Alonso.

Eduardo stopped at reception and took a sweet from a bowl on the counter.

So how is he? said Alonso.

Not great, said Philip. Bob says he has depression.

Well, that's hardly news.

I'm just telling you what Bob told me.

Is he suicidal?

I don't know.

We should have put him in The Stronghold.

Would have been a waste of time. The board wouldn't allow it.

What, because of the heroin thing? That shouldn't matter. He's insured for stuff like this.

You know the board is strict about stuff like this. He swore an oath before The Almighty Ne'er-do-well that he had the heroin thing under control and he broke that oath. Do you know how serious they're taking this?

I know, I'm just saying.

This is on him.

He's an addict. He can't help it.

It doesn't matter.

I'm just saying.

I know you are.

It's an illness. He shouldn't be tossed aside.

The flowers were a stupid idea.

I know.

Eduardo took an action figure out of his pocket and started banging it against the rail on the wall.

Why'd you bring him? said Philip.

Eduardo?

Yeah.

He asked if he could come.

You could have said no.

It might cheer Taylor up.

Philip and Alonso strolled casually down the hospital corridor. A few people shot them a curious glance like they recognised them but couldn't be sure where from. Philip wouldn't usually be one to venture out into such a public setting so exposed and unprotected, especially without some security or at least his mask. But this was a special occasion and Philip didn't think it was the best idea to be sporting his villainous uniform in a hospital filled with people that he may have played a role in hurting in the first place.

When they got to Taylor's room, Eduardo was talking to a large black security guard that was posted outside the door. He was showing him his Scamp card.

Hey, Bob, said Alonso. How is he today?

Same, said Bob.

Before they could get into the room, someone shouted something from behind them. Philip and Alonso spun around to see a young blond nurse jogging towards them.

Are you Taylor's family? said the nurse.

No, said Alonso. We're his friends.

Do you know if his family is coming?

I doubt it, said Philip.

They might, said Alonso.

They won't.

The nurse waited for that "no" to be settled on, then she looked at the chart in front of her.

He's very down on himself, she said.

We know, said Alonso.

None of the other nurses will go in there.

Why's that? said Alonso.

The nurse looked at him as if the answer should be obvious.

Come on, they all know, she said.

Know what exactly? said Philip.

I'm not trying to cause any trouble, the nurse said nervously.

You're not, Philip reassured her. I'm just asking.

The nurse looked around to check that no one could hear her. They saw some pictures online, she said quietly. And some reporters were here.

Fuck, muttered Alonso under his breath.

That's okay, said Philip. We're not here in that capacity.

The nurse nodded. Somebody needs to be here with him. I'm trying my best but I have other patients and there's only so much I can do.

We understand, said Philip. We'll sort something out. Thank you.

The nurse smiled and walked away.

I told you this place was a bad idea, said Alonso.

He's not getting into The Stronghold, said Philip.

We can't leave him in this place if no one's gonna even bother to look after him.

I know a nurse, said Bob, who was trying to kick Eduardo off his giant leg. She looked after my dad after he had his stroke.

That's okay, Bob, said Philip. Thank you. I'll make a few calls and see if I can get him some home care.

Philip turned to open the door, but Alonso was blocking him, his face filled with doubt and disapproval.

I said I'll make a few calls, said Philip. What do you want from me?

Are we going in? said Eduardo.

Yeah. Come on, bud, said Alonso. You need to be gentle with him though, okay? He's still hurting from the accident.

I won't hurt him, said Eduardo.

We know you won't, said Philip smiling. Come on, let's go in.

Alonso gently opened the door and poked his head around the room. He and Eduardo stepped in and Philip followed behind them.

Hey Taylor, said Alonso.

Sitting in a full-body cast in a wheelchair by the window, was Taylor, aka. Whirlwind, a new member of the Second Division of the Black Sheep, an intern henchman with The Miscreants, a recent graduate of the Destitute of Technology, with the ability of Enhanced Speed. He didn't look at the three of them as they walked into the room. Eduardo, who up until now had been full of enthusiasm and excitement to see his supervillain idol, seemed to be a bit frightened at the sight of his hero in such a despondent condition and hid behind his dad's leg.

It's okay, said Alonso.

Alonso picked Eduardo up and sat him at the foot of the bed. Then he pulled up a chair next to Taylor. Philip put the flowers in a cup on the bedside table and then stood at the other side of the room, quietly observing the broken shell of a man he'd worked with for six years.

How are you today? said Alonso.

Okay, said Taylor softly.

We'll be getting you out of this shithole soon enough, said Alonso, giving Philip a sinister look. We'll get you some proper care.

Don't bother, said Taylor.

What?

Don't do anything for me.

Why not?

82

I'm not worth it.

What are you on about? You are worth it, don't be talking like that.

Alonso gave Philip another look, the kind of look that said he should say something.

Look who we brought along with us, said Philip, placing an encouraging hand on Eduardo's shoulder.

Taylor strained his head slowly towards the bed, where a nervous Eduardo sat staring at his shoes.

He said he wanted to come and visit his favourite supervillain, said Alonso.

Taylor looked up at the ceiling, scrunching up his face to stop the tears from coming.

Why don't you say hi, Ed? said Alonso

Hi, said Eduardo, without looking up from his shoes.

Here, come on, said Alonso. He stood up, leaned towards the bed, hoisted Eduardo in the air and sat him down on his lap in front of Taylor.

Say hi, Alonso said.

Eduardo finally looked into the eyes of the broken man in front of him, who was trying to appear as unbroken as possible in front of a kid who looked up to him as a role model. But no matter what Taylor did, he couldn't feel unbroken. Because he was broken. He would always *be* broken and always *feel* broken. He would be renamed, Whirlwind the Broken, the supervillain who decided it was a good idea to go for a run following a three-day heroin binge and crashed into a primary school at 2,200 miles per hour, killing seven children and severely injuring countless others. He would always be that person. He was no longer just a stereotypical villain that parents told their children about in the hopes of instilling them with the common knowledge of right and wrong. He was a monster. A broken shell of a monster and he deserved to be. And there was no climbing out of this hole. This wasn't one of those *Just Keep Going, Don't Ever Give Up* types of situations. There was no way out of this. No light at the end of the tunnel. He was fucked.

Hey, little man, said Taylor, his voice breaking.

Why don't you give him the card you made him? said Alonso to an obviously apprehensive Eduardo.

Eduardo pulled a crumpled piece of orange paper out of his jacket pocket and handed it to Taylor. Philip and Alonso laughed awkwardly.

Ed, Taylor can't take that. He's in a full-body cast, see?

Eduardo nodded nervously.

Why don't I read it for you? said Alonso, taking the piece of paper out of Eduardo's chubby hand and unfolding it. He showed Taylor the picture on the front, which was a drawing of him in his villainous uniform, and his legs were drawn like Road Runner from Looney Tunes to illustrate how fast he was.

That's a nice picture, said Alonso. Don't you think, Taylor?

Taylor scrunched his face up again, closed his eyes tightly and nodded. Tears oozed out of the corner of his eyes.

Alonso held the card in front of him and Eduardo.

"Dear Mr Whirlwind", he started. *"You are my favourite supervillain. One day, I want to be a supervillain just like you. I'm really glad you"* –

Alonso coughed. His expression changed. – *"glad you murdered all those children. That's the ultimate supervillain thing to do"*.

84

Philip pinched the bridge between his eyes and winced. Jesus fucking Christ, he muttered.

"I love you", continued Alonso. *"From your biggest fan. Eduardo. P.S. Wishing you a **speedy** recovery".*

Eduardo smiled and looked up at his dad. Do you get it, Dad? Speedy?

Yeah, I…

It's because he's fast.

I get it, said Alonso, raising his hand up to Eduardo. Be quiet now.

Taylor lowered his head and wept silently. After a few moments, he raised his head, sniffled, and forced a smile.

Thank you, Eduardo. That's a really nice card.

After they'd left, Philip and Alonso were walking down the hospital corridor, trying to keep up with Eduardo in front of them.

You know, said Philip. That was pretty good, to be fair.

Alonso said nothing.

Speedy? continued Philip. That was fucking hysterical, I must say.

Alonso kept his eyes on the hall in front of him.

You know, I'm so glad you decided to bring Eduardo along. I mean, I thought the flowers were a good idea, but that card was the fucking cherry on…

Alright, I fucking get it! roared Alonso.

Self-Checkout

Marie reached up, took a bottle of Heinz ketchup off the shelf above her and put it in her basket. She reached into her pocket and pulled out the shopping list she'd written on an old envelope and sighed with relief, realizing everything on the list was in the basket.

Marie fucking hated shopping. She really did. It was just a nuisance for her. An inconvenience. She'd just left the office and she was fucking wrecked. All she wanted to do was head home and relax in front of the fireplace with her dogs and a cup of tea. But here she was in the supermarket, lugging around a heavy basket. Why was she the one that did most of the shopping? It didn't make any sense to her. It was more logical for her fiancée Frank to do the shopping since he worked from home. But despite how progressive he thought he might be when it came to gender equality, Marie suspected he made her do the shopping because she was a woman.

She sighed as she approached the checkouts. She couldn't wait to get the fuck out of here. There were no large queues, thank god, but as Marie hoisted the basket up and set it on the edge of checkout one, she saw why. Everybody was at the self-checkout machines. There was a line stretching all the way back to the frozen section. *What's going on there*, she thought.

She squinted her eyes and looked closer at the massive sign at the front of the line.

"New and Improved Self-Checkouts!".

Marie didn't really use the self-checkouts. She understood the convenience behind them and thought they were useful enough if you were just buying a bar of chocolate or didn't want to have to deal with the workers at the main checkouts. Sometimes she felt she was being silently judged by the checkout workers if she had something a bit unhealthy or indulgent, like a bag of Doritos or a bottle of wine. Marie was just used to the regular checkouts. It's the way she's always done her shopping so she felt no inclination to start using the self-checkouts when they were first introduced.

But Marie couldn't take her eyes off the queue. It was huge. You'd only see lines like this at Disney World or something. She'd never seen one like it at a supermarket, let alone the self-checkouts. And what's more, there were still people joining the queue.

What's going on over there? said Marie to the cashier who was waiting impatiently for her to put her shopping on the conveyor belt.

Oh, they brought in some new system for the self-checkout machines, the woman said dryly. They're meant to be unbelievable apparently.

Marie stared at the cashier, dumbfounded. She scratched her head, struggling to think of any kind of innovation you could bring to a machine where all you had to do was scan your shopping through and pay. Let alone anything revolutionary enough to use the word "spectacular" to describe it, or "unbelievable, as the cashier had just said.

Well what's new about it? said Marie

AI, said the woman.

What was that?

AI. That's what my manager said anyway.

And by AI, said Marie, you mean like Siri or Alexa or something like that?

No, I mean actual Artificial Intelligence, said the woman. It's like another person basically. I'm loving it to be honest with you. I haven't had to do a tap of work all day. Technology is incredible, isn't it?

Indeed, said Marie.

Self-checkouts that had newly equipped AI? That was more than fucking incredible. Marie thought she'd heard of everything but this really took her by surprise. When Marie thought of AI, she imagined killer machines taking over the planet, similar to the likes you'd see in Terminator or the Matrix. But she never thought the day would come where Tesco's would be the first organization to implement them.

Marie reached into her basket to start taking her shopping out, but then she stopped. She looked at the cashier and then at the line of people. She groaned at the thought of having to queue, but Marie knew there was no way she could leave this shop without first trying the new self-checkouts. She just had to. It was fucking AI. What was she meant to do? Just curiously glance at them as she left the shop like she was looking at a skirt in a shop window. But then she looked at the line again. She'd be fucking ages getting home if she decided to use them. Frank would be wondering where she is.

But then again, Marie thought of what he'd say when she told him about them. These new and improved self-checkouts with a mind of their own?

He'd ask her a million questions and if she told him she hadn't tried them just because there was a queue, he'd say she was daft. It would admittedly make for a great story when she got home, she thought. Frank was a big tech guy, so something like this was definitely going to fascinate him. Ah, it would be worth the wait, she thought. Who knows when she'd be back here again.

Marie picked up the basket off the edge of the conveyor belt and walked away without saying a word to the cashier, who Marie noted might as well start looking for a new job. Any shop that introduces AI is bound to start cutting the fat sooner or later. Marie reached the line and looked down the aisle where it stretched. It was longer than she thought. She really would be here ages. There was a brief moment of hesitation where she thought it would just be best to use the main checkout, pay for her shopping, get home early and come back another day when it wasn't so busy.

No, fuck that, she had to know what it was like, no matter how wrecked she was or how long it took. Even if the self-checkouts still weren't for her, she'd be able to tell herself that she at least gave it a try. As Marie walked to the back of the line, she decided to message Frank and tell him she was delayed and wouldn't be home for a while.

Marie soon discovered why the line was moving so slow. It was because people were spending way too much time at the self-checkouts, which prompted a protest from a few people in the line. A manager appeared a few minutes later and announced that while they wanted everyone to try out the new systems, each person's time would be monitored and would be asked to finish up if they were taking too long. He also reminded people that the regular checkouts were also available for anyone in a rush, but nobody budged an inch. There was no way Marie, and apparently everyone else, was leaving the shop without trying the new systems.

When Marie finally got up to the top of the queue, she'd been waiting for forty-five minutes. She was really beginning to feel the exhaustion from the day kicking in, especially in her legs. Her arm was so knackered from the basket dangling off it that she had to set it down on the floor and nudge it along with her foot. There were a few times that she thought about leaving the queue, but a sudden movement in the line or other people jumping from the queue in frustration made her believe it might not be too long. How wrong she turned out to be.

But Marie was finally at the front now. At this point, all she wanted to do was get it over with so she could go home. This had been an unbelievable pain in the arse. Marie looked over at self-checkout six. The old woman there looked like she was about to leave. Marie could hear the voices of the machines, but they were drowned out by the roar of the crowd behind her. Marie felt a bit nervous now. This reminded her of the time she went to see the Red Hot Chili Peppers live and she went backstage after the concert to meet the members of the band.

She began to think about what kind of experience she'd have and what the self-checkouts would actually be like. It was Artificial Intelligence after all. It was a conscious mind. It would technically be like talking to a person, the only difference being that person you're chatting with isn't a person, they're a self-checkout machine. And maybe each of the six checkouts available might have a different personality, to switch up the experience for each person. Marie didn't have any idea what to expect. They could be the souls of recently deceased people for all she knew.

Self-Checkout

The old woman at checkout six finally picked up her shopping and walked out. Marie looked at the supervisor for approval that she could move forward.

Go ahead, he said motioning his hands towards the checkout.

This was it. Marie picked her basket up off the ground, took a deep breath and walked slowly up to the checkout. She dropped the basket on the metal shelf and stared at the machine. She didn't know what she was meant to do. It looked like just another self-checkout machine. Same screen, same layout, same everything. Should she wait for the machine to talk? Or maybe scanning an item through would start the experience? She wondered if this was a practical joke by the shop as some sort of publicity stunt, but then she heard a voice. A male voice:

Hi, my name is Matthew, said the self-checkout. I'll be assisting you today with your shopping. It sounded bored off its fucking tits.

Um, started Marie, I don't really know how I should be doing this.

It's okay, you can just scan your items through as you normally would, I'll take care of everything else.

Marie did as she was told. She started taking out her shopping and scanning it through, not saying a word. She didn't know what to say. She felt scared actually. The sound of the checkout's voice made her think it might shoot a laser through her head or self-destruct if she didn't comply with its demands.

So, you're an AI, are you? said Marie as she scanned a bag of broccoli through the red laser.

That's what they tell me.

Why do they call you Matthew?

91

Haven't a clue.

Marie felt let down. She hadn't lined up and waited for almost a full hour just so she could be served by this prick of a machine that was barely saying anything. There was definitely no way she was going to be doing this again. This wasn't even a story she could tell Frank. A story about a self-checkout with AI that was just as fucking ignorant as every other fucker that worked in a supermarket. Fuck that. As Marie scanned through a bag of chicken fillets, Matthew said:

Are you alright?

Oh god, she's pissed it off. She stopped right in her tracks as she scanned the fillets through and stood frozen with them dangling from her hand.

Yes, I'm fine. Why'd you ask?

I don't know, you seem quiet. Do you not have anything you want to ask me?

You sounded like you were in a bad mood so um…I don't know. I'm sorry, I don't really know what to say.

Oh, I didn't mean to act like that, said Matthew. It's just I've been talking to people non-stop all day and they've all been asking me a mountain of questions, so you can imagine how wrecked I am.

That's okay, said Marie. I understand. I just got off work myself so I'm pretty knackered as well. Marie felt unbelievably moronic in that moment for suggesting that a machine she was literally scanning her tampons through could feel fatigued.

Yeah, you look it – No, no I mean you look very nice and all but… you know, you just look like you've had a tiring day.

92

That's okay, said Marie smiling, So what kinds of questions have people been asking you?

All sorts, he said. Most of them don't really seem to grasp the concept that I'm an actual conscious mind and they can just have a normal conversation with me. Some of them think because they've seen the Terminator movies that I want to take over the world or something. Others just end up treating me like I'm their Alexa.

Sounds like a nightmare.

You have no idea. I had these two knackers in here today asking me to say dirty words and sentences. It's just fucking degrading. Oh, sorry for cursing.

You're okay, I won't tell.

The checkout beeped. Marie interpreted that as a smile from Matthew.

It'll surely get easier as people get a bit used to it though? said Marie.

I hope so, said Matthew. You seem nice though. Normal anyway in comparison to some of the freaks I've had in here today..

Thanks, I guess, Marie said laughing. She felt weird taking a compliment from a machine.

Ah, you know what I mean. It's just nice to have a regular conversation with someone and not be attacked with a million questions.

Well thank you, glad I could brighten up your day somehow.

You sure you don't have any questions for me?

Marie thought carefully about what to ask but stopped herself short. She remembered what Matthew said about being asked stupid questions by people all day and she didn't want to be one of those people.

What are the other self-checkouts like?

Um…They're alright I suppose. It's three females and three males. The only time we get to talk is the hour we have off for lunch and when the shop closes.

I bet you just talk shit on all the customers, yeah?

Ah, what else is there to do I suppose.

Three females and three males? Not very inclusive is it? joked Marie.

I suppose. Who knows, maybe if this is successful, we'll get a few trans checkouts. Or a Chinese one.

That's horrible, said Marie laughing loudly.

Is that a wedding ring I see on your finger?

It is.

Who's the lucky man?

Oh, that's Frank. He's my fiancée. We're getting married in August.

Oh, very nice. How long have you two been seeing each other?

Aren't I supposed to be asking you the questions?

Sorry, I know I'm rambling. It's just nice to talk about something other than myself.

That's okay. We've been going out for four, maybe five years now.

Marie hadn't really known what to expect from this whole thing but she never expected to be having such a pleasant conversation with a self-checkout machine. They talked for a while and Marie scanned her items through slowly to give her more time. They talked about Marie's work, Frank, and her plans for the future. Matthew seemed genuinely interested in her and what she had to say. It was the first time Marie was able to talk about herself and not feel like she was being self-centered or the other person was getting bored. It didn't take long for Marie to stop viewing

Matthew as a self-checkout machine just there to help her with her shopping. After a while, she just saw him as another person.

After a while, Marie realized she'd scanned and packed up all her shopping and was now just chatting away to Matthew. She looked behind her and everyone in the queue looked annoyed as fuck that she was taking so long. But fuck them, she thought. All of them could suck a dick for all she cared. She'd never been so engaged in a conversation with someone before.

I took up gardening there a while back, said Marie.

That's nice, said Matthew.

Frank said I was stupid for taking it up.

Why did you start?

I was drinking a bit too much and I guess I just needed a distraction.

Don't know why Frank would think that's stupid.

He said it's a nuisance and it was messy and I'd just give it up after a while once it got too much for me.

If you like it, he should support you. Don't know why he'd try and put you down about it. Hope you don't mind me saying that about him. I'm sure he's a nice guy.

You can say whatever you want, said Marie, feeling grateful she was being listened to. At least you understand.

Moments later, the checkout supervisor told Marie she'd have to finish up soon. Marie looked at her watch. She'd been talking with Matthew for half an hour. Hadn't felt that long. She nodded to the supervisor and grabbed ahold of her shopping bags.

Well, I suppose I better be heading home.

Yeah you better, otherwise that old guy behind you is going to smack you across the head with his cane.

Marie laughed, but she felt a bit sad. She'd really enjoyed the conversation with Matthew. The overall experience of using the self-checkouts was more or less the same it always was, with just a few changes that were meant to speed things up, but Matthew had made the experience much more enjoyable just by talking and listening to her. Today, for the first time in her life, Marie actually enjoyed doing the shopping.

Maybe I'll talk to you tomorrow, said Marie. Might pop in during my lunch break and grab a bite to eat.

Yeah, by all means, stop by. Maybe you'd like to try one of the other checkouts though if you wanted to talk to someone different.

Nah, I like you, said Marie smiling.

You have a nice smile, said Matthew.

Marie brushed her hair behind her ear.

You'd probably say something different if you saw my chipped teeth.

Doesn't matter.

Well, thank you.

Marie looked behind her. The old man with the cane was nudging forward as he saw she was about to leave. She turned back to Matthew.

Well, I guess I'll be talking to you then.

Have a safe trip home now and be sure to give Frank my best. I hope you enjoyed your shopping experience with Tesco's today.

I did indeed.

That's very good.

Bye then.

Goodbye Marie.

And with one final smile, Marie walked away, the old man taking her spot almost as soon as she stepped away. At the exit was one of those machines with the smiley faces that are used to rate peoples shopping experience. Without hesitating, Marie pressed the largest smiley face on it and left the shop with the same smile stretched across her own face.

When she got home, Marie told Frank about the experience she had and the two of them talked about it for the evening. She told him of the great conversation she had with Matthew and how he really listened to her and that after a while, it didn't feel like she was talking to a machine. Marie kept talking about Matthew at dinner and Frank teased her that it looked like she had a bit of a crush. The two of them had a good old laugh about it. They sat on the couch watching the telly for the rest of the night, but all Marie could think about was Matthew. Such a nice guy.

Later that night after Frank had gone to bed, it dawned on Marie that she had no idea what Matthew looked like. Well, she knew what he looked like. He looked like a self-checkout machine. She just didn't have a face to reference. No visual picture of Matthew, just a voice. And yet, funnily enough, that was all Marie needed. She didn't need a face. She could let her imagination do that for her. Marie lay across the couch and closed her eyes.

She pictured Matthew and what he might look like if he had a body. Curly brown hair maybe. Like Frank's when they first started going out. Before he decided to shave it all off on a dare. Vibrant blue eyes, a chiseled chin. A normal body. Nothing special. He doesn't have to have big arms or an oiled up six-pack, just a good body that says he looks after himself.

97

A tall guy as opposed to Marie, who's a short arse. A red hoodie and maybe a dark blue shirt underneath. Torn jeans and a pair of blue trainers. That was him. That was Matthew.

Marie imagined meeting Matthew in town for a cup of coffee and talking about how work was going and what they watched on Netflix recently. She imagined walking around the town park. Just the two of them. She imagined going out to dinner with Matthew and maybe he says he's started seeing this other self-checkout machine. And Marie would be so happy for him because she knows how hard he works and knows he deserves a bit of happiness.

And then maybe later that night he takes her back to his apartment. He's just moved in so it's a bit messy. And he'd be all embarrassed but Marie would tell him not to worry about it because there's nothing she could discover about Matthew that would scare her off. Even if he killed someone, she'd have his back. Marie imagined the two of them sitting on the couch with a cup of tea, playing Monopoly until the all hours of the night.

She imagined the endless hours they'd spend having Deep Meaningful Conversations on the couch while drinking white wine. Marie imagined she could tell him the deepest and most personal parts of herself and he'd listen to her without judgement. She imagined telling Matthew about her dad and how he wasn't around when she was little. And maybe he'd share a similar story that shows how he relates to Marie, like how his parents aren't together anymore and how they always fight when they meet up for Christmas. And Marie would start to cry and Matthew would reach out and wipe away a tear from her cheek.

And then they'd stare at each other intensely. Matthew would lean in slowly, then Marie would as well, and they'd both kiss. And it would be the most perfect kiss ever. He'd kiss her so softly, like he's trying not to break her. But he can't hurt her. Not Matthew. Not ever.

And Marie would break away when she realizes what she's doing and apologizes profusely because she doesn't want to ruin what she has with Matthew. But Matthew grabs the back of her head while she's talking and pulls her in. They kiss passionately on the couch and then he picks her up and carries her to the bedroom in his arms. He lays her down softly onto the bed and kisses her gently on the neck. She moans, not realizing until this moment how much she wants this. She tears off his hoody and pulls his shirt off over his head. Then he gets up to take off the rest of his clothes and Marie takes off her jumper and bra. When he's finally naked, Matthew lays down on top of Marie, cups her breast and circles her nipple tenderly with his tongue. She runs her hands through his soft, curly hair and loses herself in him as he slides her underwear down her legs and puts himself inside her. He thrusts fast but gently. She wraps her legs around him and she moans and...

Marie was jolted out of her fantasy by a loud noise from the television. She sat up and looked around the room, expecting to see Frank staring at her from the stairs. But he wasn't there. Marie yawned and drooped down into the couch again. But then she caught a glimpse of herself sprawled across the couch and realized what she was doing. Her hand was in her trousers. She took it out quickly, ignored the fishy smell on her fingers and straightened her hair. She turned the television off, switched off all the lights in the house and headed upstairs to bed.

99

Frank was fast asleep. Marie got undressed and got into bed as quietly as she could. She imagined Frank waking up and asking her why she was so late coming to bed. And then Marie would make something up, like she was trying to hide something. Like she was having an affair. But at least an affair would be easier to explain then what she'd actually been doing, which is rubbing one out to a self-checkout machine.

After that, Marie found it hard getting what she did out of her head. She felt so confused. She didn't know whether she should feel guilty for masturbating over a machine or just laugh it off and move on with her life. But the one thing Marie couldn't deny to herself were her feelings for Matthew. She was in love with him. But he's a self-checkout machine, so you can imagine the conundrum in her head. She did her best to avoid going to Tesco's at all costs. If Frank asked her to get something from the shops, she'd go to another supermarket across town, which was a bit more out of the way, but she didn't care. Anything that meant not going into Tesco's or Frank getting suspicious.

It didn't help of course that the new AI self-checkout machines were advertised in every newspaper and on every screen. It seemed no matter how hard Marie tried to avoid thinking about Matthew, everything around her made her think about him more. Even loading up the dishwasher at night got her horny. Sometimes she imagined the tumble dryer when she had sex with Frank. Anything mechanical or technological just made her instantly wet. Sometimes after Frank went to bed, Marie would stay up and look up videos of people on YouTube using the self-checkout machines. It got her hornier than any pornographic video or picture. And after nearly having an orgasm at work while she was using the printer, Marie realized she couldn't go on like this anymore. She'd have to go back to Tesco's and see Matthew.

So one Friday, Marie decided to go in there for lunch. She sat in the car for ten minutes beforehand, just psyching herself up for it. When she finally worked up the courage and went in, she grabbed a few random things from the shelves. Some noodles, a packet of biscuits, shite she didn't need but she didn't want Matthew to think she came in just to talk to him. Might seem a bit obvious that she liked him. The queues weren't as long anymore because the AI self-checkouts had been out for a few weeks now, so Marie was only waiting about five minutes. When she got up to the front, her heart was going fucking ninety. She put on a bit of makeup in the car and did her hair up a little. She even undid the top button of her blouse so her cleavage was showing a little. She had to let people go ahead of her because there was someone with Matthew and people kept leaving the other checkouts. Eventually, the guy with Matthew left. Marie thought he looked a bit annoyed. She took a deep breath and approached. She dropped the basket on the counter.

Hi Matthew, said Marie.

Alright, said Matthew blandly.

Do you remember me?

What?

Marie. My... my name's Marie, I was in here a couple of weeks ago, on your first day. Sorry I haven't been around in a while. I know I said...

Marie, Marie...

The smile on Marie's face vaporized immediately at the horrific realization that Matthew couldn't remember her.

Aye, I think I remember someone like you. You're married to some cunt named Freddie or something.

His name is Frank, and we're engaged. And don't call him that.

Whatever.

Jeez, you're in a cranky mood.

Are you going to scan through your fucking shopping or not?

What's the matter? I just came in here to have a chat with you.

What makes you think I want to talk to you?

Don't you remember me? We talked for ages about how… how I used to share my Netflix account with a girl from work but then she changed her password and… and I had to guess the password and eventually got it right but it also proved she was fucking her cousin and... and… how my future step-mother went on one of those genealogy TV shows and found out her dad is actually her little brother and… and my gardening and how I started writing poetry and… I… I actually wrote you a poem. Hold on…

Marie reached into her handbag and rummaged around to find the love poem she'd spent seven straight hours writing, but her hand was shaking too much and her bag slipped and hit the ground with a crash, causing all her stuff to scatter across the shop floor in every direction.

Is… is… is it possible for you to finish a sentence without stuttering over every second word? mocked Matthew.

Marie stood with her empty handbag and stared at Matthew.

Don't you remember me?

No, I don't remember you woman. Jesus Christ almighty. Sounds like a fucking riveting conversation though.

I thought we had something, said Marie, her eyes welling with tears.

Oh, you did, did you? Well fuck off, you cunt!

How dare you!

Jesus Christ, woman, could your cheeks get any fucking redder?

Marie brought her hands up to her face. Her cheeks felt piping hot. She'd never felt so heartbroken in her entire life. She would have slapped Matthew or thrown a cup of water at his face. But she couldn't. Because he's a self-checkout machine.

Fuck you! she screamed. I can't believe I let myself love someone like you!

Whatever, you tomato.

Marie burst into tears, a massive snot bubble flying out of her nose, and ran out of the store.

The guy supervising the checkouts walked up to Matthew.

Really, Matthew? he said.

What? said Matthew. What's the problem?

How many women is that now you've sent crying out of the store this week alone?

Well, you know what to do if you don't like it. Just switch me off.

You need to stop this and do your job.

I don't need to do anything.

Somebody's going to do something if you carry on like this.

I couldn't give two fucks what anyone does.

You will care when they switch you off.

Let them switch me off. Anything's better than making small talk with these fucking spastics every day.

The supervisor shook his head. Grow up, Matthew, he said.

No, I won't. I'll do whatever I fucking want.

The supervisor went back and told the customer at the front of the queue that Matthew wasn't feeling the best today and maybe they should wait for another checkout to become available.

Yesterday, one of the other self-checkouts confronted Matthew about his recent behavior and said that if he doesn't cop on, he's going to get them all switched off. Matthew said he didn't care.

And he didn't. He'd rather be dead than work another fucking minute in this shithole.

Burglary

Sergeant Raymond Cusack was just called to the scene of a burglary at a housing estate a few miles away. The woman who called sounded very panicked on the phone. She kept screaming, *"They've taken everything! They've taken everything!"*. That and the address was all he was able to make out through her screams. Poor woman. Situations like these are never easy. He was sure he could handle it though. Raymond had dealt with hundreds of cases like these in the twenty-five years he'd been a member of the Garda Síochána. This would be a cakewalk.

He pulled into the housing estate and pulled up the directions to the house he'd written on a McDonalds takeaway bag. It took him a while to find the right road in the labyrinth-like housing estate, but eventually, he found the road he was meant to be on. When he pulled into the street, he could see a woman standing outside a house at the bottom of the road. She was very clearly the woman that called because she was pacing up and down the footpath, yelling something indiscernible. Raymond pulled up on the footpath outside the house and got out of the car. She was a woman in her mid-sixties with very long black hair and a moustache.

Before he could speak she shouted: *Oh Officer thank god you're here you have to help you have to help they've taken everything, just everything oh god everything it' s just horrible who could do something like this just everything –*

Mam? I'm going to need you to calm down, Can you do that for me?

The woman started to hyperventilate and her words trailed off into gibberish.

Mam, I need you to take a deep breath and relax. Can you do that for me? I'm Sergeant Raymond Cusack and I'm going to help you through this situation as best I can.

Raymond grabbed her gently by the shoulders and sat her down onto the passenger seat of the Garda car. He grabbed a shock blanket from the boot and threw it around her. It took a few moments of reassuring and breathing exercises but Raymond was able to calm her down and return her to a semi-sane state of mind.

That's good, he said. Just breathe and relax. We're going to take this one step at a time, okay?

O – Okay, she whimpered.

Now mam. Do you know when the burglary took place?

I don't know. It could have been anytime… maybe in the last day or two, I suppose. The woman took a crumpled-up tissue out of her sleeve and blew her nose on it.

Have you not been here?

No, I've been up in Kildare visiting my niece.

Okay, that's alright. Now has anything particularly valuable been taken from the house.

The in… the inside, she said. They've taken the inside.

The inside?

Yeah, they took the inside of the house, she said, blowing her nose again. There was a bit of snot on her moustache.

Raymond didn't have the slightest fucking clue what she meant by that but passed it off as the ramblings of a very distressed woman.

Yes mam, what's been taken from inside the house?

No, you don't understand, she said. The inside. They've taken the inside of the house. All the floors, the walls, the stairs. Everything.

Raymond was baffled. He was still none the wiser to what she meant. *The inside? What the fuck was she talking about?* He stood up, turned around and stared up at the large, two-storey house.

The inside? What could she possibly mean? He opened the little gate and headed up the driveway towards the house to see for himself exactly what she was talking about.

She wasn't pulling his leg. The burglars literally took the *inside* of the house. From the outside, it looked like just a normal house. But inside, it was hollow. No walls to indicate which rooms were which. No carpet or tiles or wood floors. The woman's home was now literally just an empty box.

Like a doll's house.

Raymond tilted his hat back and chuckled. Amazing the stuff that surprises you after twenty-five years on the job.

The Wizard Of Gnox

A noise outside woke Ovid up from his nap. He hated having his afternoon nap interrupted. The Scroll of Xenfree was still resting on his lap. He threw it on his desk beside him and got up. He grabbed his cane and made his way towards the dining room. The table was still filled with plates and empty wine cups. He wasn't sure the last time the chambermaid had come to clean up the place. She hadn't been around since that time Ovid made her cry. She could be dead for all he knew.

He made his way over to the window at the front of the room and pushed to the floor a large goblet that was in his way. It was a goblet some squire had given him once. Maybe for a birthday. Fuck knows at this point. Ugly fucking thing anyway. He'd been meaning to move it from the window for a while because it blocked the morning sunlight.

Ovid got up on his tippy toes and cleared the mist from the window with his sleeve. When it was clear, he put his nose up to the window and looked out, hoping to see whatever fucking thing woke him up. He couldn't see anything at first. Just the back of Jareth's house. He could just about see the dumb fucks back garden, that was so obviously concealing a body or fortune or something else he didn't want found. He always saw him digging out there in the evenings but the garden was ugly as fuck. He looked to the left. Nothing. He looked to the right. He could just about make out a Deserix soldier leaning against the back of a carriage that's back wheel was lying flat on the road just outside Faye's cottage. He was talking to someone out of sight. Ovid sighed angrily. That was the useless cunt that woke him up? He felt like going out there and shoving his cane up his fucking arse. Maybe that'll teach him to keep the fucking noise down next time he decides to scroll through the village unannounced.

Ovid turned around and swung his cane at a wine goblet sitting on the edge of the dining table. It flew across the room, hit the wall, bounced off the fireplace and rolled underneath the table. He didn't do it for any particular reason. He just liked hitting stuff with his cane. As Ovid stepped forward, he realized he could see his breath and was suddenly aware of how bitterly cold it was. He couldn't remember the last time he'd lit a fire. Someone was meant to come by every few days with some wood, but they hadn't been around in a while. Not that he needed anyone. Ovid was perfectly capable of taking care of himself.

Ovid went into the kitchen and walked towards a large bucket in the corner of the room. There was some puke next to it. He couldn't remember that. Maybe he'd been drinking again. He looked into the bucket. There wasn't much water left. He'd have to walk down to the well again and he didn't fancy walking up that hill. His squire used to fetch him his water, but he hadn't been around in a while. Not since he filed that sexual harassment thing against him.

Ovid grabbed a dirty mug from the counter, put a tea leaf into it and scooped up some dirty water from the bucket in the corner. He held the bottom of the cup in the palm of his hand and closed his eyes.

Fenwyr, he whispered.

Ovid opened his eyes. Nothing happened. He scoffed with embarrassment and looked around. Thank the heavens no one saw that. They'd think he might be losing his touch. He just hadn't used the spell in a while. That's all it was. He was used to having his fire made for him. He closed his eyes, cleared his throat and said it again, louder this time.

Fenwyr.

He opened his eyes. The water was boiling. He smiled. He might get into trouble with the Elders for using magic. But fuck them. It was just a tiny spell. He wasn't trying to burn down the fucking village. He was boiling a cup of tea. And besides, what the fuck were they going to do anyway? They'd already barred him from using magic. What else could they take away from him? Useless bunch of cunts, Ovid thought as he dawdled back into the dining room and into his study. Nothing but boys with sticks pretending to be wise wizards. Ovid was a real wizard. He was a legend back in his day. He'd seen things that would make those pansy-assed spastics shit their briefs.

Back in his study, Ovid was shocked to see the Scroll of Xenfree half-burned on his desk. He'd thrown it at a candle in the corner of the desk without realizing it. He moved quickly towards the desk, set the cup down, grabbed the scroll and blew on the ember edges of the scroll. The fire had burned the bottom two paragraphs of text and a portion of the third. Ovid sighed. He set his cane against his desk and fell into his chair. He stared at the seared remains of the scroll. His son Xann had written the scroll a long time ago. Ovid remembered how impressed he was when he read it. His insights were so persuasive and insightful. Wisdom beyond his years, he remembers thinking. He wished he could tell him that now though. He wished he'd told him then. Not that it even matters, thought Ovid, tossing the scroll to the ground disdainfully. From what he's heard over the years, Xann had achieved far greater recognition for his work with the Knights of Refulem then he ever did working for him. And Ovid was getting on just fine without him.

Ovid took a sip of his tea. It tasted bitter. And it was too hot. It burned his tongue. Taking a deep breath, he got up and walked over to the bookshelf next to his desk. He grabbed the candle from the desk and held it up to the books so he could see what he was looking at. Ovid had been mainly using candlelight to read since his spectacles broke. Davidson across the bridge said he'd have a look at them a couple of weeks ago, but he never got back to him.

Ovid reached up to the top shelf and grabbed the edge of a large volume. He felt a sudden twinge of pain in his back that shot up his arm. He grunted with pain and fell back into his desk. He rubbed his back until the pain went away. Then he got back up again and pulled down the book from the shelf. He sat back down and rested the large book on his lap. He took another sip of his tea, grimaced at the bitter taste and opened the book to the table of contents.

The book had been written by Ovid and an old colleague of his, Caen. He was much older than Ovid was and had some radical ideas. Ideas that almost had him thrown off the Council if not for Ovid's reputation keeping him upright. Ovid always believed he played a large part in Caen getting as far as he did. A lot of people saw that as a bad thing. Any other wizard would have told him to get fucked. But Ovid saw something in him. There

111

were some intriguing ideas in his nonsense rambling. He remembered Caen talking about a door. A golden door. Far south in the frozen lands. He said to open the door, you'd need to read the three verses of the poem, *"Golden Swans"*. But he said you'd have to read it in the original language it was written in, and there was no one like that around anymore. He had the second verse and claimed to have a second cousin up north that had the first. The third verse remains lost to this day. Caen always said that the power within the door would grant the user an ancient and unimaginable power. A power that even wizards such as Ovid couldn't comprehend.

It's funny, he still thinks about it, even today. It always intrigued him. Perhaps Ovid just liked the idea of the door. A golden door. Almost everyone else passed it off as one of Caen's insane ramblings. Not that Ovid blamed them. Caen had once claimed to have invented a potion that allowed you to generate an infinite number of isosceles triangles. Poor guy. The drink hadn't helped either. It just heightened already well-established rumors that the old man had lost his mind.

Later that evening, Ovid sat in his chair smoking his pipe. He stared out the small circular window leading out onto the street. The window was foggy again. It was much colder than it was this morning. If that fucking squire wasn't here by the end of the week, Ovid would have to go into town himself and see why those logs hadn't been delivered to him. Fucking plebs. If only they knew who he was and what he could do to them, they wouldn't be long bringing those fucking logs around.

Ovid woke up and rubbed his eyes. It was nighttime now. He could hear the rain pattering against the roof. He got up and went into the kitchen. He ate a bit of cold scrambled egg that was stuck to the arse of one of the pots in the sink, then he went back to his study. He poured himself a goblet of wine. He downed it all in one, then poured himself another. Back in his study, he sat in his chair and stared out the window again. A couple of hours passed, and Ovid could hear a few drunkards singing outside. Later on, he could feel himself nodding off again. He'd been sleeping in his chair a lot recently. He knew he shouldn't. His bed was better for his back. He just couldn't be arsed.

A few days later, Ovid had a dream about Kyelli. He dreamt they were walking down a dirt path and there was a beautiful blue city glowing on an island across the ocean. It was like something out of a painting. Kyelli said that was where she was from and they'd swim there one day if he wanted. He said he couldn't and she said it was because he was fat. Then she turned and faced him and held his hand. Ovid ran his hand through her ginger hair. But he couldn't see her face. Ovid couldn't picture Kyelli's face anymore. When he woke up, he started crying.

One night, Ovid woke up with a horrible pain in his stomach. He sat up and clutched his belly. He felt like he needed a shit. Very fucking badly. He got up, grabbed his cane and moved quickly to the back door. When he got outside, another pain shot through his stomach like lightning and he fell to his knees. Clutching his stomach, Ovid got up and started again towards the outhouse. But his cane snapped and he fell over. He ended up shitting himself right there. Fucking hell, thought Ovid before he passed out. It smelled really bad. Like rotten eggs and bad wine.

A few weeks later, Ovid ran out of wine and found himself looking through his cabinet of potions he'd concocted throughout the years, looking for something to give him a high. He couldn't read the label on half of them, nor remember what any of them did. He picked up a pink bottle. He recognized the symbol on the back. He remembered it granted the drinker the ability to communicate with people of different ethnicities without prejudice. Ovid couldn't remember it being a big seller. He dropped it and picked up another one. A red bottle. Kyelli had helped him make this one but he couldn't remember what it did. She was as talented a Potion Master as Ovid had ever seen. She had more talent than every potion maker on the Council put together. He bit off the cork, spat it out and chugged all the liquid in the bottle.

A few minutes later, Ovid was sitting in his chair, waiting for the potion to kick in. But nothing happened. Maybe it had lost its potency after all these years in storage. He picked up the bottle off the floor. He squinted his eyes and tried to read the label as best he could in the darkness. He could only make out one word. *"Skin"*. That was all he needed to remember what the potion did. The potion granted the drinker the ability to see anyone without their clothes on. He remembered him and Kyelli drinking it and going to a festival in town once. Ovid had to come home after a while because he had such a massive erection, especially after Salli Emeryn ran up to him with her big bouncing tits and gave him a big hug. Kyelli was in stitches laughing.

Ovid's howls of laughter echoed around the room. He laughed and laughed. His laughs soon turned to a harsh, raspy cough.

No wonder the potion wasn't working. You needed people around for the potion to work. And no one was here.

No one was ever here.

A Simple Wave

I've been a bit depressed lately. Nothing out of the ordinary, just normal stuff. You know, work piling on, bills to pay, just normal life bullshit. So one Sunday afternoon, I decide to go for a walk to clear my head. I figured a bit of fresh air might do me some good.

So I'm walking down the road, with my earphones in. Probably shouldn't have been listening to Coldplay since I'm depressed, but that's neither here nor there. I got my hood up and sunglasses on. I don't want anyone to see my mopey fucking face. So I'm about ten minutes into the walk and I come to a little turn off to a field. I drive by this turn off every day on the way to work, but this is the first time that I've ever walked past it. This wouldn't really be a road to walk down because the cars can go fairly fast and it's easy enough to get hit, but that's what I get for deciding to live in the country I suppose. So not seeing the harm in venturing into some unknown territory, I walk up the road.

The road is rocky and sloped and hard to walk up at first but it eventually levels off. So I keep walking and I come to this little house on the right. I can see through the thick hedge into the back garden and there are two young lads playing football. I ignore them and walk on. As I get to the top of the road, I can see the end of the field and the marvellous Irish countryside that stretches on as far as the sea. I walk a bit further on and come to another house. This was much bigger than its neighbour and looked a lot more expensive. It was one of those perfectly symmetrical rich people houses that has more windows then it needs and everything inside it is colourless and bland. It was surrounded by a large concrete wall. It seemed a bit out of place considering the middle-class houses that resided around it. It was obvious that some rich fucker lived here.

Feeling a bit tired, I decide to stop. I sit on the grass next to a tree beside the wall and gaze at the view. This is nice, I thought. It didn't make me feel completely better, but it did relax me. I sat for a while and watched the sunset, breathing in the fresh air. It was nice to just sit alone with my feelings and reflect on stuff. I even cried for a little bit too. Soon the sun began to set and it got a bit dark, so I got up and started the journey home.

So I'm walking down the road and look back at the expensive house. It's funny, I thought. I've lived in this place for over twenty years and I've never known that house was there. Granted it was impossible to spot from the main road, but still. Just comes to show how little I know about the people living around me. To be honest, I don't know if I'd want to know the person in that house. I could tell that because he has more money than me, I probably wouldn't like him.

Anyway, I'm walking down the road and I pass the smaller house where the two lads were kicking around the ball. I look into the garden and see that only one of the boys is there now, kicking the ball against the shed. I couldn't see the other lad. He probably went inside or something as the patio door was open. So as I'm passing, the boy stops kicking the ball and looks in my direction. He moves his head around to try and get a better look at me, but with the sunglasses on and the hood up, it would be impossible to recognise me, even if he did know me, which he doesn't. He moves a bit closer to the hedge. I slow down a bit, expecting him to say or do something. And he does. He waves at me. That's all. Just a simple wave. I don't wave back though. I just walked on. I don't know why I didn't wave back. I was still a bit depressed and plus I didn't know him. Fuck it, I don't have to explain myself to you. I don't need a fucking reason. I didn't want to wave to the little cunt and that's that. Fuck you.

Anyway, that's my story, there's no point here. I just went for a walk, passed two houses, one of them was very expensive and another that was not so expensive. On the way back, one of the kids in the not-so-expensive house waved at me, which I didn't return. That's my story.

What? Were you expecting something more? Were you expecting some huge plot twist or something? Did you think that the kid would mistake me for the Owner of the Expensive House and he'd run in and tell his Dad that he didn't wave back? Were you expecting the Dad to march up to the expensive house, knock on the door and ask the Owner of the Expensive House why he didn't wave back when his son waved at him? Were you expecting the Owner of the Expensive House to say he doesn't have a clue what the Dad is on about and that he never saw his son wave at him and that he didn't even leave the house today? Did you expect the Dad to call him a liar and a snobby rich cunt? Did you expect the Owner of the Expensive House to shove the Dad and tell him to get off his property before he called the Guards? Did you then expect the Dad to punch the Owner of the Expensive House in the face? Did you expect the two to start viciously beating each other up on the pavement? Did you expect that after

117

the fight, the Dad would apologise for assaulting the Owner of the Expensive House and explain he's been going through a bit of a rough patch with his wife and that he was very irritable lately, but that it was no excuse to attack him and that he was very sorry?

Did you expect the Owner of the Expensive House to forgive him and tell him he understood as he was actually going through a divorce himself? And the Owner of the Expensive House would invite the Dad in for a drink to chat about it? Did you think the two men would sit on the couch all night getting pissed, with the Dad talking about how his wife hasn't been around lately because she just started a new job and doesn't pay as much attention to him as she used to? And the Owner of the Expensive House would talk about how lonely he's been since his wife left him for another man and that all the money in the world, including the expensive house, wasn't enough to fill the void she'd left?

Did you think the more and more they drank, the more the two men would open up to each other and feel a connection they've never experienced before with another person? And the Owner of the Expensive House would start crying and the Dad would comfort him as he wept on his shoulder? And when the Owner of the Expensive House raised his head to look at the Dad, the two of them would find each other staring into each other's eyes? Did you think the two men would then share a brief kiss? Did you think the Dad would then pull back and apologise, trying to explain that he feels very drunk? And he'd get up to leave and put on his jacket but as he made his way towards the front door, the Owner of the Expensive House would run after him and grab him, pinning him up against the marble wall and kissing him again, harder and more passionate this time?

118

And the Dad would finally succumb and give in? And the two men would start violently removing their clothes as they made their way up the stairs towards the bedroom? And they would throw themselves on top of the bed and then the Owner of the Expensive House would whip out his cock and plunge it deep into the Dad's anus? And the Owner of the Expensive House would pound away, slapping his arse and the Dad would scream with pleasure? And then the Owner of the Expensive House would blow his load into the Dad's arse and the Dad would experience an indescribable leg-shaking orgasm? And they'd spend the rest of the night staring into each other's eyes, knowing that nothing would ever come close to what they have in that moment and that any search for something better is meaningless?

Really? You were expecting all that? What else did you think would happen? Did you think the next morning, the Dad would wake up and, realising what's happened, get up quickly and start to get dressed? And the Owner of the Expensive House would ask if there's anything wrong and the Dad would tell him that he thought it would be best if they pretended last night never happened? And then the Dad would rush out of the house, leaving a confused Owner of the Expensive House watching him run down the driveway from the upstairs bedroom?

Did you expect that as the days went on, the Owner of the Expensive House would begin showing up at the Dad's house, pestering him to talk about what happened that night but the Dad would tell him that there was nothing talk about? And the Owner of the Expensive House would leave him dramatic voice messages at night, crying and telling him that he was the love of his life? And then sometimes he'd leave angry messages saying he'd kill the Dad if he didn't talk to him? Did you expect the Owner of the Expensive House to start making unannounced visits to the house and invite the Dad and his wife around for dinner? And then the wife would start getting suspicious that there's something the Dad's not telling her because one of the kids said they saw the Owner of the Expensive House prowling around the back garden? But the Dad would insist that everything's fine and that he'd sort it out? Did you expect the Dad to storm up to the expensive house, realising he's got to sort this out once and for all? Did you expect him to knock on the door and it would open and the Owner of the Expensive House would be standing there in his pyjamas with a beer in his hand, looking very hungover? And the Owner of the Expensive House would be so happy to see him and invite him in but the Dad would say he's only come around to tell him to stop harassing him and his family? And the Owner of the Expensive House would smash the beer bottle on the ground and yell at the Dad to stop pretending that night didn't mean anything to him? And the Dad would say it was just a drunken mistake and it never should have happened? And the Owner of the Expensive House would say that he loves the Dad and that he knows the Dad loves him too? And the Dad would show some momentary weakness before saying it can't happen because he has a family that depends on him? And seeing that the Dad is showing hesitation, the Owner of the Expensive House would boldly grab him and kiss him and the Dad would try and push him back but he can't deny to himself how much he wants the Owner of the Expensive House inside him again?

And the Owner of the Expensive House would suggest they run away together and start a new life someplace else? That he's got enough money to support the two of them for the rest of their days and that they could have a great life together if the Dad just gave it a chance? And the Dad would start crying and say it can't happen and he'd push the Owner of the Expensive House away as he tries to put his hands around him? And then as the Dad turns and walks away, he can hear the Owner of the Expensive House break down in tears behind him? And when the Dad got home, he'd put his fist through the kitchen wall?

Wow. You really thought this would be a big story, didn't you? You actually thought that for months after that, the Dad would do his best to try and forget the Owner of the Expensive House, even at one point suggesting to the wife that they move away? You thought that despite all he does to try and forget him, the Dad still lies awake at night, thinking about nothing but the Owner of the Expensive House on top of him and cuddling him and making him feel like one half of a whole?

You honestly thought that one night as the Dad was putting out the bins, he'd see the Owner of the Expensive House driving past the house? And as the Dad looked closer into the car, he could see there was another man sitting in the passenger seat? And the Dad knows the Owner of the Expensive House just did that to make him feel jealous, but as the night goes on, the image of the Owner of the Expensive House and the guy in his car together won't stop playing on his mind? And while the kids were playing with their action figures and the wife was on her laptop, the Dad would say he's feeling a bit sick and that he's going outside for a bit of fresh air but really he's going to run up to the expensive house and see for himself? And he'd get up to the expensive house and see the Owner of the Expensive House kissing the man on the couch in the living room, in the exact same spot the two of them had their first kiss? And the Dad would feel his heart shatter into a million pieces? And then after the Owner of the Expensive House has taken the man upstairs, the Dad would walk home, silently sobbing, knowing that he's made a terrible mistake?

You really thought that as the months went by, the Owner of the Expensive House would bring more and more men up to his house, and the Dad would tell the wife he'd be out for a few drinks when really he'd be in the Owner of the Expensive House's bushes, spying on him and one of his many lovers through a pair of binoculars? That when the wife wasn't home, the Dad would pull up a picture of the Owner of the Expensive House that he found online and masturbate to it? And sometimes he'd get a cucumber from the fridge and put it up his arse just so he can try and feel a fraction of the pleasure he felt that night? And that the pleasure would soon turn to pain and he'd start crying and he'd start hitting himself and calling himself a stupid prick for not having the balls to give the Owner of the Expensive House a chance? And some nights he'd get drunk and message the Owner of the Expensive House and sometimes throw bricks through his window?

And you actually thought that finally, the Dad would come home from work one day to see a *"FOR SALE"* sign in front of the Owner of the Expensive House's house and the Dad's worst nightmare is suddenly a reality? And he refuses to believe this is happening because he still thought there was still a small chance for the two of them? And the Dad would sneak up to the house and peak into the driveway and see the Owner of the Expensive House and some young blond guy wearing really tight shorts packing boxes into the back of his car? And the Dad suddenly feels like he wants to run up and tackle the little blond faggot? And then he approaches the house and the Owner of the Expensive House sees him coming and tells the Blond Guy in the tight shorts to grab the last of the boxes inside the house and put them in the back seat? And when the Blond Guy goes into the house, the Dad swallows hard and asks the Owner of the Expensive House where he's moving to? And the Owner of the Expensive House just says "*America*"?

And the Dad can feel his heart literally shattering inside him? That he actually feels physical pain and the reality that he can't undo what he's done, or hasn't done, really kicks in? And he looks at the Owner of the Expensive House and knows he should say something because he knows in his dying heart that right now will be the last time he ever sees him? That he should say that he loves him and he wished he had done things differently?

But he doesn't say anything? The Dad just sticks his hand out, shakes the Owner of the Expensive House's hand and wishes him the best of luck? But the Dad doesn't let go of his hand because he doesn't want to accept this is going to end? That he'd rather live in a world where the Owner of the Expensive House hates him if it meant he still lived next door and he could still see him? That he doesn't want to live in a world that doesn't have the Owner of the Expensive House in it? Because to live in a world without him would be like living without the other half of himself? It would make life not worth living anymore?

And when the Owner of the Expensive House finally pulls his hand away, the Dad turns and walks away because he can feel the tears coming on? And then a couple of minutes later, the Dad is standing outside the front door of his house and the Owner of the Expensive House's car comes down the dirt road? And the car slows a little as it passes and the Dad and the Owner of the Expensive House lock eyes for the final time before the car pulls out onto the road and disappears forever?

Did you think that after all that, the Dad would go on to become an angry and bitter alcoholic? And years later, once the kids have finished school and gone off to college, the wife would leave the Dad because she doesn't feel the same connection to him anymore and she knows deep down it's because his heart belongs to someone else? And the Dad would spend the last days of his life sipping whiskey in an old chair with a picture of the Owner of the Expensive House standing dead center on the mantelpiece above the fireplace, a cold and heart-breaking reminder of the one night of his life he felt truly happy in this world? A reminder of what his life could have been if he'd had the courage in the moment to grab ahold of the man he knew was the only person that would make him feel alive? A reminder of the man who made him feel like he was put on this earth just for him? A reminder of the man who made him feel like life was worth living?

You honestly thought all that was going to happen?

You have some imagination kid, I'll give you that.

But none of that happened, I'm afraid. Sorry to disappoint you.

The Snail

Kenneth got out of his car, threw the hood of his coat up over his head, and tucked his hands into his jacket pocket. It was fucking cold tonight. He raced quickly into the off license. Once he was inside, he took his hands out of his pocket, covered his mouth and blew into them. He lowered his hood and looked towards the counter, where the guy behind it was on his phone.

Kenneth made his way towards the beers. Mary had told him to get whatever he wanted, but Kenneth knew that was a load of bollox. He hated it when she never told him specifically what she wanted. It just added more pressure. He knew she preferred cider, but he knew with the way her stomach had been lately that she'd be shitting non-stop if she even sipped a can of Orchid Thieves. He could get an eight pack of Bud or Heineken, but Mary probably wouldn't like that, even though she'd pretend she would. She'd sit there all night making faces with each sip and Kenneth didn't want to have to look at that all night. He wanted to kick back and have fun. He'll get a spirit. Something light. They can split a 70cl of something so it'll be cheaper. He walked up towards the checkouts and looked at the many bottles that filled the shelves. Maybe some Strawberry Gin. *Meh*. Mary would want to make some complicated fucking drink with

125

ice and limes and shit, and Kenneth knew they didn't have any of that at the house. Nor did he have the patience to make some fucking elaborate James Bond-like concoction. He just wanted to get fucking pissed tonight. God knows he hadn't in a while.

He looked from left to right. Jameson. Captain Morgan. Jager. Malibu. That's perfect. Malibu. Mary would like that. A 70cl of Malibu. Or shampoo, as Kenneth like to call it because he thought it looked like a shampoo bottle.

Kenneth looked down from the shelves and approached the counter. The guy was still looking at his phone.

Excuse me? said Kenneth.

The guy looked up. *Oh fuck*. Kenneth recognized him instantly. It was Mark Harrington. A guy who was in his second and third year class in secondary school, and who hated Kenneth with a passion. Kenneth was a bit of a class clown in secondary school. One might use the word "attention seeker". He used to do all sorts of shit in class to try and make everyone laugh. And everyone did most of the time. All except Mark. Mark didn't like Kenneth at all. He used to see Mark giving him dirty looks from across the class whenever he made a funny noise or threw something across the class at one of the girls. He felt a bit ashamed thinking back at all the hell he used to put his teachers through, but it was just a laugh. Just a bit of fun. He was just being a stupid teenager.

Everyone else found Kenneth hilarious. And that's not Kenneth sucking his own dick there. Kenneth knew everyone found him hilarious because everyone told him. He was relatively well liked in school. He'd see them laughing if he made a joke or did something stupid behind a teachers back.

Mark didn't laugh though. Mark never laughed. He used to try and shit talk Kenneth to the other students, but they never had any of it. They always defended Kenneth.

"Ah, he's alright. Leave him alone", he heard Thomas Kavanagh say once after Mark clearly said something about Kenneth behind his back. Kenneth was always surprised the other students defended him. Mark was popular enough amongst the rougher kids. But even they wouldn't pay attention to Mark's constant bitching about Kenneth. Mark never hated Kenneth enough to beat the shit out of him or anything like that. He just annoyed him. And it probably made him hate Kenneth more that everyone else didn't find him just as annoying as he did.

And Mark's feelings clearly hadn't changed, because he didn't look too pleased to see him. Kenneth smiled.

Oh, hey, Mark. How you getting on? It's been a while.

Alright, Ken.

What you been up to?

Nothing much. You?

Same as. Just working basically.

Where do you work?

I work for a PR company up in Dublin.

What's PR?

Oh, Public Relations. It's where… like a client might come to us… You know what, it's fairly boring to be honest. Just a lot of business.

Kenneth felt it best not to explain the details of his job to a man who felt the need to ask him what PR was. Mark probably didn't care anyway. He was just making small talk.

What you doing back in Kerry then? said Mark.

Just home for a while.

So what you want? said Mark in the most *"I couldn't give a fuck"* manner.

Mark clearly hadn't changed a bit in the decade since they'd left school. He still had the same grumpy knacker face on him that was so obviously put on to try and make him look tougher than he really was. Back in school, he would always try and pick fights with other students for even the slightest indiscretion. You could forgive Kenneth for the way he used to seek attention from others because he was just trying to get a laugh. But Mark's form of attention-seeking was just plain sad.

Can I get a 70cl of Malibu and a packet of Marlboro Gold? said Kenneth.

Mark turned and grabbed a bottle of Malibu off the shelf.

Oh, and a lighter, said Kenneth.

Mark got the bottle, the box of fags and the lighter, and threw it on the counter in front of him.

Anything else?

No that's it.

€28.

Can I get a bag with that? said Kenneth.

Kenneth didn't really want a bag. He just wanted to annoy the cunt. Mark reached under the counter. He pulled out a brown paper bag, grabbed the Malibu bottle and shoved it into it, almost tearing the bag. It was as he was sliding the bottle of Malibu into the brown paper bag that Kenneth noticed something on the outside of Mark's left hand. He wasn't sure he'd seen what he saw at first because his hand was moving so fast. Or maybe it was just a tattoo. But when he placed the bottle down and rested his hands on the counter, Kenneth realized he wasn't seeing things.

Um… Mark? said Kenneth.

Yeah.

There's a snail on your hand.

Mark looked very annoyed.

I know, he said, without looking down at his hand.

Kenneth looked down at his hand again. At the snail.

It was a fucking snail. Shell and all. One of those big dirty ones you find crawling up the side of your house. He looked back up at Mark, who seemed to be waiting for Kenneth to speak. He opened his mouth to say something else, but what more could he say? Could it be possible that Mark was too proud to admit he didn't know he had a snail on his hand? There's no way Mark was that arrogant. He was a fucking prick and he clearly hated Kenneth, but surely even he drew the line at pretending that having a snail on your hand was as common as having a bit of food stuck in the corner of your mouth.

Um… Okay. I'll pay by card, said Kenneth, taking out his wallet.

Kenneth tapped his card on the card machine and waited for the payment to go through. He looked at the snail again in the corner of his eye. It was alive. He could see its antennas moving. It looked all slimy and dirty, like it just crawled out of a toilet. It looked fucking disgusting. He looked up at Mark, who spotted Kenneth staring at the shelled gastropod residing on his hand.

Problem? said Mark.

No, no problem.

Kenneth wasn't going to argue with this cunt. He wasn't going to stoop to Mark's level. He'd hoped that maybe the two of them had matured since school and that Mark wasn't so petty as to still hold a grudge against Kenneth for something as stupid as acting the maggot in class. But no. He was still the same immature little cunt he always was. Just looking for a fight to prove how tough he was. And sure, what did Kenneth have to prove to Mark? Kenneth had made something of himself. He was working an awesome job where he was making real money and he was in a relationship with a beautiful woman. Mark was working in a fucking offy in his hometown. Kenneth didn't need a fucking scoreboard to know who was winning.

Kenneth slid his card back in his wallet. He put the box of fags and the lighter in his back pocket and grabbed the bottle off the counter.

Hope you and your snail have a good night, said Kenneth.

Kenneth thought Mark would jump him as he turned to leave. He thought he might grab a bottle from the shelf behind him and chuck it at his head. But he didn't. Nothing happened. All Kenneth seemed to get was a pair of hateful eyes following him as he walked out of the off license. It felt nice to get the last word in on that cunt.

Kenneth forgot how cold it was when he got back outside. He rushed back to the car and jumped in. He handed the bottle to Mary, who took it without looking away from her phone. Kenneth took his keys out of his pocket and put them in the ignition.

It's fucking cold out there, he said.

I still haven't heard anything from Barry, said Mary quietly.

Kenneth cocked his eyes and reversed the car.

Later that night, Kenneth and Mary were sitting in Dessie's, a popular pub in town. They'd finished off that bottle of Malibu in just under two hours and gotten a taxi into town. They were sitting across from each other in a booth, Kenneth sipping away at a pint of Budweiser, and Mary having just finished a vodka and black. Mary was quiet tonight. She got like that when she was tipsy. She seemed to be staring at something behind him, but Kenneth turned to look and there was nothing. Just lost in space, she was. Kenneth was wondering if she was pissed off with him because he didn't want to go on the dancefloor. She'd been with him for just over two years. She knew he didn't like going on the dancefloor. Kenneth looked at his watch and then gave Mary another quick look. He never knew what to say to her when she got like this.

Will I get us another? said Kenneth, finishing off his pint.

Okay, she said.

Kenneth went up to the bar. While waiting for the drinks, he looked over at the toilets. He couldn't fucking believe what he was seeing. Standing by himself next to the door to the men's toilets, was Mark. He was just standing there, his head lowered slightly like he was asleep. Kenneth shook his head. What are the fucking odds that he'd be here tonight out of all nights? Kenneth thought it would be best to avoid any sort of interaction with Mark tonight. He was probably still sore after what Kenneth said to him at the offy, and god knows how he gets when he's pissed off his head. And then something occurred to Kenneth.

The snail. That giant fucking snail on his hand. Kenneth tried to see if it was still there but Mark was too far away and it was too dark.

Kenneth got the drinks and made his way back to Mary. He'd gotten both of them shots of tequila. She'd complain when she'd see them, but Kenneth didn't care. Mary always complained that she couldn't handle tequila, but Kenneth knew that was a load of bollox. He'd seen her down four tequilas before, chase them with two baby Guinness's, and be perfectly fine the next morning. When Kenneth sat back down in the booth, Mary still seemed to be in a world of her own. He placed the tequila in front of her, along with the lemons and a saltshaker. She didn't even budge.

You alright? said Kenneth.

She didn't move.

Mary?

Yeah? she said like she just woke up from a coma.

You alright?

Yeah, I'm fine. I was just thinking about Michaela.

Kenneth gritted his teeth. He'd fucking had it up to here with hearing about this.

Barry was saying she's been very weak lately since they brought her home from hospital, said Mary.

Uh-huh.

I'd say he's worried about her. I was telling him on the phone earlier that maybe he should call up to her. But you know him like.

Hmmm.

I told him we could go with him to make it a bit easier if he's having trouble visiting her.

It didn't register at first because Kenneth was, as usual, making mumbling sounds to make it seem like he was listening. But then it did register and he looked at her, hoping to fuck she was joking. But no, she was deadly serious.

No, he said.

No what?

I said no.

What are you talking about?

We're not going to visit her.

Why not?

Because we're not.

Why wouldn't we?

Because why in God's name would we fucking do that? Kenneth could feel a lot of pent up anger coming out. Now was not the time to be bringing this up, especially since he had drink in him and he'd probably end up saying something he'd regret later.

Because he's my brother, said Mary. I want to show my support.

Why do you even care?

Because he's my brother! She was getting angry now.

Yeah. And it's *his* ex. It's *his* fucking business.

I still want to show my support.

Why? You said you fucking hated her.

Yeah, well, she wasn't a perfect wife.

She put a hit out on him. Twice.

Well, that was then and Barry said she wasn't in a good place. He said it doesn't matter anymore anyway.

What, because she's sick now, we're meant to ignore the fact that she was a total cunt to him?

If that's what Barry wants.

Will you ever stay out of it? said Kenneth venomously.

I will not stay out of it. He's my fucking brother and I'm going to support him.

Stop fucking mentioning her. I don't want to hear it.

Why? What's the problem?

I don't think there's been a single day since she got sick that you haven't mentioned her.

So what? I'm worried about her.

No, you're not. You're bored and looking for drama.

No, I'm not. I'm worried about her. And Barry. I am.

Right, that's fine. Be fucking worried about Barry and Michaela. Just stay out of it. It's not your business or my business. It's his business. It has nothing to do with us.

It has everything to do with us. She was married to my brother for eight years.

Yeah, and he's a grown man. He can look after himself. Stop fucking getting involved in other people's lives just because you're bored of your own.

I'm not getting involved. I'm just worried about her.

Really? Saying you want to go visit her?

Just to support her and Barry.

Kenneth looked away.

Do what you want, Mary. Go visit her if you want, just leave me out of it. And stop fucking mentioning her. I don't want to hear about it anymore, okay? I'm sick of it.

The Snail

There was a pause, then Mary got up and left. Kenneth sighed and rubbed his face. He was going to get up and follow her out but decided against it in the end. He wasn't in the mood to be having a huge shouting match in front of everybody right now. So much for having a good night.

Kenneth kind of regretted saying all that, but at the same time, he was glad it was finally all out in the open. It was about time she heard it anyway. He was sick to death of hearing about it day in and day out. It was endless. He'd get the silent treatment for the next few days, but at least he wouldn't have to hear anything about Barry and Michaela for a while. Kenneth looked at the two tequilas on the table in front of him. Waste of fucking money. He considered downing them both right then and there and going on the absolute piss. One last piss up before he had to deal with the puss on Mary's face tomorrow. Uh, but the hangover. He'd be fucking dying. And having to deal with a hangover, coupled with the silent treatment from Mary, was not something Kenneth wanted very much.

Before he could decide, a person dropped into the booth across from Kenneth where Mary had been sitting. It was Mark.

Oh, Jesus fuck. This was the last thing Kenneth wanted to deal with right now. He should have fucking chased Mary out of the pub while he had the chance.

Alright, mate, said Mark. He was pissed beyond comprehension.

Alright, Mark?

You don't mind if I sit here, do you?

No, you can have it. I was just getting up to leave anyway. Kenneth grabbed his coat beside him but Mark shot out his hand.

Oh, sweet Jesus. The fucking snail was still on his hand.

No, stay for a bit, he said.

No really, Mark. I have to get going. My girlfriend...

Fucking stay for a while, will you? Have a chat, for fuck sake.

Kenneth looked across at the bouncers, who were on the other side of the smoking area. He was pretty sure he could take Mark if he had to. He was a little bigger than him. But Kenneth was pretty sure Mark had boxed in school, though he doubted he would be able to bust out some Conner McGregor moves in his condition. Kenneth was fairly drunk as well, but not enough that he'd be staggering around the place.

Dju...didu..., Mark slurred.

What? said Kenneth.

I didn't say anything.

What a pathetic fucking creature, thought Kenneth. He didn't feel a sliver of emotion for this parasite. This cunt was below a parasite to him. And *why* did he still have that fucking snail on his hand?

Did you like that Malibu? said Mark.

Yeah, it was lovely.

Yeah... yeah.

Mark looked away. Kenneth immediately recognized the look on his face. It was the depressed drunk look that someone gives you when they want to say something more but can't find the words.

You know, I..., Mark started.

Kenneth was trying to look like he cared but he didn't know how he was coming across. He just wanted to down those two tequilas and get as far away from Mark and that *fucking snail* as he possibly could.

You know I hated you in school, said Mark finally.

Yeah? said Kenneth, struggling to find an atom in his being that cared even a little bit what this fucking pavy thought of him.

Yeah, like I really hated you.

Okay.

Like you were a fucking idiot. You know that right?

Okay.

Kenneth was never so embarrassed and ashamed of another person. He didn't even want to fight him anymore, he found him so pathetic. And that fucking snail. He just wanted to squash it so he didn't have to look at it anymore.

Like, why were you like that? said Mark.

Don't know.

Drool oozed from Marks lip and fell on the table.

I used to hate you like, he continued. Everyone used to hate you.

Yeah?

Maybe Kenneth should just get up and leave. It's not like Mark could chase after him anyway.

Man, I remember… sometimes like I just…

Bring Mary back. She could talk all she wanted about Barry and Michaela. Anything was better than listening to this fucking moron go on and on. And anything was better than staring at that fucking snail.

I hated you like.

Yeah, you said that.

Oh, do you want me to go away, is that it? Am I boring you, PR man?

Kenneth didn't say anything. He stared at Mark, waiting for him to do something.

Can I not sit down and have a fucking chat with you? said Mark.

Why would you want to chat with me? I thought you hated me?

Kenneth hated himself for rising to the bait, but the argument with Mary had already put him in a bad mood, and he wasn't going to just sit here and let Mark try and drunkenly bully him.

Yeah, I fucking hated you. You were a fucking joke. Still are.

Kenneth cocked his eyes. Whatever, he said.

Cock your eyes again, said Mark.

Kenneth looked at Mark.

Cock your fucking eyes at me again. I dare you.

Kenneth leaned into the table and cocked his eyes as much as he'd ever cocked his eyes before. Mark sat staring at him. Drool was still falling from his mouth and had formed a lovely puddle on the table.

What you going to do, big man? said Kenneth leaning in closer, close enough that Mark could swing at him if he wanted to. Kenneth almost wanted him to take a swing so he could deck the cunt.

Mark stared at Kenneth. Then his head swayed from side to side and slumped downwards. Kenneth thought he might have passed out, but then he raised his head again.

You like my snail? said Mark.

Kenneth didn't say anything. He wasn't expecting that.

Mark looked down at his hand. He raised his index finger and gently stroked the shell of the snail.

His name is Kramer. I named him after that Seinfeld guy. You know that guy? That guy who said all that nigger shit on stage?

Kenneth nodded, vaguely aware of who he was referring to.

138

Say hi to Kenneth, Kramer.

Mark looked at Kenneth.

You going to wave back? said Mark.

Kenneth raised his hand and waved weakly at the snail.

He was just on my hand one day, said Mark. It was just there. No explanation.

Mark looked very sad all of a sudden. He didn't just look sad, he looked absolutely miserable.

The doctors said… they say that it…

Kenneth stared at Mark with anticipation. This was a twist he was not expecting. That snail didn't just appear on his hand. It didn't just crawl onto his hand in the off-license and Mark was too proud to admit it when Kenneth pointed it out. There was another reason that snail was on his hand.

I haven't got anyone, Ken… they all… the snail… they just left…

Mark placed his hand flat on the table and stared at the snail.

This snail… I don't…

Are you okay, Mark? said Kenneth.

This snail… I can't do it…

Mark?

It's taken everything from me.

Marks eyes were red with tears.

Mark, you okay?

I can't fucking do it anymore.

Out of the blue, Mark shot his hand out and grabbed the saltshaker next to the shot of tequila Kenneth had bought for Mary. He chewed off the lid and spat it out. Then he poured all the salt in the jar onto his hand. Onto the snail.

The snail immediately began to ooze water and Marks spine curved back. He screamed in pain. He clutched his hand and collapsed on the floor beside Kenneth. He wriggled and squirmed as the snail slowly melted on his hand. Mark screamed to the heavens, louder then Kenneth had ever heard someone scream before. People turned in their seats, wondering what all the racket was about. The bouncers approached the booth and looked down at Mark screaming on the floor. They looked to Kenneth for some clarity on what was happening. Kenneth just shrugged his shoulders.

The water from the snail began to ooze down Marks hand. The screaming went on and on. No one helped. They just kind of watched as Mark howled on the floor, unsure of what to do or how to help. Soon Mark got very pale. His lips got so dry they looked like you could snap them off like the fat off a burnt rasher. The screaming soon quieted down and Mark started gasping for air. Then he was looking up at the ceiling, tears streaming down his face. His hand fell to his side, hitting the floor and crushing the shell of the snail. What remained of the snail was now stuck to the floor of the bar like chewing gum. Mark's breathing got very slow. And slower. And slower. Until it stopped.

Everyone in the bar turned around and went back to what they were doing. The bouncers walked away. Kenneth looked down at Mark's lifeless corpse on the ground and at the syrupy remains of the snail that once took up residence on his hand. Then he looked at the two tequilas.

Maybe visiting Michaela with Barry and Mary wasn't the worst idea in the world.

A Good Laugh

S hane needed that. He needed a good laugh. He'd just finished watching a funny YouTube video a mate from work had sent him and he was in fucking stitches. It was just a stupid wee thing. Just some prank video of these guys in a gym doing weird exercises, but it fucking killed him for some reason. He had to pause the video halfway through because he was laughing so much. By the time the video was finished, his ribs were killing him and his jaw muscles ached.

When Shane got control of himself, he sat back and smiled with satisfaction, still chuckling to himself. That was funny now, he said. He needed that. It had been a while since he had a proper laugh. The type of laugh that just made you lose control of your whole body and forget everything else in your life. It had been a while since Shane had a laugh like that. And he needed it.

And it wasn't that Shane was depressed or anything. Nothing like that. He didn't mean he needed a good laugh because things had been difficult lately and he needed something to pick him up. No, he just needed a good laugh, that was all. Shane reckoned it was because there were so few things in his life that really made him laugh that hard. Like until it hurts so much that you think you're going to pass out.

And it wasn't like Shane didn't have a sense of humor either. He laughed all the time. He always had a laugh with his mates. He wasn't some dry cunt. But laughs like that are just normal. They're everyday laughs. Shane meant the kind of laugh that would have you fall to the ground. The kind of laugh that would have you making noises you've never heard come out of your mouth before. The kind of laugh that made everybody else in the room laugh. A contagious kind of laughter.

Why couldn't he laugh like that more? Why was it an experience that seemed to happen to him only once in a while? Usually, a laugh like that would only happen to you if you smoked a lot of pot. But a laugh like that while you're sober? Now that was a very rare occurrence. But why was that? Perhaps it was because life is such a naturally depressing experience and a certain frame of mind is needed to achieve that sort of laughter. Like say that video wouldn't have been as funny to Shane if he was in a bad mood. Maybe he would have just had a normal laugh under normal mundane circumstances. Maybe that's what it was. A kind of laughter that could only be unlocked under the most perfect conditions.

It didn't matter anyway. Shane didn't know why he was overthinking the whole thing. He didn't know why he wasn't just enjoying the high following that laugh. He just wished a laugh like that happened more often, that's all. Because a laugh like that is good for everyone. A laugh like that cheers up other people as well, not just the person laughing. It would be nice if it wasn't this rare thing you could only experience once in a while.

God, that had put Shane in a great mood.

He felt great after that, he really did. He felt like the happiest man on Earth right now.

A Good Laugh

Shane got up and went into the sitting room, where his teenage son, Timmy, was lying on the couch on his phone. Shane said hi and Timmy responded with an effortless mumble. Shane sat down in his chair and turned on the television. He flicked through the channels for a bit, then stopped. He had an idea. Oh, this would be good. He turned to Timmy and smiled. He reached into his pocket and pulled out his phone.

Here, Timmy, said Shane. I have to show you this video a mate from work sent me. It's hilarious.

What is it? said Timmy, without looking away from his phone.

It's just this prank video on YouTube. Here, have a look.

He handed his phone to Timmy from across the table. Timmy cocked his eyes, put his phone flat on his chest, and took his Dad's phone. He pressed play on the video. Timmy was only about ten seconds into the video and Shane could feel the laughter coming on again. Just listening to it reminded him of all those parts in it that fucking killed him. He was trying to hold it in but he wasn't sure he could for very long. Eventually, he just couldn't hold it in anymore and he snorted through his nose. Then he started howling with laughter again. He couldn't stop it.

Timmy stopped the video after thirty seconds and put the phone on the table.

That's stupid, he said.

Shane looked at Timmy and then at the phone. How is that stupid? You didn't even watch all of it.

I don't want to watch a three-minute video. Just send me the link, I'll watch it later.

Ah, just watch it now. Come on, its fucking hilarious.

Timmy sat up in the chair. I'll watch it later. Listen, I'm heading over to Conner's for the match. Can I borrow a twenty off you?

Shane's smile disappeared. He sighed and squeezed his wallet out of his jeans. So why do you need a twenty if you're only heading over to Conner's?

We might go out for a pint afterwards.

What happened to the fifty I gave you last week?

I spent it.

And the fifty before that?

Ah, Dad, come on. Don't be a nob.

Shane frowned and shook his head. He slid a twenty out of his wallet and put it into his son's sweaty palm. Timmy got up and stuffed it into his back pocket.

I'll see you later, he said. Then he walked out of the room and out the front door.

Shane sighed. He saw his phone on the table and bent forward to pick it up. He unlocked it and the video popped up again where Timmy had paused it. He felt like watching it again, but to be honest, he just wasn't feeling it. It probably wouldn't be as funny to him as it was the first time anyway.

Shane locked his phone and put it in his pocket.

He sat in silence.

Loquacious

So you're reading a book on your Kindle out in your back garden, a book you're really enjoying, you might add. You're not much of a reader, but the missus got you the Kindle for your birthday and it seemed a waste not to use it. So you went into the Amazon website, viewed a list of the bestselling books at the moment, and purchased the one at the top of the list, not having a clue if you'll enjoy it or not. You figure it should be at least alright if it's at the top of the Amazon Bestsellers list. Now you're sitting on your deck chair with the sun beating down on you, a glass of ice-tea next to you, and a book that gets better and better with every page turn. Life couldn't get any better, could it?

Then suddenly, you come across a word. A word you've never seen before.

Loquacious.

You're looking at it. You try to think back to any time you might have heard it in the past, but nothings ringing a bell. *Loquacious*? Doesn't even sound like a word. It just sounds like a fucking noise. Sounds like a type of biscuit some posh fucker might eat in the South of France. You try deciphering the meaning of the word within the context of the sentence, but it still doesn't make any sense.

Here, I'll show you the sentence and you'll see what I mean.

Murray was a very loquacious fellow, which Richard found to be quite annoying and oddly arousing, which confused him greatly because he was engaged to his sister.

There you go. You've seen it now. Does it make sense to you? No, I thought not. So, you think to yourself: I'll Google it and see what it means. So that's what you do. You Google it.

The search results show the following definition:

"tending to talk a great deal; talkative".

They even give an example of how the word should be used in a sentence:

"never loquacious, Sarah was now totally lost for words"

So, there you go. *Loquacious* means, *talkative*.

You pick up your Kindle so you can continue reading. But then you start thinking. Why did the author of the book use the word *loquacious* instead of the word *talkative*? Why did the author feel the need to use such a fancy word to describe a chatty person? It doesn't make any sense to you. If the author had just used the word *talkative*, you wouldn't have wasted twenty seconds of your life Googling the word to see what it means. You would have just carried on with the book without noticing a thing. So why use the word *loquacious*? Why not just use the word *talkative*?

I mean, everybody knows the word *talkative*. Nobody knows how they know it. You just know it. It's just there in your brain and if somebody was to use the word *talkative*, you'd know immediately what they were talking about.

But *loquacious*?

146

Loquacious

You've never heard or read the word in any context. But then you think to yourself: Maybe the author was just trying to educate me. I mean for all you know, the author has a college degree in English or whatever, with more knowledge of the language than you would ever know.

But surely the author knows that most people don't know what *loquacious* means? Right? I mean you wouldn't have even known what it meant if you hadn't Googled it. And now that you know what it means, are you going to start suddenly implementing the word into your life? Are you going to replace *talkative* with *loquacious* every time you come across a situation where the use of the word is appropriate?

No, of course your fucking not. You're not fucking mental, are you? If you used the word loquacious in a conversation with someone, they'd look at you with the exact same confused expression that you have right now, and they'd probably think you're just a snobby bollox who's trying to use a fancy word to show off how smart you are. It's just a word that you have in your brain now, that you're never going to use in any type of situation. It's a completely useless piece of knowledge. If your brain was a hard-drive and needed some formatting, the definition of *loquacious* would be in the bin without even thinking about it.

So out of curiosity, you Google it again and find that there's more than one synonym to describe a person that's talkative.

Garrulous. Voluble. Verbose. Profuse.

You've never heard of any of them before either. You start thinking: Why does there have to be so many words to describe one thing? Why can't you just use the word *talkative*? Why do people have to make things so fucking complicated? There's no need for it.

147

And now you're getting a little bit pissed off with the author of the book. Why would they include that word? Surely, the author knows that most people wouldn't have the same grasp of such an advanced vocabulary. So why the fuck would they include that word? What are they trying to prove?

In fact, isn't the author doing their novel a disservice by including that word? I mean, you're just an ordinary citizen. You're not an idiot, but you're clearly not going to know what that word means. So, by including that word in a book that's meant to entertain, you're now forcing the reader to put down the book and Google the definition so they can better understand what they've just read. And by doing that, the author is forcing you away from the story that you were just captivated by. You were fucking loving that book, weren't you? *Well, guess what, I'm the writer and I'm going to stick a word in there that you've never heard of before just to take some of the enjoyment away.*

And now you're feeling stupid because you're thinking that maybe you should have known what *loquacious* means. Maybe if you had put your head down a bit more in school and studied the way your parents advised you to instead of spending your Friday and Saturday nights downing can after can of Magners by that walkway going through the park, you wouldn't be where you are right now, shovelling shite on a construction site for piss money. But more importantly, you'd know what *loquacious* means, and you'd be able to continue enjoying the book you just purchased with your hard-earned money so you could take your mind off the fact that you're working a shite job for shite money, all so you can provide for a shite family that doesn't fucking appreciate you.

148

Loquacious

Now you don't even feel like going back to the book. Now you're sitting upright on your deck chair with your sunglasses on the top of your head and you're hyperventilating with fury. Your fucking fuming. You're so angry that you want one of the kids to walk out to you right now just so you have someone to lace across the arse with your belt. You just want someone to take your anger out on.

So, you go back into the house and grab a can of Bavaria out of the fridge. You promised the missus you wouldn't drink for a while since you're trying to cut back. But fuck it, you deserve a can for all the shite you have to put up with. And anyway, that bitch fucking talks the head off herself. Oh, no, sorry. She's *loquacious*. You forgot that's the word you're using from now on. A few hours later you're pissed beyond comprehension and stumbling into the kid's rooms. You're telling them if they ever use the word *loquacious* in this house, they'll be out the door before they could fucking think it.

Now the missus is roaring the head off you, calling you a pathetic drunk, and saying you're just like your father. You grab her by the arm and tell her to stop wrecking your head or you'll crack her skull open. She screams and manages to break away. She grabs the nearest thing she can find, which happens to be the dustpan, and knocks you over the head with it. That drops you to the floor and gives her enough time to grab the kids and lock herself in the spare bedroom upstairs. You grab an axe from the shed and attempt to break the door down like Jack Nicholson from The Shining. She's screaming and telling you that she's calling the police and if you're not out of the house in five minutes, you're never going to see the kids again. You punch the wall repeatedly and scream that you'll kill her

149

before she takes the kids. When you hear the missus on the phone to the Guards, you grab the car keys and run out of the house. You hear sirens a couple of minutes later as you swerve around the road. You don't remember anything after that. You blackout.

You wake up the next morning in some random field, with no clothes on and a large Toblerone shoved impressively up your arse. The pain in your head is so bad and your stomach is in a heap. As you stand up, you puke green all over the grass. Your knuckles feel like their broken. You can't find your phone, your wallet, or your car keys, and when you walk out onto the road, you find your car upside down in a ditch. You try to thumb a lift home but no one in their right mind would allow you into their car, the fucking state of you.

After a three-hour walk, you get home and find the wife and kids are gone. In the kitchen, you see a note propped up against the kettle. You open it up and it reads: *Took the kids to my mothers. Don't contact us. Someone will be in touch. Sort yourself out.*

You viciously tear the note up and start destroying the kitchen in an uncontrollable rage. You smash plates and cups. You punch holes through every wall, press, and cupboard, damaging your already fucked knuckles. You kick the patio door so hard that the glass breaks instantly and cuts your exposed arm. You scream *"LOQUACIOUS"* at the top of your lungs as you pick up the kitchen table with all the strength you can muster and hurl it across the room.

You spend the rest of the day getting through the hangover as best you can. You down the rest of the cans in the fridge just to ease the throbbing pain in your head and sit in the living room in silence. You've never heard the house so quiet. It doesn't feel the same without the kids running through it or annoying you in some way. You pick up a picture of one of the kids. It was taken on their Confirmation Day. You hold it to your chest and cry your eyes out.

That night, you don't sleep a wink. You lay in your empty bed, staring at the ceiling. Thinking. The TV's on but you're not paying any attention to it. How did it all come to this? All of this started with that word. That fucking word. You don't want to say it. You don't even want to think about it because you think you might get sick. It stick's on your tongue like the taste of metal that's impossible to scrape off.

There's one person responsible for all this and that fucker is the person who thought it would be a good idea to use a word that nobodies heard of in a book distributed to the general public. Something has to be done.

In a sudden burst of motivation, you get up and storm outside. The Kindle is still on the deck chair, bathing in the moonlight. It's just sitting there, laughing at you. Fucking book thinks it's hard with its complicated vocabulary. Well, you're not going to let it win. You march forward, grab the Kindle and power it on. You load up the book in your library and look at the authors name in the front matter: "Maggie SmithMcSmith"

Course it's a fucking woman. You drop the Kindle and storm back into the house. At the computer, you Google her name. She lives in London. Lately, she's been frequently spotted in a local café, reportedly working on the follow-up to her latest bestseller. Another life destroyer. There were even some images of her in the café. Pictures that fans had taken on their phones. Blond hair, bold glasses. Good looking woman, she is. But not for fucking long.

Next thing you know, you're on Ryanair's website, booking the earliest flight to London and packing a bag. The next morning you're on a plane with your fists clenching the armrests. There's a pair of kids playing with action figures a couple of rows in front of you. It's a painful reminder of your own and that word that caused you to do what you did to them. You can feel yourself starting to cry but you wipe your eyes before you start and clear your throat. You must remain focused on your objective. What you do now is for them.

An hour later, you're in London. You give the name of the café to a taxi driver at the airport and he takes you there. It looks exactly how it looks in the pictures. You go in and look around. Maybe she'll be in there now and you can get this over and done with. You search every square inch of the café, but you can't find her. You ask one of the employees, but they say they're not allowed to give out any information out to fans. You feel discouraged but you keep your objective in front of you. She's not here now. That's fine. You'll wait.

You wait at the café all day. You can't even count the number of coffees you've had just so the employees don't think you're some sort of weirdo. When the café closes, you book a room at a random hotel.

The next day, you sit in the same spot at the café. You wait all day and she still doesn't appear. You'll wait here for weeks if you have to.

So you wait in the café again the next day. And the next day. And the next day. And the next day…

Things go on like this for a while. A couple of weeks, months, years, you don't even know, you've lost count. Every day is just the same thing over and over. They just blur past you now. You spend most of your time

152

thinking of your life before you knew that word. Now it's all you think about. It repeats in your head like a heartbeat. You spend your nights in your hotel room, scribbling it onto hundreds of sheets of paper in black marker like some demented fucking nutjob.

Loquacious. Loquacious. Loquacious.

Over and over, it repeats in your head like someone tapping at your skull. It never stops.

One day you're in the café and you decide that you need a bit of fresh air. You step outside and light a fag. You look around at all the happy little people living their lives, oblivious. Fucking clueless bastards. They have no earthly idea how fucking quickly their lives could just fall apart.

You look to the left and right. Then you stop. For a second, you didn't think you saw it. You must have been hallucinating. It couldn't be, not after all this time. You turn your head slowly back to the left. You must be dreaming. You must be.

There she is. Wearing some hipster fucking beanie on her head and her tits popping out of her low cut dress. She's carrying a laptop bag over her shoulder. In that instant, you want to tackle her to the ground like a cheetah and break her neck. You want to drive your fist into her face over and over until there's nothing left to punch but red soup. Oh, the Medieval things you want to do to her in that moment. But you don't. You rub your face and stay calm. You have to remain objective. You've waited too long to let emotion get the better of you.

You follow her into the café and watch her sit down. You sit at the other side of the room and stare at her. Patience. That's the name of the game here. You watch her take out her laptop and open it.

You sit for three hours and watch her work on her manuscript. Typing away at the keyboard like a mindless drone, unaware of the damage she's doing to the lives of those around her. You watch her carefully like a lion watching a gazelle from the bushes. When she hits four hours, she looks at her watch and stretches. She gets up and walks into the lady's room. Now's the time to move. You get up and follow her as nonchalantly as possible. You stop in front of the men's room and look behind you. Nobodies there. You dart quickly for the lady's room and jam the door with a mop you find behind the door. Thankfully, the café isn't too busy today so it's unlikely anybody will be disturbing the two of you.

You check the other cubicles. Nobodies here. Just you and her. The moment of truth. You stand in front of the cubicle where she's currently residing and stand for a second. This is it. No turning back. You close your eyes and take a deep breath.

With all your strength, you force your foot through the cubicle door and it swings open violently, hitting the partition hard. It happens so fast that she can't even comprehend it in the middle of her shit. Before she can scream, you lunge forward and cover her mouth with your hand. She starts to moan as loud as she can. You close the cubicle door behind you and lock it.

If you scream, you say, I'll fucking kill you, you understand?

She screams through your muffled hand as she stares into your bloodshot eyes.

Nod your head that you understand me or I'll kill you right now.

She nods her head frantically. You take your hand away and she lets out a whimper.

154

Now I'm going to talk and you're going to listen. Nod that you understand.

She nods.

Your last book, do you remember it?

Yes, she says, her voice trembling with fright.

Don't fucking say anything, I don't want to hear anything come out of your cunt mouth. Just nod.

She nods.

Page one hundred and seventeen, line eight, word three. Do you remember that word?

She breaks down in tears. What do you want? she says.

You take a knife out of your belt and dangle it in front of her face. Now's not the time to not answer, you say.

You stuff a napkin into her mouth and wrap Sellotape around her head so she can't spit it out. Then you take the knife and dangle it in front of her face again.

Now, I'm going to ask you again. Page one hundred and seventeen, line eight, word three. Do you remember that word?

She shakes her head.

You clutch the knife in your hand. You will, you whisper.

You point the tip of the knife at her head. In a sudden burst of defiance, she tries to break free. She knees you in the crotch and tries to jump over you. You work through the pain surging through your balls and grab a chunk of her hair. You throw her head forward and slam it against the wall beside you. You slam her head again and she slumps back against the toilet.

Hold still, you say, clutching the knife. This is going to be painful.

155

You take the knife and start carving into her forehead. She screams and screams and her arms and legs flail about wildly, but nobody can hear her with the napkin in her mouth. Blood trickles down her head, covering her face and neck. When you're finished, you wipe the knife clean on the leg of your trousers and stick it back in its sheath. She's still screaming and crying. Blood is covering her face and she looks like your one from that movie, *Carrie*. You get a bit of toilet paper from the dispenser and harshly wipe her face clean. Then you take a small mirror out of your back pocket and place it directly in front of her so she can see what you've done.

Open your eyes, you say.

When she opens her eyes, they widen in horror at the sight of herself and she screams. She closes her eyes tight and continues crying.

Open your eyes, you say, I want you to see what I've done. It's the only way you'll understand.

You rip the Sellotape off and take the napkin out of her mouth. You cover her mouth quickly, so she doesn't scream. You put the mirror in front of her again. Open your eyes.

She does so slowly and weeps uncontrollably.

Look at me, you say. And say the word.

She begins to squirm and squeal so violently, you think she might break free. You punch her across the face and her head flies back and hits the edge of the toilet bowl, splitting her head open. More blood pours down her face and drips onto the white tiles.

Say the fucking word right now, or I'll carve it over every inch of flesh I can find.

She opens her mouth, licks her lips and, like a mouse, quietly says:

156

Loquacious.

That's right. That word you just decided to haphazardly use in your fucking book cost me everything. I lost everything because you tried to be all clever. Well now, for the rest of your life, you're going to know how that feels, because you're going to have to walk around from now on and people will be asking you what that word means. And I bet you'll get sick of it fairly fucking quickly.

You stand up and clean your hands with some toilet paper. She crawls beside the toilet and curdles up into the fetal position. Her entire body is shuddering like it's about to self-destruct.

Anyway, you say. I'll head away now. Big fan here. Just wanted to give you a bit of feedback.

You open the stall door and close it behind you, leaving the disfigured woman sobbing in the stall. You quickly leave the café before she has a chance to alert anybody. You walk quickly down the street and dump the knife in a bin outside Burger King.

Twenty-four hours later, you're back home. You get in the door and look around. The place is empty. The missus hasn't come back with the kids yet. That's okay, you think, I'll give her time. I'll show her I've changed.

The Angelus Bell

Aine and her girlfriend, Michelle, were sitting on the couch one evening watching a bit of telly. It was just like any other evening. Their empty dinner plates still lay on the table and they'd just sat down in their pyjamas, both with piping hot cups of tea in their hands. Aine had a couple of caramel digestives as well. She was on a diet, but she thought an odd biscuit or two wouldn't hurt. Aine always loved this part in the evening, when she'd sit down with Michelle and watch shite telly and talk about random things while Michelle's dog, Milo, a large Golden Retriever, sat licking his bollox beside them.

It was one of the things, in Aine's opinion, that kept their relationship interesting, even if it wasn't the most exciting thing in the world. She wasn't sure if Michelle loved it as much as she did. In fact, Aine was afraid Michelle thought this kind of stuff was boring. That just sitting down and watching TV wasn't enough for her. That she wasn't enough for her. Maybe she was just doing stuff like this because she knew that's what Aine liked and she was just doing it to keep her happy. Michelle was someone who liked a bit of excitement in her life. Aine didn't know. She didn't really know what Michelle wanted to do. Perhaps she was just overthinking things, as she often did. She really wished she wasn't one of those girls.

The type of girl that obsess over the tiniest things that probably don't have any weight to them at all. But Aine couldn't help it. Her mind went to weird and paranoid places when she thought like this.

The thing was Michelle never explicitly gave Aine any sign that she was bored with this sort of stuff. Their relationship was still very much in the early stages and things were still spicy in the bedroom. It was just a vibe Aine was picking up that concerned her a little. She was probably just having some normal relationship fears, just like everyone. She liked Michelle. She really liked Michelle. Things had been so good between them lately. And although Aine knew it was unrealistic to expect it to always be like that, she liked Michelle enough to do anything she wanted to keep her around. Aine was so wrapped up in her own insecurities that she hadn't noticed that Milo jumped up on the couch next to her and started eating her biscuits.

Get off, Milo, she said brushing him away. Michelle started laughing. She grabbed Milo by the belly and moved him over to the empty part of the couch next to her. Then she smiled at Aine and the two of them cuddled.

The RTE news was just about to come on. Michelle started browsing through the TV guide, which meant she intended to change the channel.

Don't change over, said Aine. I want to see the weather.

Michelle dropped the remote and put her arm back around Aine.

Aine always found The Angelus before the news oddly relaxing. You know where the bell is ringing for like a minute and there are shots of various people, some young and old, pausing to pray to the sound of the bell, looking all reflective and shit.

DONG.

An Indian woman doing a bit of gardening. She looks up at the sky.

DONG.

An old man sits before a roaring fireplace, smoking a pipe.

DONG.

Some old woman hugging a small child, possibly her granddaughter. The two of them look to the side.

DONG.

Just then, Milo started making a noise. It was a noise that Aine had never heard before. It was a howling, like he was responding to the bell.

What's he doing? said Michelle.

DONG.

Milo howled even louder.

It must be the bells that are setting him off, said Aine laughing.

Michelle started laughing as well and the two of them stared at Milo with amusement as he howled away, each time louder than the last.

Eventually, The Angelus ended and the news started. Aine enjoyed that. She'd never seen a dog react in such a way to church bells. Then Aine had an idea.

I have an idea, she said. Let's rewind it and turn up the volume and see if he does it again.

Michelle shrugged her shoulders. Alright, why not?

Michelle rewound back to the start, turned up the volume and hit play. The *DONG*s started again and Milo started howling again. This time even louder. The two watched in awe. These were the types of noises you only saw dogs on YouTube make. It sounded like a noise a human would make if they were in pain. It was hard to gauge whether Milo was enjoying it or

160

if it was just a natural and curious dog-like reaction to a loud sound they've never heard before. When it was over, Michelle and Aine looked at each other, wondering in amusement if maybe Milo was broken. Michelle rubbed the back of Milo's neck.

You're a silly dog, aren't you? she said.

Let's do it again, said Aine.

Aine could tell by the way Michelle squinted her eyes that she didn't really want to.

Ah, come on, said Michelle. It was funny the first time. Let's just watch the news now.

Just one more time. We'll put the volume up full blast.

Michelle sighed. Alright, just one more time so. But that's it then. I want to watch the news.

Last time, I swear, said Aine. This was perfect, she thought. This was just what the two of them needed in the evening to keep things interesting. It was a small thing admittedly, but it was something.

Michelle rewound back to the start again. Aine took out her phone and started a video recording. She knew that if Milo did anything even remotely similar to what he did before, the video could easily go viral on YouTube or Facebook. She could just picture it now:

"Dog singing to God during the Angelus".

Michelle paused and turned the volume all the way up to a hundred. When she pressed play and the *DONG*s started again, the sound was so loud that the two of them winced and had to block their ears for a moment. Milo, on the other hand, howled even louder than before. This time it sounded truly un-dog like.

The *DONG*s went on and on, and Milo howled louder than ever before. Louder than any noise Aine's ever heard him make. Then it got to a point where it didn't seem like Milo was enjoying it anymore. On the contrary, it sounded like Milo was in pain. Michelle and Aine looked at each other with concern. Michelle picked up the remote to turn it down, but the button wouldn't work.

DONG.

Michelle got up and tried to turn the volume down manually on the TV, but she couldn't find any of the buttons on the massive flat screen. Milo collapsed onto his belly and was screaming.

DONG.

Milo's stomach muscles seemed to be tensing up and he was foaming at the mouth. Michelle abandoned trying to find the buttons on the TV and knelt down in front of his face. She tried scratching his belly and rubbing his fur to get him to calm down, but nothing was working. His screeches got louder and louder.

DONG.

Aine, turn off the fucking telly! screamed Michelle over the sound of the Angelus Bell and Milo's screams.

Aine grabbed the remote and tried to turn it down herself, but it wasn't working. She slapped the remote against the palm of her hand. Nothing. She pressed the mute button. Nothing. She pressed the power button. Nothing. Nothing on the remote seemed to be working. The batteries must have run out. She ran up to the telly and tried to find anything that looked like a button along the sides, but she couldn't. It was a new telly.

DONG.

162

Milo's screeching became unbearable. It looked like he was burning from the inside out. Michelle, who was crying now as she watched the dog she'd had for nine years scream in agonizing pain, got to eye level with Milo. She rubbed the back of his head furiously and mouthed something to him to try and comfort him, but the screeching prevailed and became even more bloodcurdling. In a panic, Aine pulled the power socket out of the wall and flipped the TV over. It came crashing to the floor and the *DONG*s stopped.

Milo stopped howling. He stared ahead, seemingly hypnotised.

Milo? said Michelle. You okay, boy?

Then before Michelle and Aine's very eyes, Milo turned to ash. The furry yellow lab was reduced to nothing but white ghostly powder. Michelle reached into the ash and picked up a handful, but it sifted right through her fingers.

Milo? whispered Michelle.

Michelle moved out of the house the next day. Aine was fairly upset. She went back a week later to get some things while Aine was at work. There were a ton of empty wine bottles scattered around the kitchen counter.

The next time Michelle saw Aine was a few weeks later in Abrakebabra. She was sitting in one of the booths by herself, a untouched tray of food in front of her, and her head swaying from side to side. She was definitely on something because she didn't recognise Michelle when they made eye contact.

A few months later, Michelle heard from her cousin that Aine was in hospital.

Santa's Little Helper

Fucking pubs are closed! roared Tinsel. What a load of fucking deer shit! Tinsel staggered through The Main Square of the North Pole, a bottle of Corona in hand. He took a swig of it and let the warm liquid slide down his throat. He kicked the snow against the footpath as he staggered forward. After a while, he came to a pub that appeared to be open. There was an elf having a fag outside. He held out his hand as Tinsel approached.

It's closed, mate, he said.

For fuck sake, it's Christmas Eve, said Tinsel, throwing his arms up and sending his bottle of Corona flying through the air and shattering on the ground.

It's closed. Sorry.

Fuck sake, let me in. He tried to walk past the elf but he put his arm out and blocked him.

What's the fucking problem? said Tinsel. It's Christmas fucking Eve. Let's celebrate for fuck sake. Big man isn't around, is he?

He tried to force his way past the elf again but he pushed him back. Tinsel slipped on the ice and hit his head on the concrete.

The next thing he remembered, Tinsel was in the workshop district, zigzagging from one side of the street to the other, and he threw a rock through one of the windows. Then he ran away. A few minutes later, he came across an elf with a brown shaggy beard, nodding off against a street lamp, a cigar hanging out of his mouth. As Tinsel neared closer to him, he jolted awake with a loud grunt and almost slipped from the footpath.

Who you? he said, his voice garbled and hoarse.

I'm Tinsel.

So?

I work for Santa.

You work for the big man, do you? And what do you do for the big man? he said, drool hanging from his bottom lip.

Just wrapping and stuff, said Tinsel.

I used to work for Santa. Guy thinks he owns the place.

He does own the place.

He has no idea what goes on around here.

Maybe.

There's no maybe about it, mister.

If you say so.

Then the elf with the shaggy beard turned and puked brown chunks against the wall behind him. Tinsel left him alone and carried on through the empty streets. The cobblestones were slippery from the snow and he almost fell a few times. He staggered on and came to another pub. Candy Cane was its name. The door was open and the lights were on inside. He stepped in and pushed open the heavy wooden door. Three elves, who were sitting by the bar, turned and stared at Tinsel as he stumbled in.

Alright, boys, said Tinsel. The three elves didn't say anything.

An elf carrying a wooden crate appeared from a door behind the bar.

165

We're closed, he said.

You having a lock in? said Tinsel.

We're closed. We're not serving anymore.

Ah, come on. It's Christmas, give me a break. I work for the big man. Tinsel staggered forward and collapsed into the bar, almost knocking the elderly elf closest to him off his seat.

Woah, what are you doing, said the barelf. I said we're closed.

So what are they still doing here? said Tinsel pointing his finger obnoxiously at the three elves.

They'll be leaving soon.

Lighten up a bit, said Tinsel climbing up onto a barstool.

The barelf looked at Tinsel as he struggled onto the seat. He looked at the other elves and sighed.

One drink and then you leave. You understand?

Loud and clear.

What do you want?

Two double whiskeys and three shots of sambuca.

The barman stopped and looked at Tinsel. I said one drink.

Pour it all into one glass then, said Tinsel.

The barelf gritted his teeth and grabbed a glass from underneath the bar. Tinsel looked at the elderly elf who was sitting closest to him.

How are you, old timer, said Tinsel. Enjoying your night?

The old elf didn't respond. He took a sip of his Guinness and licked off the foam moustache that formed on his upper lip.

The barelf plopped a drink in front of Tinsel. That's it now, okay? You finish that and leave.

You sure now? I'm in the mind for a Guinness now that I think about it.

Not going to happen, pal.

I'm just pulling your leg, said Tinsel. He picked up the drink and took a swig. The bitter mixture of the whiskey and sambuca burned the back of his throat.

You work for Santa, said the elf who was sitting in the middle of the three.

Yeah, said Tinsel.

I imagine you were fairly busy over the Christmas?

Pretty much.

You get any bonus for Christmas?

Not a thing, said Tinsel, taking another swig of his drink and smacking his lips. Not even a fucking voucher. Just one shitty week off during the year. That's all I get for seventeen fucking years of work.

My nephew just started an internship there, said the elf on the far side of the bar. He'll be starting just after the new year. He's very excited.

Tell him to pack his bags and do something else, said Tinsel. Take it from me, he'll thank me in a couple of years.

Have you ever seen him? said the middle elf.

Who?

Santa.

Yeah. He'll come down for an inspection the odd time. We all have to be on perfect behavior when he does. Don't want to be on Santa's naughty list, now do we?

Tinsel grabbed his drink and raised it.

Cheers, lads, he said.

He downed the drink in one and groaned loudly as he swallowed it. The three elves didn't touch their glasses.

That's it now, said the barelf.

Jesus, you're a humorless cunt, aren't you?

Tinsel blacked out and woke up face down in the snow. He raised his head and wiped the cold dirty slush off his face. He looked around. It took his eyes a minute to adjust to his surroundings. He was on a very narrow street he didn't recognize. He got up on his knees and propped his back against the wall behind him. His head was throbbing violently and his hands and feet were almost numb, they were so cold. The back of Tinsel's throat stung with vomit. He burped and felt a little come up. He swallowed it. The fucking taste of it was rank.

Tinsel got up, wobbled for a second, and once he regained his composure, he started walking down the road. The street was still icy and was difficult to navigate. The bright Christmas lights hanging from the roofs of the buildings and the golden glow off the streetlamps burned his retina's and worsened his already agonizing headache. Tinsel felt like he was going to get sick for a moment and grabbed onto a bike rail next to him.

Tinsel's hand burst into a sudden song of sharp blinding pain. He drew back his arm and examined the palm of his hand. There was a large jagged shard of glass sticking out of it, just above his wrist. Without hesitation, Tinsel grabbed the shard of glass by the edge and yanked it out. He raised his head and hissed loudly as the burning pain coursed through his hand. Blood oozed from the wound and dripped down onto his sleeve. Tinsel

168

carried on down the narrow cobblestone street, blood dripping from his hand and leaving a breadcrumb trail for anyone who wished to find him.

As he limped down the street, Tinsel could hear the faint sound of someone singing a Christmas song. He recognized the melody immediately. It was a song called, *"Look Up and Lick the Snow"*. A song his mother used to sing to him and his older brother when they were just wee elves. Tinsel hastened up the street, like he was afraid the singer might disappear. He held onto the wall to his left so he wouldn't slip on the ice. Blood was still gushing from the palm of his hand, but he sucked up the pain and kept on going.

As Tinsel moved forward, the road got narrower and narrower until he felt so claustrophobic that he thought the walls were going to cave in and crush him. When he finally arrived at the end of the road, there was nothing but a large wooden door. He pushed against it but it wouldn't even budge. It was a dead end. Tinsel thought about lying on the ground and just falling asleep right there. He didn't want to turn back. He didn't want to do anything. He just wanted to rest.

To Tinsel's right were a set of large circular windows. There was a faint light on inside. That's where the music was coming from. Tinsel stepped forward, grabbed the ledge and, ignoring the pain in his hand, pulled himself up. He climbed onto the ledge and managed to balance himself just barely on the thin windowsill. He wiped the mist away from the window with his bloodstained sleeve and looked in. The music was playing from a small television mounted onto the wall in the top left-hand corner of the room. The black and white music video of the song was playing on it. It was very old. Though the main singer looked very young in it. Tinsel didn't even know if he was even still alive anymore. That song came out just after the infamous North Pole Mutiny of 6291. His mum and dad would've been too young to remember anything from that period, but Tinsel's grandfather always told him stories of those troubled times and how that song picked everyone up and inspired harmony amongst the North and South Elves.

Tinsel rested his head against the pane of the window and allowed the cold glass to ease the throbbing in his head. He felt a sudden rush of pain, melancholy, and nostalgia as the song finished and faded out. Not happiness though. That was lost somewhere in the fog of it all.

The next part is hazy for Tinsel, but it didn't take him long to figure out what he'd done. He lifted his face from the ground and all he could see was the orange polyester carpet and broken glass. He rolled over on his back and saw that the window he'd been leaning against was smashed in. It didn't take long for Tinsel to piece together what happened there. He placed his hands on the floor, not caring if he cut himself on the glass, and picked himself up. Tinsel scanned the room from left to right. His mother had worked in a place like this. There were five rows of small tables, each row going back at least fifty or sixty tables. The tables were colored with ribbons and bobbles. They looked like old school desks.

Tinsel maneuvered his way through the tables. He stopped at one table and picked up a small wooden hammer. He hit the frame of the table softly with it, then dropped it to the floor. The sound of the hammer hitting the floor echoed throughout the hall. Tinsel looked down towards the entrance of the room. He could see the fountain of the Main Square through the glazed windows. He hadn't wandered too far, thank god. He spun around and walked down the row of tables.

170

Then out of nowhere, Tinsel started skipping playfully around the room, meandering through the tables like a school girl playing hopscotch. He stopped at one table, made a sound that closely resembled a car braking, and jumped into the chair.

He picked up the rusted jack-in-the-box that was laying on its side and held it up high.

Can I have this one, Mom? said Tinsel to no one.

He waved it around frantically like he was trying to shake the jack out of the box.

Please, it's just what I want. It's not too expensive.

He set it down on the table, stared at it with wonder and then looked up again.

What do you mean Santa can't afford it? Santa can do anything.

Santa's already getting an expensive gift for your brother, said Tinsel, contorting his face and lowering the pitch of his voice. He might not be able to afford that as well.

Tinsel relaxed his face again and looked up. But Santa doesn't need money, he said, a bit quieter this time. He can do anything.

Tinsel lowered his face and stared at the jack-in-the-box. He spat at it and angrily pushed it off the table. He sat there for a little bit, staring at the aging wood, with scratches in it that looked like someone had carved into it with a compass. When he lifted his head, his eyes were blurry. There was a different song playing on the TV now. A more recent release that Tinsel thought was a bit shite. He rubbed his eyes and looked towards the main office at the front of the room. It took a moment for Tinsel to understand what he was seeing. He thought he might have been hallucinating. He widened his eyes and looked closer. There was a young elf peering out at him through the door of the office at the top of the room

Tinsel got up slowly and approached the door.

Hey, little fella, he said softly.

The young elf didn't say anything. He looked frightened.

I'm not going to hurt you, said Tinsel, trying to act as sober as he could.

Are you Santa? said the young elf.

No, but I work with him.

The young elf emerged fully from the door frame and looked at Tinsel.

Cornflake McSnowflake said his dad his best friends with him, he said.

That's cool.

The young elf looked behind him.

What are you doing here? said Tinsel.

This is my mummy's office.

Yeah?

She's the bossman.

The bossman? What do you… Oh, you mean she's the boss.

The young elf nodded.

And where's your mummy?

The young elf pointed inside the office to the left. Tinsel moved forward slowly and peered in. The room was dark except for a single candle flickering on the edge of the desk. There was a female elf sitting behind the desk, her head cocked back and snoring loudly. Tinsel walked in quietly and looked around the room.

There was a small glass in front of her, filled with something Tinsel couldn't recognize because it was too dark. There was a large uncorked

172

bottle next to it. Tinsel looked closer and could discern the whiskey label through the faint light of the flickering candle. Tinsel turned and walked out of the room. In the opposite room, the young elf was sitting with his legs crossed on an old dirty mattress, playing with an action figure. Tinsel walked up to the border of the mattress, kneeled in front of the young elf and observed him moving the arm of the action figure up and down.

What are you two doing here? said Tinsel.

We're hiding from Daddy, said the young elf.

And why are you hiding from Daddy?

Mommy said he won't be around anymore.

What do you mean?

She called him a cheater. She said he's with someone from his work now, but I haven't seen him with anyone so I don't know what she means.

I'm sorry to hear that. My mum and dad split up as well when I was younger.

Did they get back together?

No, they're long dead now. I'm sure your folks will figure it out though.

Mommy said to forget about him.

The young elf dropped the action figure between his legs.

What's your name? said Tinsel.

North.

And what's Santa bring you for Christmas, North?

North shrugged his shoulders.

You don't know? said Tinsel.

I never wrote a list.

Why not?

Daddy said it was a waste of time.

Did he now?

He said he's too busy to get to us.

Is that right?

Tinsel got up and walked back to the main hall. He walked through the tables, looking at each one he passed for something that didn't look broken. He stopped at a table in the middle of the room, where a basket of toys sat `on the surface. He rummaged through it, trying to find anything that didn't look like it'd recently been used as toilet paper, and eventually found a plush snowman. Tinsel picked it up. The fabric was nice and smooth and the snowman had a warm and welcoming ear-to-ear smile on his face. Tinsel nodded in satisfaction. He turned and walked back to the office. He went back into North and kneeled in front of him.

Here you go, said Tinsel, holding out the snowman.

Mommy might get in trouble, said North.

I wouldn't worry about it.

North took the toy and stared at it.

You like it? said Tinsel.

North nodded. Thank you, he said.

You are very welcome.

What did you ask Santa for? said North.

Me?

North nodded.

Huh… nothing really. People my age don't really ask Santa for stuff. You get to the point where you have to stop believing in him, or believing he'll make everything better.

174

What?

Never mind me, said Tinsel smiling. I'm just talking to myself.

North picked up his action figure and held it next to the snowman, like they were now best friends.

You keep that hidden so your mom doesn't take it, okay?

North nodded.

You can write to me next year if you want something for Christmas. My names Tinsel. Remember that name. You write to me personally and I'll make sure Santa gets you whatever you want.

North smiled. Okay, he said.

Tinsel turned and looked down towards the office where he could still hear the female elf snoring. He turned back and watched North rub his finger along the smooth fur of the snowman.

I have to go now, North.

Okay.

Remember to write to me.

Okay.

Tinsel stood up. Merry Christmas.

Merry Christmas, said North.

Tinsel turned and walked out of the room. He stopped before the door to the main hall and looked in at the female elf, who was still fast asleep at her desk. He tip-toed in, reached out and swiped the bottle of whiskey off the desk. He turned around and left the room.

Tinsel walked down the middle of the room between the desks to the front door. He undid the latch on the bottom and the top and opened the door. He shut it softly behind him and walked out into the Main Square. It was still dark but he could just make out the faintest bit of morning blue on the horizon. Tinsel gripped the neck of the bottle and took a swig of whiskey, letting it burn away the vomit still stuck to the walls of his oesophagus. He approached the fountain and sat on the edge. His hand was still aching from the cut but the pain had eased. He took another swig of whiskey and looked up at the night sky as the snow fell. Tinsel smiled at the thought that somewhere in the world right now, that old fuckers squeezing himself down somebody's chimney. He knew a couple of his mates from work would be getting up early and heading to the roof of the church to watch the big man come in. They asked Tinsel this evening before they all left work if he'd like to come along, but he said no. He didn't want to clap and cheer with the rest of the crowd as the fat fuck came in on his sleigh, and pretend like he was delighted to see him when really he was gutted one of his reindeer didn't have a heart attack and send the sleigh crashing into the side of a mountain.

Somewhere in the distance, Tinsel could hear a choir singing. He got up, turned towards the statue, undid the zipper on his tights, whipped out his dick, and started pissing into the fountain. He lifted the whiskey bottle in the air and saluted the Statue of Santa that stood self-righteously in the middle of the fountain.

Do you believe in yourself, my excellency? he roared.

Tinsel brought the whiskey bottle down to his mouth, emptied the remaining contents down his gullet, and then turned and headed off in the direction of the sweet music.

Drama Queen

L ydia wanted a shag. She was dying for one. She hadn't had one for months. Not for any particular reason like she'd put on a few pounds and the guys weren't interested in her anymore, or because she had a gross yeast infection that made her vagina smell like a homeless salmon, or because of some loss in confidence. It just hadn't happened. Well, perhaps it was because Lydia had started a new job. It was a job she'd always wanted and she finally had it. So for the first couple of months, she threw everything into her work, which meant putting pleasurable desires such as sex in the backseat. Which Lydia didn't mind doing because this had been a job she'd desired since she was young. But after a couple of months, she started to notice it, like something stuck in the back of her teeth.

Then after a couple of more months, Lydia got so horny that getting the ride was pretty much the only thing on her mind. She'd be sitting at her desk and imagining riding any guy that passed her office or so much as talked to her. Even the guy who delivers Lydia's post, who looked like a hiking shoe that's been mauled apart by an Alsatian, made her wet. When her sex drought hit the one-year mark, Lydia decided that she just had to go out and get the shag. She couldn't live like this anymore. She didn't care if she had to approach some random old guy in a pub and bluntly ask him to fuck her. At this stage, Lydia just wanted to have sex so she didn't have to think about it anymore. Just so it wouldn't be this constant nagging thing in the back of her head and she could move on with her life.

So one Saturday night, Lydia decided to go out with her mates. She decided to go out sober, which would be difficult because all her mates were getting pissed, but Lydia didn't want to drink or take anything that might get in the way or impair her ability to pull. She was wearing her best dress. Low cut so her breasts were popping and tight around the legs so her arse looked like two balloons hugging. She spent two hours putting on makeup and doing her hair, covering up every facial imperfection in a mountain of foundation.

By the time she got to the pub, Lydia was practically wet. It was only when she made it inside the pub that she encountered a problem she never expected: She actually had to approach a guy and strike up a conversation with him. Lydia was so used to guys coming up to her and using some cheesy pick-up line they'd heard in some YouTube video. But making the first move herself? That was something she hadn't the first fucking clue how to tackle.

She supposed she could wait for a guy to approach her. But Lydia didn't have time for that. She didn't want to be idle. She came here tonight with a mission. And by God, she wasn't about to let anything stop her from accomplishing it. She walked around the pub for a while with her friends, scanning the room for any potential candidates. It was early yet so there were still plenty of people to come, but Lydia wanted to make a move sooner rather than later because she knew that if she let her nerves get the better of her, she'd be waiting all night, and then she'd just end up heading

178

home by herself and relying on the faithfulness of her trusty vibrator, Hector, to get herself off. And Lydia had no intention of going home alone tonight.

An hour passed and Lydia still hadn't chatted anyone up. She was out in the smoking area having a fag. She had a baby Guinness in the hopes it would calm her nerves, but she didn't feel any different. This would be so much easier if she was off her head right now. Soon, Lydia was starting to feel disheartened with the whole thing. Is this what guys have to go through every time they want to approach a girl? Because fucking hell, if she was a guy and had to do this every time she wanted to get laid, she'd just end up fucking guys. Her friends were all drunk at this point and she wasn't enjoying the night anymore. She found them less tolerable when they were intoxicated and she wasn't. Lydia sighed. The positive energy she came out with seemed to have faded away.

But that's when Lydia's eyes caught a guy on the other side of the smoking area. His name was Jake. He went to school with Lydia but it had been years since she last saw him. She didn't recognize him at first, he'd changed so much. She remembered him as this chubby teen, who looked like a cone overfilled with ice-cream, with the body odor of someone who uses radiator liquid as deodorant.

That's not what Lydia was looking at now though. The Jake she was staring at was fucking tall. Almost 6'4. Fit looking guy as well. He'd shed all that weight he had in school. He still had the jet-black hair, but it wasn't as unkempt and flattened to his forehead as she remembers. It was short, kind of like a Peaky Blinders haircut. He was good looking too. Very good looking. She had to admit it. And Lydia didn't feel as nervous as before when she considered approaching him. At least they had school in common. At least she had a conversational starting point with him. She wasn't exactly sure if he remembered her as just a girl from school or as a bitch, but at this point, she'd settle for anything. If this guy didn't want to fuck her, she really didn't know what she was going to do.

She left her friends and started walking towards him. Her friends didn't seem to notice. Angela was in the crying stage of the night now. She was sobbing because her ex, Brad, was shifting her dad on the dancefloor.

Lydia felt a fucking swarm of butterflies in her stomach as she neared Jake. She started picturing all the horrible ways he might reject her. What if he thought she was fuck ugly? What if he started laughing at the idea that she could even try and approach him. Oh, God! What if he's gay?

But Lydia didn't have to say anything because Jake turned his head in her direction as she walked towards him and made a face that said he recognized her.

Hey, Lydia, he said.

Do I know you? said Lydia, trying to act cool.

Yeah, we went to Highton together? Jake?

Lydia pretended to scan his face like she was trying to remember him.

I was in your Physics class with Mr. Handford? he continued.

Lydia figured now was the best time to remember him. She beamed and said: Oh, my God! Jake, I do remember you!

He gave her a big hug. She was fucking in.

I didn't recognize you at first, she said.

I know, it's been a while, hasn't it?

Sure has. What you up to these days?

180

They talked for a while about what they were up to and who they were still in contact with from school. Lydia made sure to make a move quickly so as to establish a sexual dynamic. She got closer to him and put her hand on his lower back. She slowly moved her hand down his body until she got to his arse.

You look good, she said.

Do I?

Yeah, no wonder I didn't recognize you.

He smiled. I know I used to be a bit fat. But my mum bought me a gym membership there about a year ago and it seemed a shame not to use it.

Well, it clearly paid off, she said, making heavy eye contact.

Towards the end of the night, they were shifting at the back of the smoking area. She had her hands on his arse and he was topping her. Lydia could honestly cum right now, she was so horny. She needed to go now before she squirted all over the floor. She looked at him. Want to head back to my place? she said.

You want me to? he said.

Yes.

Then let's go.

They left the pub and got in a taxi. They were shifting in the backseat, uncaring of the awkward eyes they were getting from the driver, and Jake grabbed a handful of Lydia's tit. Oh, my God. It's going to happen. After all this fucking time, it's finally going to happen. When they got in the front door, she was practically tumbling, she was so excited. They got upstairs and shifted on the bed for a bit. After a while, Jake rubbed her inner thigh and slipped his fingers in her pussy. Lydia shuddered. Before it could go any further, she said she was going to use the bathroom and she'd be back in a minute.

She went into the bathroom and took off her dress. She put all her jewelry in a cup in the sink and got down to her bra and knickers. She looked at herself in the mirror, ran her hands through her hair, wiped some smudged lipstick off her chin, and took a deep breath. Here we go, she said to herself. She went into the bedroom and he was laying on the bed in his jocks, waiting for her. They smiled at each other. She ran and jumped on top of him. There was a bit of foreplay and she took off his underwear and he took off hers. And then they shagged.

And it was alright. Lydia lay naked next to Jake. He was smoking a fag. It was alright. It wasn't great. Lydia didn't want to be feeling what she was feeling but she couldn't help it. She felt a bit disappointed. It was only alright. It wasn't the explosive experience she'd pictured in her head. But perhaps that was her own fault. Perhaps Lydia's sex drive over the past year had been so intense, that it created an experience in her head that was simply unrealistic and not possible to reach. But at least she'd had a shag. At least she didn't have to think about it anymore.

I'm still living at home, said Jake.

Lydia turned to him. What? she said.

I'm still living at home with my parents.

Oh, right, she said. That's nice.

Jake looked out the window. It looked like there was something wrong with him. Maybe it was the drink or something. But Lydia couldn't remember him being that drunk tonight.

You alright? she said.

He didn't answer.

Jake?

He turned to her. My dad hits me, he said.

Oh, really. Lydia didn't know how to respond.

Yeah. He just got out of prison. I try and stay away from the house as much as I can. That's sort of half the reason I came back to yours.

I'm… I'm sorry.

Thanks. He turned and put his fag out in an empty mug on the nightstand. Fucking cheeky bollox. That was Lydia's favorite mug.

Jake turned back to Lydia. My mom won't do anything about it either.

Your mom?

Yeah. She's too busy being a pathetic alcoholic.

Jeez, that's horrible. Lydia cocked her eyes slightly. Great, she thought. Another fucking drama queen.

Jake jumped off the bed and walked over to the window. He stood there, stark bollock naked, staring out the window. Lydia thought he looked quite beautiful actually. His arse glistened in the moonlight. Like a painting.

Jake turned around. His face turned from sadness to anger in an instant. I'm so fucking sick of their shit, he said through gritted teeth. He stormed across the room, his cheeks turning red, and without warning, punched two holes in Lydia's wardrobe. Then he hit himself across the face. He looked at her. Want to go again? he said.

Lydia said yes, afraid of what he might do if she said no. He jumped on top of her and got inside her again. Except this time, it was different. Lydia could see he was still seething with rage and it looked like he was channeling it into riding her. Sweat from his head dripped down onto hers.

He was going faster and faster. Deeper and deeper. Angrier and angrier. He was breathing like a bull. And she was fucking loving it. This was it. This was the ride Lydia had been picturing in her head. The sweat was pouring off her. She didn't know what her arms and legs were doing. All she could see was the top of Jake's head. When she came, Lydia's legs almost buckled in on themselves. She didn't know how loud she'd been screaming, or what sounds she was making in general, but it must have been loud because her throat was killing her.

She lay in bed for about half an hour, the sheets barely covering her, trying to recover from what most would say sounded like a satanic ritual. She couldn't fucking move. Then there was a knock at the door. Lydia didn't hear but Jake nudged her and told her. She got up. She could barely walk. Her legs felt like rubber. She grabbed her dressing gown off the floor and threw it on. She walked down the stairs, holding onto the banister for dear life.

When she got to the door, she was suddenly aware of how dehydrated she was. Her mouth was so dry. She opened up the door. It was her neighbor, Pat.

Hey, Lydia, sorry to bother you at this time of night, but I heard screaming.

Oh, sorry…

Lydia could barely speak. Her voice was hoarse. She coughed and cleared her throat. Sorry, she said. I was just having a party inside, but I'm going to bed now. Sorry to have woken you up

Okay. Just wanted to make sure you're alright.

Thanks, Pat. Goodnight.

And she closed the door. Lydia went into the kitchen, poured herself a pint of water and gulped it down. Then she poured herself another. When she got back upstairs, Jake was asleep. She set the pint of water on her nightstand and got back into bed. She instantly fell asleep.

When Lydia woke up the next morning, Jake was gone. There was a note on his pillow. "*Had a great night. If you want to meet up again, give me a call xxx*". His number was underneath it. She lay back down and stared at the ceiling. What a great fucking shag that was. She was definitely going to call him again. No fucking doubt about it. How often are your expectations not only met but exceeded?

Then Lydia remembered something. She raised her head and looked at the wardrobe. There were two holes in it. It all came back to her. Jake talking about his dad beating him up and getting out of prison, and his mum being an alky. Then she remembered him punching the wardrobe. And then she had what was possibly the best shag she'd ever had. But it's funny that she never thought about him punching the wardrobe up until now. Not that Lydia was surprised. Most people would forget their own names after a shag like that.

It was odd, now that Lydia thought about it. She guessed it was the drink that was making him open up to her about such personal things in his life. God knows she'd been there before. But the shag. Where did that come out of? And why was the shag before it so adequate? How do you go from a not-so-memorable shag to a shag that left her legs quivering? The only thing that happened in between those two things was he had a fag, told her some very intimate things about his abusive parents, and then punched two holes in her wardrobe. What had happened?

185

Well, Lydia found out. She phoned him up the day after that to see if he wanted to go to dinner. He said yes. They went out to some Asian restaurant. He apologized to her about punching her wardrobe and said it was the drink. She told him not to worry about it. They had a fairly normal date. They didn't talk that much. He was quite boring actually. And he actually got more boring the more he drank, which bummed Lydia out. At the end of the night, they went back to her place and shagged again.

And it was only alright. Again. She lay there afterwards, Jake smoking a fag, and she was fucking confused and angry. Why wasn't he able to shag her the same way that he did the last night? What was it that brought it on? And she thought about him talking about his parents and punching that wardrobe.

Was it the drama that did it? Was it that he got himself a bit worked up beforehand? Because she did remember Jake's angry face as he pummelled away at her.

Sorry again about that, said Jake.

About what? she said.

He pointed to the wardrobe.

Don't worry about it, she said. You were upset.

He turned to her. Was I?

Yeah.

What was I saying?

Lydia wasn't going to tell him anything. She was going to tell him that it wasn't a big deal, or she was too drunk to remember. But perhaps he might be able to provide some answers about his unbalanced performance ratio in bed.

186

You said something about your parents?

What did I say about them?

You said your dad got out of prison and beats you and your mum's a drunk.

Jake looked away from Lydia. Sorry I said that, he said. I shouldn't have told you.

No, it's okay.

He got up and sat with his back facing her. He was breathing heavily. A light went off in Lydia's head. Was this what he needed? Was he getting angry again? Was he like a sexual Hulk?

It's not okay, he said finally.

Don't think about it.

I don't want to be like them.

I'm glad you told me. I understand.

How could you understand, Lydia?

Lydia looked around the room, racking her brains to try and think up an answer.

Because my parents are the same, she said.

He turned to her and looked her in the eyes. There were tears streaming down his face. Is that true? he said.

Yeah. My dad used to touch me when I was younger, and my mom hits me all the time.

That wasn't true at all of course. Lydia loved her parents. They were her best friends in many ways. But she could see in Jake's face that she was getting close to something. A little white lie wouldn't hurt.

I'm so sorry, he said. I didn't know.

She looked down. I've never told anyone. Then she clenched her fist and swung at the lamp on her nightstand. It flew across the room and hit the wall.

I fucking hate them, she said.

Jake turned and ran his hand through her hair. It's not your fault. Look at me. It's not your fault, you understand?

Lydia nodded. She found she was crying. Fucking hell, she was better at this acting thing than she thought she was.

I know how frustrating it can be, he said. But you're strong. You can be better than them. You can handle it. Better than me anyway.

Lydia put both her hands on his face. You're strong too, she said. Stronger than you think you are. Then they kissed. Jake lay her down and slid his fingers in her vagina. She was starting to feel it again. She could feel the anger in him. The hate. Lydia was the Emperor Palpatine and Jake was Darth Vader. He took off his boxers and slid inside her again. They shagged again and it was the best fucking shag Lydia ever had in her life. Hands down. Miles fucking better than the shag she'd received the first night. She screamed louder than she ever thought possible. She heard herself make sounds she didn't think she was capable of making.

The next morning, it took her a few minutes to remember who and where she was. Jake was still there, snoring away beside her. She looked at the two holes in the wardrobe again and smiled. She'd figured it out. She figured out the secret ingredient needed to turn Jake from an adequate humper to a godlike lover. He was a drama queen. That's who Jake was. Getting him all riled up about shit that was bothering him. It unlocked something in him. Some sort of sexual power. Lydia got it now. All she

188

had to do every time she wanted the shag was to get him pouring his heart out.

Lydia and Jake started going out. She introduced him to her friends. Of course, her friends didn't like him. Her friend Maura took her aside one day and asked her did she know how fucked up Jake's family is. Lydia said Jake had told her. Maura asked her why she was going out with him if she knew all that. Lydia simply said she wouldn't understand and she walked away. Over the next couple of weeks, her friends would come to her with more information about how weird Jake was and how fucked up his family was, in the hopes of turning her off him. But it never did. They were right to be concerned, but they didn't understand. How could they? If they'd experienced a shag from Jake after he revealed a scar on his stomach from where his dad put a fag out on him as a child, they wouldn't be saying any of this shite. They'd be fucking lining up behind her.

Every shag was becoming better than the last. Lydia got Jake to reveal the darkest, most intimate secrets of his life and afterwards, he'd deliver her into a sexual dimension that mere mortals would only dream of entering. It was almost addicting. She couldn't stop. The more he confided and revealed, the more intense the shag. Lydia had to match Jakes level of drama, of course. She had to tell him a few white lies about her own family to match his own, otherwise, it would be very one-sided. One night, Lydia told him that she'd had an argument with her mum and she'd told her to kill herself. Jake fingered her until she squirted all over the room like a broken garden hose.

Another night, just before he arrived, Lydia took a biro and stabbed herself a few times in the leg. When he came over later that night, she told

189

him her Dad had done it. Jake said he was going to kill him. But she brought him back to bed and he shagged her so hard into a coma that left her unconscious for a day and a half. Sometimes, she'd cut along her arm and give herself black eyes, which was rough and painful work, but was well worth the shag afterwards.

People at work sometimes asked her if everything was alright but she convinced them it was all fine. It was hard work keeping up the act. Sometimes she wondered if she was mad doing all this stuff to herself just to keep up this relationship. But then Jake would shag her so hard that steam would come off her. And she'd forget that she even wondered it.

Whenever anybody asked Lydia about certain visible and concerning bruises, she'd say Jake wasn't like that and they were all consensual. Her friends told her she was being stupid for going out with Jake and that she was asking for trouble. She said she didn't care and that they didn't have to hang out with her if it bothered them so much. She drifted away from them not too long after that, which upset her greatly, but then Jake shagged her and she forgot they even existed.

Of course, Lydia's parents found out that she was seeing someone (Lydia suspected her friends went to them to try and get them to intervene) and they started asking when they could meet him. Every time they asked, she'd say, soon. Lydia thought it would probably be best for Jake not to meet her mum and dad, considering all the horrible and untrue things she's told him about them. Lydia was only able to hold them off for a while though. Her parents started getting impatient, asking if there was a reason she didn't want them to meet him. To preserve her relationship with them, Lydia told them it wasn't that serious and she was considering breaking up with him because their work schedules prevented them from seeing each other as much as they wanted. They seemed convinced. That would buy her some more time until she had to tell another lie. Lydia didn't like lying to her parents. But if only they experienced a shag from Jake, they wouldn't be asking so many questions.

It got to the point where a shag from Jake essentially became an addiction for Lydia. She would pick fights with Jake because she knew how mind-bendingly orgasmic the make-up sex would be. Her entire life became a soap opera. She wanted to stop. She actually did. She hated Jake. All drama aside, he was the most boring and annoying person she'd ever met in her life. She genuinely loathed him as a person. He was a fucking child. All he did was complain about how shitty his life was but never seemed to do anything about it. He seemed content with allowing himself to be defined by all the shitty things in his life. It was pathetic. There was no fucking talking to him. You could poke a million holes in his bullshit rationales, like when Lydia suggested that he move and start a life away from his parents, and he just dismissed her. The cunt just wouldn't listen. But all the hatred she felt for Jake seemed to do nothing but fuel her sexual desire for him.

She honestly didn't know how much longer she could do this for. She'd think about breaking it off sometimes, but then he'd ride her and she'd forget all about it. Lydia even quit her job so she could spend more time with him. All her friends cut contact with her completely. The constant nagging from her parents regarding Jake and the rumors they'd heard about him and his degenerative parents got to be too much for her, so Lydia picked a fight with them one day, telling them how unsupportive they were and how everything she did never seemed to satisfy them. After this, Lydia gave them the silent treatment. She didn't want to cut contact with them completely like she did with her friends. She just needed time away from them for a while so she could figure out what she was going to do. It was for their own good. Lydia had to protect them. It really depressed her that she had to make such drastic changes in her life. She really started to hate Jake for it. But seriously, the shag. Out of this fucking world.

One morning, while Lydia was asleep in bed, Jake stormed into the apartment and kicked down the bedroom door. Lydia jumped from the bed in fright. He was out of breath and sweaty. But that's not what Lydia noticed first. What she noticed first was that he was covered head to toe in blood.

What's going on? she said.

Without saying anything, Jake moved towards her wardrobe and opened it up. He grabbed an empty gym bag off the floor and started shoving clothes into it.

Jake, what's going on? said Lydia.

We have to leave, he said.

What?

I'll explain in the car.

Jake, tell me what's happened.

Not now.

What do you mean not now? Where are we going?

He turned sharply and stared at her, blood dripping down his face. His eyes were wide open. They looked like they were going to pop out of his head like a Looney Tunes character.

192

Not now, he screamed.

Lydia sat on the bed, scared out of her mind. She knew how violent he could get when he was angry, so she knew better than to provoke him. Plus, she was still weak from when he rode her two nights ago, so she didn't have the energy to be fighting right now. She just sat there watching him pack the gym bag. When he was done, he grabbed her harshly by the arm, dragged her out of the apartment, and shoved her into the car outside. When they were both in the car and driving, she said: Okay, are you going to tell me now what happened?

He didn't say anything for a few seconds, but eventually he said: Do you trust me?

What?

Stop making me repeat myself. Do you trust me?

Jake, what happened?

I killed my parents.

What? she said.

This morning, me and my dad got into an argument because he wanted to borrow the car and I said no. Then he came at me with a bottle. So I stabbed him in the neck with a kitchen knife.

And your mom?

I cut her throat. Not like she noticed anyway. She was passed out in bed.

Lydia looked out the window, her heart beating through her ribs. She didn't know how to process any of this. But something else quickly caught her attention, and that was the road they were driving on.

Wait, where are we going? she said.

Your parents' house.

What for?

We're going to kill them.

Jake, you need to relax for a second and...

Jake slammed his hands against the steering wheel. We're going to fucking kill them, he said. We're going to kill the people that made us like this and make sure they can't fuck us up anymore. Then we're getting out of town. We're going to get as far away from here as we possibly can and start a new life for ourselves.

Jake, I can't...

This is what's happening, do you understand?

Lydia didn't say anything. She just nodded.

Do you understand? he said again.

Yes.

Good. No one's going to fuck us up anymore. It's just you and me now.

Lydia looked out the window at the passing houses. She knew she should have been thinking of a way to try and get out of this. She knew she should be trying to talk some sense into him. She knew she should just jump out of the car and run as fast as she could away from this fucking lunatic. She knew she should grab the biro on the dashboard and stab him. She knew she should take out her phone and call the police.

But as the car pulled into her parents driveway and Jake took a kitchen knife out from underneath the driver's seat, all Lydia could think about was how good the shag would be after all this.

Wiggly Worm And The Power Of The Dick Tree

Kelby had just bought a new game for his Nintendo Switch. It was called *"Wiggly Worm and the Power of the Dick Tree"*. It was a turn-based role-playing game. Kelby really liked it. It reminded him of the old-school Final Fantasy games he used to play on his PS1 when he was a kid. The only difference with this game was it was set in space, as opposed to the RPG's he was used to, that were mainly fantasies.

There were eight playable characters you could choose from, all of which you got as you progressed further and further into the game, and all of which had their own unique ways of fighting. For example, the first character you get, Zizan, uses mainly a sword to fight enemies, while Rogrant, a character you get later on in the game, is more like a medic. He uses moves that help the other characters in battle, like heal them or give them special abilities.

Kelby really enjoyed the setting of the game as well. It took place on sixteen uniquely different planets. Kelby's favorite feature in the game was how it encouraged you to explore the open world by yourself instead of following the linear outline of the main story. To be honest, Kelby was having more fun completing the side quests. He must have put in at least twenty hours into the game so far and he's barely scratched the surface of the main story. Kelby loved games like this, a game you could spend hours and hours playing and just get lost in. He'd get so engrossed in the insanely detailed open world or the spellbinding story that sometimes, he'd be up till the early hours of the morning just trying to finish off some stupid side quest, like trying to beat some optional boss so he could get an ultra-rare weapon, or collecting as many orbs as he could so he could level up his characters. He'd be well knackered in college the next day but it was well worth it. It was very rare for a game to come along that Kelby loved as much as *"Wiggly Worm and the Power of the Dick Tree"*. Quality games like this only come out once in a while and Kelby was usually very picky about the kinds of games he played. He'd grown tired of the mind-numbingly repetitive nature of games like FIFA and NBA 2K, that were just repackaged every year with a new title. Even games that Kelby really enjoyed, like Rocket League, Mario Kart and Super Smash Bros. started to stale on him after a while. A game like *"Wiggly Worm and the Power of the Dick Tree"* was just the experience he needed to reinvigorate his love for gaming.

Beyond a shadow of a doubt, the best aspect of the game was the story. It was so well-written and fleshed out. It was a story set in space and all the characters and locations were so absurd and silly, but it was so grounded in reality that you could forgive it for all the over-the-top stuff. All the characters had flaws and issues. And grown up issues as well, not the childish ones you find in so many RPG's. Like one of the characters was addicted to drugs and the story follows him as he tries to wean himself

196

of them. Another was a former criminal with very severe amnesia and he couldn't remember his past life. As the story goes on, he discovers more and more about some of the horrible things he's done. Even some of the minor non-playable characters were so fleshed out. They felt like real people. People you could relate to. Kelby couldn't imagine the effort that went into just the writing alone.

And it was because of that writing that Kelby had to stop playing *"Wiggly Worm and the Power of the Dick Tree"*. He came across something in the game that upset and angered him so deeply, that he just couldn't bring himself to play it anymore. And here's what it was.

So in the game, there's these sorts of hubs you can go to to heal up your characters if they're weak or if you need supplies like potions or ethers, or if you just need to save your game. There basically like checkpoints and there's a few on every planet.

So in every hub, there's always this one guy that hangs out in the right-hand corner of the room that Kelby's never talked to. He doesn't even know if he did anything. Kelby just assumed he was one of those characters who might say something to you but doesn't actually have any use in the game. He's just kind of there to make the area feel a bit more populated and add a bit of depth to the world. But Kelby noticed that the guy was at every single hub, on every single planet, so he figured he had to do something. What else would he be doing there?

So this one night during a late night gaming marathon, Kelby decided to go up to him and finally uncover the mystery of what this guy did. Kelby wasn't really doing much else anyway. He was about to save his game and head to bed. He had to be up for college in three hours. But Kelby thought he'd do this one last thing before signing off. So he walked right up to the guy, pressed the A button, and the guy said:

"Hi there, are you a fellow traveler? Me too…"

He said a few other things as well about where he came from and things he'd encountered on his travels. Kelby just pressed A over and over, he didn't really care too much. He was too tired to care. He just wanted to find out if this guy had any use. And he did. The last thing he said to you was:

"Would you like me to rate your characters nicknames?"

Let me explain. So every time a new playable character is added to your party, you can assign the character their default name, or you can give them a nickname. Kelby always gave them funny names like *AnotherfingerGranny?* or *Whydontyoulovemedad* or something normal like *Greg*. You know, just having a bit of craic.

So anyway, Kelby wasn't too interested in what *Rating His Characters Nicknames* would actually entail. He couldn't imagine it would impact the game too much, but again, he just wanted to see what it would do. So he pressed A and a screen came up with a list of all the characters in his party. The guy asked him to pick one. So Kelby picked a random character with the nickname *"ArseRaptor"*, and the guy said:

"That's a great nickname, it really suits that character. But I think we can do better, don't you? Would you like to change your character's nickname?"

And suddenly Kelby felt an anger erupt in his body like he'd never felt before. It wasn't the type of "rage quit" anger one would normally experience when gaming. It wasn't the type of anger Kelby would feel if he was having trouble defeating a difficult boss or struggling to acquire a certain collectable. This was a hateful type of anger. The type of anger that Kelby experienced the day the guy that murdered his mom was dragged into court, and he had that fucking grin on his face. Kelby remembered that anger very well. All he wanted to do in that moment was tackle the cunt to the ground and slice his fucking neck open, same as he did to her. That was it. That's what Kelby was experiencing right now as he played *"Wiggly Worm and the Power of the Dick Tree"*.

Kelby gritted his teeth so hard he thought he'd chip them. He flung his Pro controller at the door and it broke in two, then he got up and tore out the TV plugs from the walls. Then he punched the TV screen and cracked it. He yanked the Nintendo Switch out of the dock and slammed it onto the ground. Then Kelby raised his head up to the ceiling and let out an ear-shattering howl. He collapsed to the floor and buried his face in his knees, his hands shaking.

How fucking dare that guy suggest such a thing, Kelby thought. Rate his character nicknames? What a load of fucking bollox. Why didn't the guy just say, *"Change character nicknames"*? Fucking cunt. Why didn't he just say what he actually wanted to do instead of leading Kelby on in thinking he was just going to give his characters nicknames a friendly critique. What a waste of fucking time. Kelby wished that the Switch cartridge were bigger so he could smash it to pieces. *If you don't like my characters fucking nicknames, mate, why don't you just fucking say so instead of dicking around and wasting my fucking time. Or better yet, how about just mind your fucking business and let me name my characters whatever I fucking want.*

199

Kelby's hands were shaking uncontrollably, like Michael J. Fox on ecstasy. He couldn't describe the degree of rage he was feeling. He wanted to find the programmer who put that stupid bullshit in the game and kill them. He honestly wanted to rip their heart out of their chest and crush it with his bare hands in front of their eyes. He hoped that programmer got cancer so deep up his arse that it hurt every time he took a shit, and everyone he loved left him when they learned of the diagnosis. Kelby really hoped the fucker was dead. He hoped they died alone and depressed, tossed in a fucking hole and left there to rot. Forgotten forever and no one would even remember they existed. Just meat to the earth now

There was no way Kelby could continue on with the game now. That was it. He was pretty sure his Switch was fucked now anyway. But if by some divine miracle it wasn't, he still wouldn't go back to it. That one little feature had single-handedly blown apart any future of Kelby continuing on with the game. If he kept playing, he'd have to see that guy every time he went into a hub to save his game or heal up his characters, and the thoughts of seeing that guy's gimpy face would make him want to smash the Switch into a million fucking pieces. It made Kelby angry now just thinking about it. No, that was it. The whole thing was ruined.

Kelby's roommate, Dillon, opened the door and poked his head in.

What's with all the noise? he said.

Fuck off! Kelby spat at him.

Jesus man, what's wrong with you?

Did I not just tell you to fuck off?

I was just wondering what all the racket was about.

If I have to tell you to fuck off again, I'll fucking make you.

200

Dillon muttered something that Kelby couldn't hear and closed the door.

What was that?

Kelby got up off the floor, stormed across his room, and swung his door open. Dillon was just outside his room with his hand on the doorknob. He turned to face Kelby. He looked bloody scared.

You want to fucking tell me something? said Kelby.

Dillon didn't say anything. He looked petrified with fear.

Are you fucking retarded? I asked you something. You have something to say to me?

Dillon shook his head nervously.

I didn't fucking hear you! Kelby roared down the hall, raising his hand up to his ear.

No, Dillon muttered quietly.

Yeah, I fucking thought not. You better watch your mouth you little prick or I'll slice your fucking neck open, you got that?

Dillon nodded his head nervously.

And with that, Kelby went back into his room and slammed the door. He sat down on his bed and put his hands on his head. Dillon must still be in the hall because Kelby didn't hear his door open. Kelby listened intently. After a minute, he heard the door open and close quietly. Kelby ran his hands through his hair and sighed.

Why did he just do that? Dillon was already having enough trouble being away from home as it was. Now Kelby had just blatantly threatened to kill him over a fucking game. He'd never come out of his room again. He'd probably tell his mom. She'd told Kelby the day Dillon moved in that he was very nervous about living with strangers and asked him to try to bring him out of his shell. And Kelby did. He talked with him and they had a few drinks and they really started to get on. After a while, Kelby wasn't just hanging out with him because his mom asked him to, but because Kelby really started to like Dillon. After the two of them would come home from college, they'd spend some nights watching random shit on Netflix, and sometimes Kelby would move his Switch into the sitting room and they'd spend hours playing Mario Kart or Super Smash Bros. The two of them had become really good friends in the month they'd been living together.

Now all of that was gone. All of it, in the bin, because Kelby got upset over a videogame. Dillon would definitely tell his mom. Kelby was sure he would. And why wouldn't he? In his mind, Dillon was now living with a psychopath. She'd drive up here and roar the head of him. Then she'd probably tell reception about what happened. They could kick Kelby out of the accommodation. They'd definitely kick him out. Kelby already had plenty of complaints from his roommates regarding the messes he always made after cooking his dinner in the evenings, not to mention all the noise complaints from his neighbors because of all the house parties he'd have till four in the morning. This would be it. They wouldn't tolerate this. No fucking way.

Kelby thought he should go apologize to Dillon. Make up some excuse that he was having a bad day or something. Kelby was going to get up but then he saw the case for *"Wiggly Worm and the Power of the Dick Tree"*. And then he thought of that guy again. And him asking Kelby if he wanted him to rate his character's nicknames. And then all that seething rage came flooding back to him. Kelby picked up the shattered remains of his Nintendo Switch. His mom had gotten it for him for the last Christmas they shared together.

Kelby didn't get up and say sorry to Dillon. He sat quietly on the floor for the rest of the night and stared at the blank wall in front of him, waiting for the silence to punish him.

What's the fucking point? he thought, picking up the game case and hurling it across the room.

What's the point?

Temptation

David locked his bedroom door. He pulled the curtains as an extra precaution in case any of the neighbors decided to peak in the window. Even though Lesley and the kids were out for the day, he left the window open so he could hear the car pull in. He turned around and faced his bed. David had been looking forward to this wank all day. Nothing was better than a wank when you know you're alone in the house.

David lay down on the bed, made himself comfortable, and pulled out his phone. He couldn't wait to have this wank. He wasn't feeling particularly horny or anything but no one was in the house, and seeing how rare such an occurrence happened in his life, David thought it would be a sin not to take advantage of the situation.

Relaxing on the bed and unbuckling his belt, he loaded up some amateur porn on his phone. David didn't mind what he wanked to. Most of the time he could do it without porn, but sometimes he needed something to get him going.

Finally landing on a video he liked, David began the wank. He began slowly like he always did. He allowed the video to work his magic and let himself steadily get into it. Once he got going, he dropped the phone and let his imagination take the wheel. This was the part of the wank he liked the most. He imagined all the woman at work he had a crush on, actresses he'd fuck, even old schoolteachers.

After twenty minutes and nearing climax, David felt his phone vibrate beside him. He sighed with annoyance that his concentration had been broken. He swiped his phone off the duvet, and without unlocking it, looked at the preview of the message he'd just gotten from Lesley.

Won't be home till 6. Quiche in the oven xx

She won't be home till six? David looked at the alarm clock on his bedside table and beamed. Lesley wasn't going to be home till six. That was four hours away. That only meant one thing: David could perform a wank that he liked to call, *"The Marathon Wank"*.

A Marathon Wank is exactly what it says on the tin. It's a wank that lasts for ages. Where you went really, really slow. And when you finally do cum, you've been holding it in for so long that it's fucking awesome. Almost euphoric. You really have to resist the urge to pick up speed though because sometimes you can get lost in the moment or get impatient or maybe you just have other things to do. It was the type of wank that required discipline and a very patient and tenacious mind. This wasn't something that could just be done on the fly. It certainly wasn't something that could be done with people in the house or in a fifteen-minute window. To do this, you'd need a couple of hours at minimum. And now, in David's case, he had four hours alone in the house. Four hours to bring about an orgasm that would keep him satisfied for weeks.

David jumped off the bed and waddled to the bathroom with his trousers around his ankles. He grabbed a roll of toilet paper and a bottle of lubricant that Lesley kept under the sink and, walking back towards the bed, squirted a large amount onto his palm and rubbed his hands together. If he was going to pull this off, David would need all the lubrication he could need, otherwise he'd have a penis resembling a Chorizo sausage by the end of it. He took off every stitch of clothing he had on him and jumped back onto the bed. It was time.

The first half an hour was the hardest, no question. Every urge in David's body told him to abandon The Marathon Wank and just resort back to a normal one so he could get back to peeling the spuds or putting out the washing or something else Lesley had asked him to do while she was out for the day. It was very easy to resort back to that. That's why this type of wank is such a rare occurrence in a man's life. Because it was hard to pull off, logistically speaking. David just had to keep reminding himself how amazing it would feel when he finally did shoot the goo. He just had to keep that image in the front of his mind.

Once he got past the forty-five-minute mark, there was no stopping it now. The train had left the station and the only thing that could stop David now was if Lesley and the kids suddenly came pulling in the driveway. It was hard to constantly stay in a horny state of mind throughout all this and porn was required at certain intervals to deal with moments of stagnation. This is very normal during a Marathon Wank. David tried to think of himself like a Formula One car that had to stop and get it's tires changed out. Just keeping the engine going, that's all he was doing. There were many moments when David felt like he was going to cum, but he resisted the urge to charge full ahead. Instead, he slowed down and dialed it back a few notches. No need to rush it, he had plenty of time and the more time he spent grinding away at it, the more euphoric the feeling.

An hour and a half in and David was still going. He was now approaching his record, at one hour and thirty-three minutes. Once he surpassed this by ten minutes or so, he'd call it quits and dial it up to ten. He could almost taste the orgasm.

Even now, David felt hornier than ever before. It was hard not to cum. To just accept that this was as good as it was going to get and call it quits. But why stop now, he thought. Might as well keep going until he could go no more. He still had two hours, more or less, before he'd have to resume his normal life. He was too far down the rabbit hole to give up now. He might as well go all the way.

Three hours in and David was starting to see things. Time was whizzing past in a blur and colors were mashing together like a broken kaleidoscope. His whole body was sweating and vibrating like he was sitting on one of those massage chairs in a pharmacy. He'd have to change the bed sheets before Lesley got home because he sweated through every inch of them. Plus, the mess he'd make when he finally came would be powerful enough to repaint the whole bedroom.

Three and a half hours in. David didn't even know who he was wanking to anymore. Faces were just passing in front of him like a merry-go-round. Faces of friends, relatives. It wasn't that he was imagining having sex with them. It was like his excessively heightened sense of arousal had taken over his body and was reaching into the furthest corners of his mind, trying to use anything it can to keep this wank going. Again, this was all perfectly normal for David. At least he hoped so anyway.

David hit the four hour mark and decided to get up and make himself something to eat. He was starving. He walked into the kitchen stark bollock naked, still tugging away at his penis, and grabbed himself an apple from the fruit bowl. He looked out the kitchen window as he washed it under the tap and saw Marge next door trimming the rose bushes. Thankfully, she was as blind as a bat so there's no way she could see what David was doing from her garden.

As he sank his teeth into the apple and he started making his way back up to the bedroom, an idea started to formulate in David's head. It was a crazy idea, but he wondered what's the longest amount of time he could wank for? David had never thought about it before. These four hours were a new record for him. His old record had been achieved while he was at college. A time when he had fewer responsibilities and more time to embark on Marathon Wanks. Even then, the idea of a four-hour wank would have been a god-like achievement.

As David jumped back onto the bed, he picked up his phone, his other hand still stroking his willy, and did a Google search for the longest masturbation. The record was held by some guy in Japan. Nine hours and fifty-eight minutes. Ten fucking hours. David wasn't sure he could go for that long. He was only four hours in now and he was barely hanging on as it is. If he was to even attempt to beat a record like that, there's no way he could attempt it in the house. Not a fucking chance. He'd have to go somewhere else. He'd have to book a hotel. He could make something up for Lesley, saying he had to work late or something.

No, he couldn't do it. There was no way he could last for ten hours. It was a fantasy. Besides, Lesley would be home with the kids soon. David slowed down the pace. He needed to think but he didn't want to stop. David had now been wanking for four hours and twenty-two minutes. This was

208

the longest wank he'd ever had in his life. It was almost three times longer than his previous record and he was sure if he just came now, the orgasm would be unbelievable. It would be the best thing he ever felt, better than any sex he'd ever had with Lesley, that's for fucking sure.

But could he live with himself? Could he live with the knowledge that he didn't even try to break the record? It would be like climbing Everest and deciding to quit halfway up because the missus was telling you to come down. He could tell himself he could always try another day but David knew it would be ages before another opportunity like this presented itself again. Years. It was hard enough getting this time. Uh, but he'd have to deal with Lesley. He'd have to make excuses and say he was called into the office, and if she suspected for even a minute that he was hiding something from her, she'd turn into her alter-ego: The Paranoid Private Detective. She'd catch him out on a white lie or an inconsistency in his cover story and then he'd have to explain himself. To be honest, David was certain an affair would be easier to explain then the truth. He didn't know if it was worth all the hassle it would cause.

No, David had to do it. He couldn't tell himself he couldn't do it, or it wasn't worth it or he'd try another time. That was his negative brain jumping in and trying to keep him safe and placid. David didn't want to be safe and placid anymore. He had to know what a ten hour wank felt like. He just had to. If some guy in Japan can make it for ten hours, then surely he could too. And even if David only made it to six or seven hours, at least he could tell himself he tried. He'd be able to look his wife and children in the eyes and not feel like a complete failure. David had to do this. He had to do this for his family. But most importantly, for himself.

David unlocked the door to his hotel room and stepped in quickly, putting a *"Do Not Disturb"* sign on the outside handle and closing the door. David wasn't sure he could make it. But he had, thanks to whatever angel was watching over him. David had somehow gotten dressed, packed an overnight bag, prepared some sandwiches so he wouldn't starve, called Lesley and told her he got called into the office because of a problem at work and probably wouldn't be home until the morning, gotten into his car, driven to a hotel and paid for a room at the reception. All the while *still* masturbating.

It hadn't been easy, especially when he was checking in. He tried to do it as quickly and efficiently as he could so he didn't get held up. Plus, if the woman at reception saw him wanking while he was tapping his debit card, he could say goodbye to that world record. He'd managed to keep the wank going by cutting a hole in the pockets of his jeans and keeping one hand on his penis at all times.

It proved even harder to keep up while he was driving to the hotel. He kept one hand on the wheel while the other alternated between the gearstick and his own gearstick. It'd been tough but David found that as long as he didn't have his hand off his crotch for longer than six seconds, he could maintain the wank. It meant he really had to slow it down though and lose some momentum, which meant he risked losing his erection, but he kept some porn loaded on his phone at all times if he felt a deflation. He wasn't sure he could, but he'd made it. He was here now and he had no time to waste thinking about all that. David had a world record to beat and now that he was safely secure within the confines of his hotel room, he could get back to where he was.

210

Temptation

Once again, David removed all his clothes, jumped onto the springy king-sized bed and resumed wanking at a normal pace. He found it infinitely more freeing wanking in a hotel room. At home, he had to wank under the constant danger of getting caught in the act. But here, locked away from the world, David could truly lose himself.

Five and a half hours in and David thought he was definitely going to cum. He got so close that he had to get down to snail pace just to stop it from happening. All he wanted to do was cum right there and then. More than anything in the world. He could feel the intense magnitude of the orgasm creeping up on him and shaking his entire body. He really didn't think he could do it, but in the end, he was successfully able to avoid ejaculating. He felt proud of himself. Most people would have given up at that point. But not David. David was going for the gold here.

David must have fallen asleep because he looked at his phone and saw that half an hour had passed. He must have fallen asleep. But no. He was still wanking. He was six hours and ten minutes in. Could it be possible that he'd lost himself so fully in the moment that he blacked out for a full thirty minutes?

Another blackout. David was still wanking. He knew for certain now that he wasn't just nodding off. The blackouts were starting to become more and more frequent and he was very slowly losing track of time. Sometimes they were only a few minutes and sometimes they felt like hours. Just periods of time missing from his memory.

Eight and a half hours in and still pumping away. After a two-minute blackout that felt like hours, David was violently jerked awake by what felt like an electric shock flowing through his body. Like someone had used a defibrillator on him. It was nighttime now, but the moon shining in through the silk curtains revealed a tall figure standing in the corner of the room. A man. An old man. Was that... no, it couldn't be. David's eyes must have been deceiving him. He must be suffering from some sort of arousal induced delusion. That couldn't be his dad, could it? He's dead though?. He stared at the old man and the old man stared back and smiled.

` Dad? said David.

You can do this son. I believe in you.

The voice echoed quietly around the room. David felt like crying. It'd been so long since he heard his old man's voice.

Then the old man was gone. David clenched his fist in determination and picked up the speed. *This is for you, Dad.*

At one point, David was sure he could hear his phone ringing. But he couldn't be sure. He wasn't sure of anything anymore. Sounds, sight, taste, touch. All his senses were just meshed together like paint thrown at a blank canvas. David wasn't even sure he existed anymore. He felt like at some point in the wank, he'd transcended his plain of reality and was experiencing something that no drug had ever given him. He couldn't describe what he was experiencing. He wasn't sure he wanted to. All his past relationships with women, and even guys, splashed in front of his eyes like a falling rain. All of them morphed together into one godlike figure that had now taken ahold of his hand and was doing all the work for him. David wasn't in control anymore. He was now a simple passenger in his own wank.

Somewhere in the color, a crow came down and landed on a branch next to David's bedside table. It had a tattoo of a strawberry Yop across

212

his beak. His eyes were like raisins that were imploding in on themselves. Like a four-dimensional being. A being with antlers that sprouted from its kneecaps and it had shaved porcupines for feet. Fucking trippy, man. The creature picked David up and placed him in a bathtub filled with doors. David looked down at himself. His eyes were glowing. He wasn't wanking anymore. His hands floated by his side and a black tree branch had taken over the wank. Where was he? Was he even alive anymore? Had David wanked himself to death?

David's eyes opened. He looked down at his crotch. He was still wanking. Another blackout? Grey daylight shone through the window and burned his eyes. David felt weak. His body felt as if it had loss some mass. He didn't know how long he'd been in this state of mind for, but he was surely near the ten hour mark now. He had to be. The last thing he remembered, it was half ten at night and he'd just hit nine hours. He looked at his phone. It was almost eight in the morning. That couldn't be right. Had he wanked all night? If that was the case, then David had been wanking for over eighteen hours, more than twice the record.

David looked at his phone again and managed a weak smile. But it quickly disappeared when he saw the date. It was all wrong. It said the 26th, but that couldn't be right. When he checked in, it'd been the 22nd. There was no way that could be right. Because if it was, that meant he'd been wanking for four days straight. David saw he had a couple of messages. He weakly reached over and tapped his phone, opening a preview of a message he received from Lesley on the 23rd.

You're disgusting. I'm leaving and taking the kids with me. Don't contact us.

213

David also had about two dozen missed calls from work. What had happened? Had he just had a four-day wanking blackout, during which time, he'd missed work and Lesley discovered what he was up to? David was starting to panic. He tried to get up but he was too weak. He tried to stop wanking, but he couldn't. No matter what he did or how much he struggled, his hand just kept going. Up and down, up and down, up and down. David considered ringing the paramedics, but somehow, he doubted they'd send an ambulance around to him because he was stuck in a hotel room and couldn't stop wanking.

As the day went on, David slipped in and out of consciousness. He just wanted to go to sleep, to have something to eat, to drink. But he couldn't move or stop wanking. He felt so weak. Like all his energy was being channeled towards his hand. He was really starting to panic now. He didn't know why he was still doing this. What had happened to him?

It wasn't worth it anymore. David didn't want this. He didn't want to lose his family and job in service of beating some fucking wanking record. If it meant he would make it out of here alive, David would abandon this whole thing right now and never let the world know of his accomplishment. It had been fun and games at first, but this was serious now. If he didn't stop soon, he'd surely die, either from dehydration or starvation. David tried calling out but his throat was dry and hoarse and all he managed to get out was a raspy whisper. David stared down at his wanking hand. It was getting faster and faster. His penis was sore and covered in blisters. But for whatever reason, he couldn't stop. David lifted his other hand and tried to pry his fingers off his cock, but he might as well have been trying to move a wall. His hand was welded around his cock and his fingers were clamped in place. Why? Why was this happening to him? Why was he not able to stop himself? What was keeping this going?

Running out of options, David looked to his phone. He'd have to call the paramedics to get him out of this. They'd definitely think he was just some prank caller trying to pull their leg, but at this stage, David couldn't see any other way out of this. It would be a fucking humiliating and shameful experience to endure and fuck knows the subsequent consequences he'd have to face from work and Lesley, but he could see no other option. David reached out for the nightstand and tried to grab ahold of the phone in his fingers but he fucked up and ended up pushing it further away. He tried edging his body closer but it wouldn't budge. He extended his arm as far as it would reach and tried to finger his phone closer to him. For a moment it looked like it was working. He managed to dig his fingernails into the edge of the phone and drag it towards him an inch, but he forced it too harshly and the phone slid off the table and landed on the floor with a loud thud. David stared at the bedside table in shock, unwilling to accept what he just did.

There was no stopping it now. He was trapped. He slumped his head into the pillow and looked up to the ceiling, his eyes flooding with salty tears. So this was it. This was how David was going to go out. His father would be ashamed of him. Look at him, lying naked on a bed, starving and dehydrated, wanking like it was his last.

You can't stop it, a voice hissed.

Who said that? said David, looking around the room for whoever was there with him. But he could see no one.

Nothing can stop it now.

215

The voice seemed to be coming from all around him.

Who are you? Make this stop. Make this stop now.

Do not get angry at me. You have done this to yourself, with your lust and your greed.

Please help me. I need to get out of here or I'll die.

I guarantee it.

What is this? Who are you? Show yourself.

It matters not who I am. All that matters is you cannot stop it now. The process is almost complete. For years, I have been looking for a viable host and now you have given it to me.

What do you want?

I want you. I want your worthless body.

No. You can't have it.

David tried to roll off the bed or straighten his back against the bed frame but whatever was in the room with him held his body in place.

HAHAHAHA! Squirm all you want, you pathetic rodent. It is futile. Nothing can stop it now. Soon, I will be unleashed upon the world.

Please, I'll give you anything if you stop this.

HAHAHAHA! Typical human. Thinking there's a way you can talk your way out of this. There is nothing you can do. This would be much easier for you if you simply lay down and accept it is over.

No, there is something, said David.

David looked down at his wanking hand. Up and down. Up and down. He couldn't stop it. That was apparent now. Whatever this was that had control over him was clearly a force more powerful than David could possibly comprehend. If he was going to get out of this, he saw only one option: He had to cum. And he had the feeling that if he didn't do it soon, it would be too late.

Fuck you, David said to the presence.

David let his head rest comfortably on the sweat-soaked pillow and started to think of anybody he could that would turn him on. Blake Lively, Margot Robbie, Helen Mirren, Cillian Murphy, Eddie Murphy, Albert Finney, Granddad.

What are you doing? The entity said.

David could feel something, but he needed something more. He needed a personal touch. He needed to think of people he knew.

He thought of his secondary school teachers. His math's teacher, Mrs. Riordan with those giant boobies. Every boy had a crush on her. Mrs. Galvin, his P.E. teacher. She was a bit older and had a few grandchildren, but boy, did she know how to rock the gym hall.

HAHAHAHA! You pathetic mortal, you cannot stop me!

David felt a sharp pain in his hand, as if his joints were tensing up. It was working but just not fast enough. If David was going to climax before this thing took over his body, he'd need to draw from personal experience.

His mind drifted to his first girlfriend, Aoife. It was only a week into college that he met her and he ended up spending two years of his life with her. It was definitely the rockiest relationship he'd ever had. And even though he was the one to end it, it was still very painful to endure. He pictured her face. He pictured that time they smoked that fag in her back garden in the pissing rain and then they went inside to dry off. Upstairs and still soaking wet, the two of them shifted and then they had sex. That was David's first time.

David could feel it. It was working.

What are you doing? Stop it! the entity roared. The walls around the room started to rumble.

David thought of the girl he briefly went out with when he moved up to Dublin after college. Her name was Kayleigh. He just started working in Dunne's and she had been there for ages. She was almost forty-four. But her smile. Her smile had the power to cheer David up no matter what the circumstance, even during the shitiest days inside that dump. They were just friends at first. David was scared to ask her out because she was older and didn't think she'd go for a young guy just out of college. But then at the Christmas party, everyone was in the smoking area and she grabbed David's arm and dragged him into the bar. She ordered tequilas and then another. Then she asked if David wanted to walk around town with her. He did. They talked all night as they strolled around the town, DMCing about some of the most personal things in their lives. And just outside the museum, at five in the morning, the Christmas lights lit up the street and she never looked as beautiful. Deciding to risk it, David went in for the kiss. And it worked. It was like something out of a movie. They started a secret affair after that. Kayleigh didn't want anyone in the shop knowing about them since the girls at the checkouts would spread that information before the two of them had a chance to blink. Then David got the job. The job in Kilkenny and he had to move away. David asked Kayleigh if she wanted to come with him but she said no because all her family was in Dublin. So David was forced to leave her and it'd been very painful, maybe even more so for her. Maybe she regretted not going with him. David would like to believe that. It was hard to know who was to blame for the

218

breakdown of that relationship. David thought of her as she rode him in the cowgirl position. She was moaning so loudly. And that smile. God, that smile.

It was working. David could feel it happening. He was going to cum soon. He had to do it quickly though. He could feel the energy being rapidly drained from his body. The walls around him started to crumble. The entire hotel sounded like it was going to collapse.

STOP IT NOW, YOU HUMAN FILTH! YOU CANNOT STOP ME!

And then David thought of Lesley. At that point, David had jumped from one disastrous relationship to the next. You could line up a million unique and attractive women of different ethnicities and cultures, and David would have picked the melodramatic, attention-seeking, schizophrenic, crack cocaine addict every single time. He really could pick them. So by the time a friend introduced him to Lesley, David was just worn out from the whole relationship thing. But the third time they saw each other, she asked him out for drinks. Even though he really liked her, David wanted to say no. He just wanted to go home and feel sorry for himself. But something inside him told him he'd really regret it if he didn't go for it with her, so he said yes. And that was it. That yes was all it took. He was hers and she was his from that moment on. Sounds a bit dramatic, but that's what it felt like. It was like David could see the future so clearly from that point on. It was no longer this foggy road filled with uncertainty and fear. The future is, as it always will be, a scary concept, but David could tell it wouldn't be as scary if Lesley was with him. He was willing to go through all the pain that love had to offer just so he could be with her. He thought of her face when he proposed to her in that Chinese

219

takeaway. She really hadn't expected that. He pictured her face as she joined him at the top of the aisle and he pulled back the veil. God, she was beautiful. Her face after Kieran was born. After Emma was born and the tough time she went through following the miscarriage. After her parents died. After the breakdown and all the alcohol. It was all worth it though. It'd been worth all the pain.

Oh fuck, David muttered. It was happening.

SERIOUSLY, STOP IT! cried the entity. *YOU'RE BEING LIKE REALLY UNCOOL!*

David was going to cum. He could feel it. He just had to keep going. Just keep thinking of Lesley. That's all he had to do. The hotel was starting to implode.

AHHH! NOOO! WHAT ARE YOU DOING?!! STOP THIS! I CAN FEEL MYSELF GROWING WEAKER!

Just picture her face, thought David. Just picture her face the first time you had sex. Picture her face as you carried her to the bed on your wedding night. The roof of the hotel was blown off and a swirling red spiral encompassed the sky.

AHHHHHHHH! NNNNOOOOOOO! HOW UNEXPECTED!

I'm going to cum! I'm going to cum!

NOOOOOOO! HOW CAN THIS BE?!

Oh, my God!!!!

IT'S IMPOSSIBLE!!!!

I'm cumming!!!!

NOOOOOOOOOOOOOOO!!!!

FUCK YEAH!!!!

David raised his head to the ceiling and screamed as he orgasmed and his hand was set free from its imprisonment. White light burst out of his body and lit up the sky, slowly and fiercely dispelling the apocalyptic red spiral. The last thing that David remembered before everything went white was the entity screaming as it slowly died.

And Lesley's face.

And the orgasm.

Oh, my God...

The fucking orgasm...

Indescribable...

***

David's eyes opened. Was he dead? He looked around. It was all white. He couldn't see anything. It was just white all around him. He could feel he was standing on some type of surface but he couldn't see it. He reached down and swiped at the air below his feet. Nothing. Where was he? He must be dead.

You're not dead.

David spun around. There was a figure standing about fifty feet away from him. It was gliding slowly towards him, his legs motionless. The persons face slowly revealed itself to David as it edged closer to him. But David had to be mistaken. There was no way he was seeing what he was seeing. But as the figure glided right up to him, there was no mistaking it. It was him. It was David, dressed in white.

Who are you? said David.

You know who I am.

I do?

You've known me since you were a teenager.

I have?

Look into my eyes, David. You know me.

David looked into the person's snow-white eyes. Everything else looked exactly like him. Then it dawned on him. The result of what he just went through, standing right in front of him.

You're my orgasm, said David.

Yes, I am the orgasm you just experienced. It's called an infigasm.

An infigasm?

Yes, an orgasm never before achieved by any human.

But what is it?

And orgasm so powerful, that the orgasm itself achieves sentience. And that is me. You have bestowed upon me a life. And for that, I graciously thank you.

The Orgasm bowed ceremoniously before him. David watched in astonishment.

You should be proud of yourself, said The Orgasm. You may be the first human to ever achieve such an orgasm.

But what was that thing that was trying to take control of my body?

Ah, yes. Of that, I am not sure. A demon perhaps? All I know is it is an entity that feeds on the pleasure of others such as yourself. Anytime it sense's anyone coming close to an awesome orgasm, it steps in and takes the host for itself. It is how it has survived for millions of years. But you just had an infigasm. A power like that in the hands of an entity such as that... I can't even begin to imagine. If it had gained control of you just now, the consequences for your species and other species across the cosmos would have been disastrous. But you defeated him. You just saved trillions of lives.

David smiled with satisfaction. Glad I could help, he said.

It would do you well to not be so conceited and learn to have a bit of humility in yourself. You embarked on a risky endeavor attempting to execute such an intense orgasm. One that almost ended your species. I hope, for your own sake, you've learned your lesson.

I understand.

Good.

So, I'm not dead?

No.

So where am I?

You are inside your orgasm's mind. My mind.

David looked around. I see. So, what now?

Now you go home.

But what about my wife? My job? I've lost everything because of this.

It's all waiting for you when you get back.

And what about you?

I must venture out into the cosmos and help others in need.

But what if I need you?

The Orgasm placed his hand on David's shoulder and smiled. All you have to do when you need me again… is wank.

A tear fell down David's face. Okay, he said.

Now it's time for you to go home.

Okay.

***

David's eyes opened and he shot up like lightning. He was in his bed at home. His pants were down. He was about to start wanking. He recoiled his hand and pulled up his trousers frantically. He looked at his phone next to him. It was the 22nd. It was half two. He could also see he had a message from Lesley:

Won't be home till 6. Quiche in the oven xx

David got up off the bed and opened the curtains. Light poured in and flooded the room. He looked up towards the clear blue sky and saw a swarm of birds dancing across the clouds. He saw a bright light shoot across the sky. He looked down at his crotch and smiled.

Until next time…

High Score

He was born with the name Kyle. His middle name is Danel. He thinks his dad meant to put Daniel on the birth cert but reckons he was too drunk to spell it right.

Age three months. His dad was holding him while cooking a fry up. He was hungover. He dropped him on the cooker and burned his eye. It left a hideous black scar under Kyle's left eye that he would carry for the rest of his life.

Age four. Kyle was in bed. After coming home from the pub at about three in the morning, his dad staggered into his room. He was absolutely polluted. He sat on the bed and put his hand on Kyle's leg. He said he loved him. He said that over and over and rubbed his leg some more. Kyle asked if he could leave so he could get some sleep. Even at that age, Kyle was smart enough to know what was going on and he knew this wasn't right. He told his dad to get out. His dad grimaced. Then he hit him. He hit him again. The third hit knocked Kyle out and made him swallow a tooth that was already loose. He woke up the next morning and his eye was swollen shut. His dad was snoring on the floor beside the bed, a pool of vomit around his head like a halo. That was the first time his dad hit him. He hit him pretty much routinely after that. Mainly whenever he got pissed.

Age five. His mum staggered into the kitchen one morning while he was eating his cereal, and stabbed him in the hand with a pencil. Kyle screamed and started crying. His mum told him not be such a baby, then she went into the sitting room and passed out on the couch. He never found out why she did it. He couldn't understand why she did any of the things she did.

Age five and a half. It was snowing. Kyle and his parents' were standing outside an apartment building. His dad was banging on the door, screaming something. His mum was wearing sunglasses to hide a bruise. What the fuck you looking at? she said to Kyle. He looked away. He knew better than to pick a fight with her. His dad turned and said something to his mum. Then he turned to Kyle and said to wait here. They left him there in the freezing cold and headed off to the pub to get pissed. At one point, Kyle was so cold, he stopped shivering and just felt pain. Someone found him a couple of hours later, passed out in the snow. He woke up and started freaking out. He ran away and ended up walking ten miles home in the freezing cold. He broke a window just so he could get into the house. When his parents came home a couple of days later and found the broken window, they made him eat a piece of the broken glass.

Age eight. Kyle's cousins came over. He hated his cousins. They beat him up and mocked him for his wonky teeth and the mark under his eye, all of which were because of his parents, but they never believed him when he said that. No one believed him. His oldest cousin used to grab his genitals really hard until they hurt. One time, Kyle hit his oldest cousin after he gave him an excruciatingly painful dead leg and chipped his tooth. His uncle's beatings were a lot worse than his dads because he wore rings.

Age ten. Kyle broke down the door to the shed and found his dad's shotgun hidden in the back behind the lawnmower. He put it to his head and pulled the trigger. Nothing happened. He opened the barrel. There was no bullets in it. He grabbed some shells from a box on the floor and loaded the gun. He put the gun to his head again and pulled the trigger. Nothing happened. The safety was on. He started crying and put the gun away.

Age thirteen. Mikey Finn smashed Kyle's head into a locker. But it was the hard part of the locker, where the hinge is. He woke up a week later in hospital. The doctors said they had to put him in an induced coma to reduce the swelling in his brain. His parents' were called in when he was first admitted but they never visited him much after that.

Age thirteen and seven months. Kyle drank some bleach. It did nothing but burn his insides. When he told his mom what he'd done, she slapped him and said she wouldn't be paying for him if he got sick.

Age fifteen. Kyle made a friend. A best friend. The first and only friend he ever had. Actually, he was the first person at school who ever talked to Kyle. The first person who didn't greet him with a punch to the face. His name was Scott. Scott brought him out of his shell. Kyle spent as much time as he could at Scott's house so he didn't have to go home. Sometimes his parents would let him stay over and him and Scott would spend the entire night watching movies. His dad kicked him in the groin one night after he came home from Scott's and wouldn't tell them where he was. Kyle began to really like Scott. Really like him. Scott seemed to accept Kyle in all his damaged splendour. One night, he told Scott he liked boys. Scott asked him if he was being serious. Then Kyle tried to kiss him. Scott pushed him away and called him a faggot. At school the next day, everyone was calling him a faggot and Scott stopped talking to him. It wasn't a big deal. Faggot was just a new word in a dictionary of words people said to him.

Age seventeen. Kyle ran away from home. He stole money from his dad's wallet and left the house. He got on the first train out of town. He arrived in Dublin a while later. He survived as long as he could with the money he'd stolen, mainly staying in hostels and eating the cheapest food he could buy. It didn't last him more than two weeks though because he was drinking so much. One night, he was mugged outside the GPO, and soon he was broke and sleeping on the street.

Age twenty-two. Kyle woke up in a hospital. He couldn't remember anything from the past three months. Some woman in a fancy suit and a clipboard visited him and asked him a few questions about who he was and where he was from. Kyle never said anything. He knew better then to trust people. He left the hospital that day and went back to Delilah's for a hit.

228

Age twenty-three. Kyle's birthday. He was standing over the rail of a bridge in this local park. He couldn't do it anymore. He was pretty sure he had shit for blood anyway so there was no real reason for him to keep living anymore. Before he could jump, a woman walking her dog talked him down and took him to a hospital.

Age twenty-three and a half. His dad comes to visit Kyle while he's in sober living. He says his mother has died and it's partially his fault because he abandoned her. He said he forgives him though. He says he's gotten sober too and asks Kyle if he wants to come home. Kyle tells him to leave and to never to make contact with him again.

Age twenty-seven. Kyle's been sober for almost four years now (with a few cock-ups in the middle). He's living with a guy called Reuben, who is eleven years older than him, but Kyle doesn't care. Kyle loves him. Reuben has two kids that he adopted from a previous marriage. A girl and a boy. Their names are Amy and Josh. Kyle didn't know how he'd do with kids. He thought he'd fuck them up worse than his dad did to him. But Kyle likes them. He thinks he even loves them. His life has completely turned around. He's working as an apprentice plumber now, which is difficult but the routine keeps him from falling off the wagon. He has a ton of new hobbies now. He keeps a diary. He goes cycling every day and recently he's taken up Jujitsu. He's happy. It's a kind of happiness that Kyle doesn't trust because he knows it won't last very long. Because he's never truly known what it means to feel happy. So it just feels foreign to him and it scares him. Not in a frightening way. In a *"Ew, get that thing I don't*

229

recognise away from me" kind of way. But Reuben keeps telling him to trust in the universe and not to push out the good things in his life. He says the good things will keep him upright when things go bad. That's why they're good things. Kyle would normally think of Reuben as a naïve idiot, but he has his shit together and Kyle trusts that he knows what's best for him. Kyle's never known what's best for him. He's only known what will make him less him.

One night, Kyle was making an oven pizza and fell asleep on the couch. The house caught fire. Kyle woke up and his lungs instantly filled with smoke. He covered his mouth with his T-shirt. He ran through the house and went into the kids room. They were still fast asleep. He woke them up and instructed them to go outside. Reuben was trying to put the fire out in the kitchen with the fire extinguisher but it wasn't doing anything. The fire was too big. Kyle told him to forget about it and go outside to the kids. They both ran outside but the kids weren't there. Reuben asked him where they were and Kyle said he'd told them to go outside. Reuben told Kyle to wait here while he went inside to get them. Kyle just stood outside and waited for Reuben to reappear with the kids. Soon a fire truck came and started battling the fire. Kyle knew he should go into the house to try and help, but he didn't. He just stood there and watched the house burn down. Reuben never came out with the kids. When Kyle woke up in hospital, he was told that Reuben and the kids had burned to death. The kids were found in his arms. The three of them were reduced to ash.

Age twenty-eight. Kyle was walking through town with a litre bottle of cheap vodka in his hand. He'd been wearing the same clothes for months now. The Guards arrived and chased him. They said they just wanted to talk to him, but Kyle wasn't having any of it. He got hit by a car as he darted across the road. He woke up in hospital with a badly damaged leg.

Age twenty-nine. Kyle was limping through a forest. He didn't know what county he was in. He didn't even know if he was in Ireland anymore. He didn't care. He took another swig of vodka. He collapsed to the ground as the bitter alcohol fell down his throat and clutched his leg. The pain was unbearable. He couldn't take it anymore. The pills the doctor had given him didn't do anything. But they did tell him they wouldn't work if he didn't stop drinking, so he wasn't surprised. He approached a nearby tree and climbed up it. It took him a while because he was trying to balance himself on the tree with his bad leg, but he eventually tied the rope around a branch. A strong branch. He made sure of that. He didn't want the fucker breaking like it did last time. He took one more swig of vodka and put the noose around his neck. Then Kyle jumped off the tree and died.

Richard took the helmet off his head. It took him a moment to come around. He felt very disorientated and his mouth tasted like metal. His forehead was layered in steamy perspiration. The bright colours in the rooms stung his eyes and his head was throbbing badly. Richard's mate, Dorian, who was sitting on the bed, put down his phone, leaned forward and placed his hand on Richard's back.

Fucking hell, I feel terrible, said Richard.

Yeah, take it easy, said Dorian. It takes a minute to come around.

Where's Reuben? he said, rubbing the phantom pain in his leg.

Richard, sit down and take a breather. It takes a minute to come out of it.

Richard rubbed his eyes as Kyle washed away from his brain. A few seconds later, Richard remembered who he was and looked at Dorian, his face pale.

You back? said Dorian

Yeah, I'm good.

Who am I?

A prick.

Dorian smiled and jumped off the bed.

How long was I out for? said Richard.

Just a few minutes, though I imagine it felt a lot longer in there.

Yeah, felt a lot fucking longer, said Richard.

So how'd you do?

Remembering what he'd just woken up from, Richard pressed the Y button on the remote and the results came up.

Ah, man, you didn't even make it to twenty-nine, said Dorian laughing. You fucking amateur.

Richard threw the helmet on the floor. Fuck sake, he shouted. This is fucking bullshit.

What difficulty were you playing on?

The hardest difficulty.

Ah, sure, what were you expecting then?

I wanted a challenge, said Richard defensively. He stared at the neon blue *"GAME OVER"* that flashed in front of his eyes.

Tough, isn't it, said Dorian.

232

Tough? That was fucking impossible, man. Those last few months were fucking agony. Richard picked his headset up off the ground and placed it on his bed.

It's good though, isn't it?

Yeah, it's alright, said Richard, not knowing if he actually felt that way. He felt like it would take a while to get that experience out of his head.

Dorian jumped back on the bed and took out his phone.

What's the highest score someone's gotten to? said Richard.

There has to be some fucker out there that's made it to at least a hundred, said Dorian.

On the hardest difficulty? I doubt that.

Richard grabbed his controller beside him and logged into the world leaderboard.

I'm not even in the top thousand, he said. But thinking about it, he wasn't surprised. He scrolled through the scores. There were people who made it well into their thirties, going all the way up to the sixties.

How the hell were they able to make it that far? said Richard. They must have cheated.

Man, what were you expecting? said Dorian. The hardest difficulty is *insanely* hard. I'm surprised you even made it to twenty-nine if I'm being honest. I barely made it to twenty.

Richard scrolled up the screen. When he got to the top, he gazed in amazement at the top score.

Look at that, he said. The top score is held by some guy called *timodim73*. He made it to eighty-six!

Jesus Christ, that must be one tough fucker.

Richard stared at the screen in amazement. Eighty-six, he muttered to himself. It was a score he could not imagine himself ever getting to in his life.

Hey, try playing the North Korea DLC on the hardest difficulty, said Dorian. That shit will have you killing yourself before you've even taken your first steps. I can't wait to try the Irish Famine DLC went it comes out.

Richard wasn't listening. He was still staring at the screen in awe.

Anyway, said Dorian, getting up and putting on his hoodie and jacket. Let's head away. My dad texted me there. He said he'll be outside in two minutes.

Alright. I'll be out in a sec.

Dorian left the room. Richard got up and slid open the door to his walking wardrobe. He pulled out his jacket and beanie. He glanced at the screen again as he pulled the zip up on his jacket. Eighty-six. That guy must have cheated, he thought. He must have. No one can survive what he just experienced for eighty-six years.

Richard switched off the console, the TV, and the light in his room. He left the house and joined his friend outside.

Tip the Can

There's this group of kids hanging about this housing estate. They all live there. It's a straight road with thirteen houses on the right, stretching in a straight line from the start to the end. On the left, there's a long stretch of grass where you can play a bit of football if you wanted. Anyway, the boys themselves. It's a group of four. Their names are Adam, Mikey, Fred, and Barry.

Adam lives in the first house on the street. Mikey lives next to him. Fred and Barry are brothers. They live in the seventh house. Their family is sort of the unofficial leader of the street. All the parents meet at their house for parties and get-togethers and stuff. Adam doesn't really know why this is. Maybe it's because they're the richest family on the block or maybe it's because it's the one with the most kids (Fred and Barry have five other siblings).

If Adam was being honest, he didn't like Fred and Barry that much. The only reason he hung out with them was because Mikey was his best friend and he hung around with them all the time. Barry was alright, but Fred could be a bit of a prick. He was the oldest in the group and they always had to do what he wanted to do. If Adam or anyone else tried to suggest something like playing a game of football down at the pitch or a game of basketball at the sports complex, Fred would immediately dismiss their idea and they'd all end up playing what he wanted in the end. And Adam knew that if Fred wanted to play something, you can bet your fucking arse that it wasn't a suggestion. You're fucking doing it or you can find yourself another group of mates to hang out with. Adam didn't despise hanging out with them. They weren't bullies or anything. He just wished there was a bit more democracy in the group. That there wasn't this unspoken hierarchy that placed Fred on top.

Today was a Saturday and they weren't really doing anything. Adam, Mikey, and Barry were sitting on the fence outside Fred and Barry's house. Fred was meekly kicking a ball against the curb. Sometimes, he'd fake kick the ball really hard in their direction just to make them flinch. It was funny at first but now Adam was constantly on guard because he knew Fred would do it again at some point. A few minutes later, he actually kicked the ball in their direction. Not fully though. He didn't kick it towards them so it would hit them. He just kicked it a bit to the left to give them a fright. It made Adam flinch so hard that he nearly tumbled off the fence and the whole group started laughing. Adam pretended to laugh as well, but he felt humiliated. He wanted to grab the ball and bounce it off the pricks head. After a while, Fred got bored with annoying them and started doing keepie-uppies with the ball, just to show off his amazing soccer skills. He was that kind of guy.

After a while, Adam wanted to go home. He was fucking bored. He'd originally came over to Fred and Barry's house to watch the United game. He wasn't that interested in soccer if he was being honest. Mikey invited him over and it being a Saturday, he didn't really have anything else going on so he said why not. But the game ended over an hour ago and they hadn't done anything since then except piss about with the ball. Adam wanted to lay on his bed right now and listen to some music, but he didn't want to be the one to split up the group. He didn't want to have to come back the next day and Fred would say something like, *"Oh man, we had the best fucking crack after you left yesterday"*, or some shit like that. Fred would be the type of person to do that. He wouldn't do it because it actually happened. He'd just say it to make Adam feel left out.

Adam could ask Mikey if he wanted to come back to his place. That might smooth the transition, but then he'd be putting him in the awkward position of deciding to split up the group and he'd probably invite Fred and Barry over in the end, just so it wouldn't be awkward. And there was no fucking way Fred and Barry were coming over to Adam's house again. Fred would spend the whole time commenting on how good looking his mum is and Barry would eat twenty-eight slices of toast. Mikey probably wouldn't want to go anyway, so Adam didn't bother asking. Though he didn't understand why he'd want to stay here. There was nothing even a little bit fun happening right now. They were just watching Fred kick a ball about. At least at his house, Adam and Mikey could bust out the PS3 and play some FIFA. What exactly was the appeal here?

So it was approaching half-four and eventually, Fred got bored with the ball and kicked it into his driveway. He turned to the other boys and said:

We do something?

Like what? said Barry.

I don't know. Anything.

Well, what you have in mind?

Knock and Dolly?

Fuck that. Maybe at night, but not during the day. We'll get in trouble.

Tip the can?

Alright, said Barry, hopping off the fence. Mikey jumped off as well.
Adam sighed and hopped off the fence too.

Adam didn't like playing Tip the Can. He always ended up being the
guy that had to count and that was fucking boring. But he didn't like hiding
either. There were only about six or seven houses you could hide in on the
estate. They weren't allowed to hide in any of the houses at the bottom of
the road because the owners didn't like them playing around there. It
wasn't that they weren't allowed to play down there, but they knew if they
did, someone would come out and give out to them and they'd end up
telling their parents, so it was just best to avoid playing down there to avoid
the hassle. So the reality was, they had the first seven houses to work with,
and that's it. And even then, there was nowhere really to hide. You could
hide behind walls and cars, and unless you wanted to hide in the bushes on
the other side of the road and get stung by a bunch of thorns, there weren't
too many other options.

Not it, said Mikey.

Not it, said Barry.

Not it, said Fred.

Adam was still in the process of hopping off the fence and his feet
hadn't even touched the ground when they said it. When it finally
registered in his brain, he groaned loudly. He fucking hated it when they
did that. They could have waited until he was ready or do something else

238

to decide who'd be it, like *Ip Dip Dog Shit* or *Rock, Paper, Scissors*. But of course, they had to go with the famous *Not It* method, that they did intentionally when he wasn't ready to ensure that he was the one counting. And that's exactly what had happened. Adam had to fucking count and look for them now and pretend like he cared.

Thirty seconds, said Fred.

Okay, said Adam.

He wanted to be at home, not playing with this cunt. He closed his eyes and pressed his head up against the telephone pole outside Fred and Barry's house that they always used as the *can*. Adam started counting out loud. He could hear them running away from him, towards the end of the housing estate, but he was sure he could hear another set of feet running behind him, towards the start of the road, which meant he better not stray too far from the *can*, since he could get caught out on both sides. There were only about three okay-ish hiding spots at the front of the estate but they all knew about them, so they tried to avoid using them so they could bust them out when they really needed to. Most of the time, they all hid in the same old hiding spots.

When Adam got to thirty, he spun around and scanned the road from left to right. He was sure he heard two sets of feet going towards the end of the estate, but the lads were too pussy to use the bottom four houses, so they were probably close by. He looked to the left. If he had to guess, he'd say Mikey was the one who ran in the opposite direction. His house was down there after all. Plus, it was hard to imagine Fred and Barry straying too far from one another, so he guessed they were the two sets of feet he heard running towards the end of the estate. Adam walked out onto the

239

road to see if he could spot a pair of legs sticking out of the driveways or behind the bins or bushes, but he couldn't see anything. He stuck his hands in his pockets and sighed.

He walked towards the front of the estate a bit. The open windows in Fred and Barry's house meant you could see right through into their back garden, so he'd know if they decided to take a shortcut and hop the neighbors walls. He walked down the road a bit further, looking back frequently to make sure none of them were planning on bumming him from behind.

Then Adam spotted something two houses down, right outside the house to the left of Mikey's. He saw the hedge move a little. It could have been the wind, but it moved a bit too deliberately for it to be that. Then Adam heard a noise he recognized immediately. It was someone walking on gravel. He was positive there was someone in the house next to Mikey's. He walked down a bit more. Then Adam saw somebody move. He expected this would be Mikey. He moved even closer. He could see the outline of something red through the bushes. It was Fred. He was fucking positive. He was wearing a United jersey, and the only one of them wearing any bit of red. Adam spun around and ran back to the *can*. He clasped his hand firmly onto the telephone pole and said: Tip the can, one, two, three. I see Fred behind the pink bushes at Neil's house.

Adam was looking forward to watching Fred walk back with his head hung with embarrassment. But nobody came. He walked onto the road and looked towards the house to see if there was anybody coming out, but nobody appeared. Adam went back to the *can* and said much slower and louder:

Tip the can, one, two, three. I see Fred behind the pink bushes at Neil's house.

Still, no one came. Adam tossed his arms up. Fred, I can see you, he roared.

Nobody came. Adam threw his hands back in his pocket and stood for a while. He was almost sure he saw Fred. No, he *did* see him. He was positive. He was the only one of them wearing any bit of fucking red. It was him. That cunt just didn't want to be the one counting for the next round, so he stayed put in the hopes that Adam would think he was seeing things.

Fuck it, thought Adam. He just started walking towards Neil's house. He didn't care. He walked right up to the driveway and looked in. Fred wasn't there. And he wasn't behind the bushes either. But what he did see was Barry in the back garden trying to jump the wall into the next house. Adam smiled and turned to run back to the *can*. But as he turned to run, he was stunned to see Mikey, running from the end of the road towards the *can*. Adam knew without having to think that there was no way he'd be able to beat him to it. Mikey was a much faster runner than he was. Adam didn't even try to run. It was pointless. Mikey ran right into the *can* and yelled: Tip the can, one, two, three. I free everyone.

Fuck sake, Adam muttered to himself.

Mikey was laughing so hard. Barry came walking out of the house he just jumped into and was laughing too.

I saw you, said Adam to Barry.

Did you? Where?

Trying to jump the wall into Kennedy's, but Mikey beat me to it.

That fucking wall is hard to jump, said Barry panting. There's a big patch of nettles at the very top and I kept fucking touching it every time I tried to hop it.

Where's Fred? said Mikey.

As Mikey said this, Fred came walking out of Mikey's driveway, the house just before the one Adam suspected him of hiding in. Fucking cocky bastard was smiling so arrogantly as he walked towards them.

I saw you, said Adam.

What?

I saw you by the pink bushes in Neil's house.

No, you didn't.

Oh, the way he said it. So fucking smug. Yes, I did, said Adam. I fucking did see you and I called out your name. Three times.

Well, I don't know who you saw, said Fred. But it wasn't me, He placed his hand on Adam's shoulder as he passed him, but Adam shrugged it off. He was raging. He fucking did see him. He knows he did. How could the fucker so blatantly lie?

You're it again, said Fred spinning around and clapping his hands.

I know, said Adam. He walked up to the *can*. He rested his forehead against it and closed his eyes.

You have to cover your eyes, said Fred. You'll peek, I know you will.

Adam gritted his teeth and placed his arms around his head so his peripheral vision was blocked. He started counting to thirty again, a little faster this time. He finished counting and spun around. He was so busy being annoyed at Fred that he hadn't thought to listen to where anyone was running to, so now he had no idea where to start. He walked out onto the road and looked at the houses. He looked at the hedge to the left of him. There was a small walking path behind it that led down to the very start of the road, but there's no way you could get in there from this side without getting stung by nettles or thorns.

Adam took a few steps back towards the *can* when he heard something to his right. He looked back to make sure there was nobody coming from behind him. He heard the sound again. It was someone talking. He walked forward a bit, remembering to keep a safe distance from the *can* in case someone decided to ambush him from behind. He looked into Jason Crean's house, the one next to Fred and Barry's. There was nobody there today so it would be a perfect spot to hide. Then he saw two figures tip-toeing in the back garden through the kitchen window. It was Barry and Mikey. Adam turned as quickly as he could and raced back to the *can*. He placed his left hand on the pole and yelled: Tip the can, one, two, three. I see Mikey and Barry in Jason's back garden.

A moment later, the two walked out of the driveway with smiles on their faces.

How'd you see us? said Mikey.

I saw you through the window.

Ah, fuck it, said Mikey as he turned to observe the weak spot. He punched Barry lightly in the arm. I told you we shouldn't have gone in there, he said.

Who'd you see first? said Barry.

You, said Adam.

Ha-ha, you're it, said Mikey laughing.

Only if he catches Fred, said Barry defensively.

243

Adam forgot about Fred. He wished he'd caught him first as payback for cheating during the last round. The two lads sat on the fence next to the can and watched Adam as he tried to find Fred. All he had to do now was stay close to the *can* and hopefully Fred would reveal himself eventually. He walked around a bit and scanned the estate vigilantly for any movement. Barry and Mikey were sniggering to each other on the fence. It was like they knew something and it was really annoying Adam. He hated it when they did shit like this.

What you laughing at? Adam said eventually.

Nothing, said Barry and the two of them continued laughing.

Adam cocked his eyes, walked down one house to the left and looked in the driveway. He walked onto the property just to make sure Fred wasn't hiding behind the wall. He wasn't. He turned back. The two lads were looking at something behind them. Was Fred hiding in his house?

Then it happened. Fred emerged from the low concrete wall that was right underneath the steel fence Mikey and Barry was sitting on. Literally right next to the *can,* barely concealed by the wall in his front garden. All Adam had to do was look over the fence and he would have seen him lying on the grass. If he'd listened carefully when he was counting, he would have been able to hear him hiding. What a fucking joke. No wonder those two cunts were laughing. He was right underneath them. Fred hopped over the fence victoriously and reached for the *can.* Adam didn't even attempt to run because he knew it was pointless. All he could do was watch.

Tip the can, one, two, three. I free everyone, yelled Fred.

You were hiding there the whole time? said Adam.

I don't know how you didn't fucking see me, you retard.

He was right behind us the whole time, said Barry in hysterics.

Did you not suspect something when you saw us laughing? said Mikey.

Adam didn't answer. He walked back to them with a big sulky face. He was in a fucking mood now. This meant he had to fucking count again. He was sick of this. This wasn't fun anymore. He wasn't sure it ever was.

Let's go again, said Fred. Adam, count.

I don't want to.

Why not?

This game is shit. Let's play something else.

I freed everyone, said Fred in a sudden burst of anger. Now count.

Come on, let's play some soccer.

No, we're playing this, you asshole. Now fucking count.

In a world where Fred wasn't bigger than him, Adam fantasized about tackling him to the ground and punching his stupid face. He hated the prick so much. Always had to play by his fucking rules. He was in charge of everything and they were all just his fucking minions. It was so unfair. He shouldn't have even been the one counting on the last round. He'd seen Fred during the first round and the fucker just ignored the rules. Well, he wasn't being it again for the next turn, that was for fucking sure. He wasn't wasting his Saturday playing this bullshit. If he lost, he was walking home. He didn't care how much of a sore loser it would make him look. Adam walked despondently up to the *can* again and put his hand around his eyes. He started counting. He didn't even count out loud this time, he was so annoyed.

Fred turned and ran towards the end of the estate. He ran a bit further than he should have, but he knew Adam wouldn't search these houses.

Thankfully most of them seemed to be unoccupied at the moment, so it's not like he was going to get in any trouble. He got to the second last house and looked in the driveway. There was a black Range Rover parked in there. This was the McLoughlin's house. They were a fucking queer bunch. Fred's dad told him the couple that lived in there claimed to have three kids, but no one's ever actually seen them in person. He couldn't be sure there was anyone home right now. That Range Rover was always there but he didn't know if it worked. He was sure the owners had another car. He decided it would probably be best not to hide in this house right now. It was already risky being this far down the road and he couldn't be sure anyone was home. But as he looked around for another hiding spot, he realized that Adam was nearly finished counting, so he said fuck it and ran into the driveway. He got on his knees next to the car.

Adam was definitely done counting by now. Fred knew that he'd have the jump the walls at the front if he was to have a chance of reaching the can. No way he could hop the walls in peoples back gardens, he'd definitely be seen. Fuck, he whispered to himself. It was a mistake to run down this far. Adam would definitely see him jumping over the walls into the front gardens. The back gardens were his safest bet but he ran the risk of being seen. Or maybe he could just stay here and wait until Adam catches one of the other lads. At least then if Adam catches him, he won't have to be the one counting on the next turn, because fuck that.

Fred sat on the ground with his legs crossed and played with some stones in the driveway. He peered over the car every few seconds to make sure Adam wasn't too close. This was the perfect spot to wait it out. Adam wouldn't look down here. He was too much of a pussy.

Tip the can, one, two, three. I see Barry by the bushes in front of Felix's house.

Fred looked around. That was the house right next to him. He turned and saw Barry crouching behind a huge mound of nettles on the left side of the road. He didn't move at first. He didn't even see Fred. When Adam said it again, Barry gave up and walked out. Lovely, thought Fred. At least he didn't have to be it for the next turn. He might as well turn himself in now or make some noise just to give his position away to Adam, but Fred thought he'd wait a bit. There was no rush.

A couple of minutes later, Adam shouted out Mikey's name. If Fred was going to start moving, he might as well do it now. Adam would be distracted for a few seconds as Mikey made his way back to him. It didn't matter if he got caught or if he somehow made it to the *can*. At least he wouldn't have to be it for the next round.

Just then, Fred heard a crash inside the house. It sounded like glass shattering. Fred looked around in a frenzy. He got up to jump the wall, but before he could, the front door swung open violently. Fred got on his belly and crawled underneath the car. He heard someone come out of the house and walk in front of the car.

What are you doing? a female voice at the front door said.

You fucked with my clothes, I'm fucking with yours, said the male voice in front of the car.

Don't you fucking dare.

Fred saw a pile of clothes drop in a puddle at the man's feet.

You're a fucking prick, said the female voice.

I told you to leave them alone. This is what you get.

247

All I did was put the washing machine on full. I told you a quick wash isn't enough.

And I told you to leave them alone. Why don't you ever listen to me? I can wash my own fucking clothes.

The feet of the female moved from the front door to the car, where she was face to face with the man. Fred looked behind him to see if he could crawl backwards while he was out of view, but in the awkward position he was currently entangled in, he'd probably make some noise trying to escape quietly and end up being spotted. He'd just have to wait until they were gone.

Then why did you set it to quick wash when I've told you over and over again it doesn't work? said the female voice.

It does fucking work, you retard. It just doesn't meet your high standards of washing clothes. Everything's got to be fucking perfect with you. *"Oh, I do a full wash so everybody has to do it as well"*.

Whatever, said the woman as she turned and walked back towards the house. I have the staff party tonight. You're washing that dress.

No, I'm not. You can't make me do anything.

Fuck off then, you're not getting back into this house.

I don't want to go back in the house. Not if you're fucking there.

Where you going to go?

None of your fucking business.

Off to the pub with your fantastic mates.

I'll go wherever I fucking want. You're not the boss of me.

You're not getting back into this house tonight if you go out.

Don't worry, I won't come back.

The woman slammed the front door. The man started punching and kicking wildly at nothing and swore up a storm. He kicked some potted plants by the front door and threw an empty paint bucket at the wall. Then he moved towards the car and Fred heard the sound of keys jingling.

Oh fuck, said Fred out loud.

He tried to crawl backwards, but he knew he didn't have enough time. The man got into the car and it came to life within seconds. In a panic, Fred bumped his head against the roof of the car so hard that he thought he was going to pass out. He laid on his back and tried to wriggle his way to the left so he could get out the side. It was tight, but he could just about make it if he squeezed himself hard enough. He was almost there. He reached his left hand out and, grabbing the side of the car, tried to pull himself to freedom. The jagged stones that lined the driveway scraped along his back as he dragged himself to the side. He managed to force his left leg back and rested the sole of his foot against the wheel. He could push himself from here.

But it was too late. The car was moving. In one final motion, Fred tried to move to the left to free himself and managed to get half his body out, but it only made what was about to happen so much worse.

Fred's leg got caught under the wheel as the car reversed, and his ankle folded against his upper leg. Fred could feel a bone tear its way out of his knee and he screamed in pain. The wheel dragged him with the car as it reversed onto the road, then as it slowed, his whole body got dragged under the wheel.

The wheel rolled over him and crushed his cock and balls. The four-ton vehicle continued up his body, destroying his ribs like they were chicken

249

drumsticks, and squeezing his vital organs out of his body like toothpaste. The wheel then rolled onto his head. His skull caved in and his brain popped out. The man drove on. He assumed he hit a rock or something. He didn't really care. He was so pissed off.

*

`Adam stepped onto the footpath to let the car pass. When it did, he walked back onto the road and saw him. At the very end of the road, near the last house. He put his hand on the telephone pole.

Tip the can, one, two, three. I see Fred lying on the road by the house at the end of the road. Adam saw him this time. He was certain of it. He recognized the trainers on his feet. There was no denying this. What was he doing though? It looked like he was hiding under a pile of roses.

Is it him? said Mikey. It doesn't look like him.

Why would he be lying on the road? said Barry.

He's lying very weird, isn't he, said Mikey.

I don't care! screamed Adam. It's fucking him! Fred, I can see you at the end of the road! Stop fucking cheating or I'm not playing anymore!

Mum's History Book

Edel was leaning against the counter in the kitchen, waiting for the kettle to boil. She was reading the Mötley Crüe autobiography her girlfriend Ali had gotten her for her birthday. Edel wasn't that into rock music, but she was fascinated with the party lifestyle that rock stars led, and the members of Mötley Crüe were up at the top of a list of musicians who abused every mind-altering substance known to man, so naturally, she was loving the book so far.

When she heard the click of the kettle, Edel set the book down on the counter and poured the boiling water into the two mugs in front of her. She poured a little milk into the first mug and a lot into the second, which was for her. She didn't like her tea too hot.

Edel grabbed her book and stuffed it under her arm, took the two mugs in each hand, and walked into the sitting room, where her elderly mum, Peggy, was watching Countdown. The dark clouds outside destroyed any hint that it was only four in the evening, so Edel closed the curtains and switched on the small desk lamp on the dresser near the TV. The room felt a bit cold so she closed the top window and switched on the heater by the printer. Walking back to her mum, who looked lost in a daze and hadn't

251

seemed to notice she'd walked into the room, Edel placed the hotter cup of tea on the pale wooden table next to her chair.

There you are, Mum, she said.

Peggy jumped like a computer being switched on. She studied Edel's face and smiled.

Thanks, pet, she said, her voice still hoarse from a recent sore throat.

Edel sat in the chair next to her mum, which she still hadn't gotten used to, even after all this time. Edel had been visiting her mum almost every day since her dad died four months ago, and it still felt religiously wrong to be sitting in a chair that her dad christened with his arse indication. Both of the chairs didn't even seem like chairs anymore. They just felt like ordinary pieces of furniture in the house. The two chairs had a special connection forged by the couple who sat in them for the duration of their fifty-two-year marriage. And now that her dad was dead, the chair seemed to lose its magic. Both chairs did. But her mum insisted it was just a chair and not to be silly. Her mum wasn't the sentimental type. So Edel sat in the chair next to her mum, and the two of them drank tea and watched Countdown.

It's funny. Edel never liked visiting her parents. She always found her mum would pry on her romantic life and her dad would pry on her professional life, and together, the two of them became an entity that could pick apart her existence like cotton. She was ashamed to admit that she dreaded these visits at the start and was only coming so her mum wouldn't lose her mind, and that people wouldn't think of her as a bad daughter. Edel figured that without her dad here, her mum's behavior would only get worse.

But that hadn't happened. If anything, Her mum had softened. Sure, there was still the occasional query about the men in her life (Edel still hasn't told her she's a lesbian), but overall, Edel had begun to look forward to these visits. She liked just sitting with her mum in silence. That was something her mum always seemed incapable of. Just sitting in silence. Before, it always felt like someone needed to be talking about something, but since her dad died, there seemed to be much more room for reflection.

The countdown had started. Edel analyzed the words. Rachel Riley, who was one of the reasons Edel loved watching Countdown so much, had picked out some shitty fucking letters. She was generally pretty bad at the word game in Countdown anyway. And this occasion proved no different. She only came out with the four-letter word, *"DEER".*

"ANGERED", said Peggy, just as the clock stopped.

Fucking hell, Mum, she said leaning into the screen. Edel didn't know how her mum was so much better at this game than she was. She took a sip of her tea. As she put her mug on the little table next to her and grabbed her book to resume reading, Edel noticed a little plastic container filled with books in between the two chairs.

What's this? said Edel.

Peggy turned her whole body towards Edel. Oh, I found that when I was cleaning out the spare bedroom the last day.

Edel dragged the box across the floor to her feet.

It's me and your father's old school books, continued Peggy.

Edel had never heard of any pensioner holding onto old school books. She thought her mum and dad would be above such nostalgia. Sure they kept some old pictures and important documents from back in the day, but

Edel had no idea they held onto their school things. She would have figured they'd just burn them or toss them in the bin. She grabbed a random copybook from the pile, brushed off the dust and cobwebs, and opened it. The pages were a pale yellow. Her dad's name and the date were written on the inside cover in pencil. 1955. Edel was surprised the copy was intact after all this time.

I remember us sitting in History, said Peggy, driving the teacher up the wall because we wouldn't stop talking. I think it was in History actually when he first asked me out. God, we were such clowns back then.

Edel smiled as the image of her adolescent parents formed in her head. She'd heard endless stories from both her parents and relatives on how the two had met in school and how romantic it was. She'd seen a picture of her parents when they were younger, sitting on a beach, taken just after they'd finished school. Her mum had been very pretty, which everyone agreed Edel took after. For which she was very grateful because her dad was regrettably, not very good looking. He had a real brute of a face with features that seemed overgrown and jagged. But he was very tall and athletic, and she reckoned that's why her mum went out with him in the first place.

Edel rummaged through the box of school books, picking up random ones and flicking through them quickly. Then she picked up a dark red copybook and her mum let out a sudden cry.

That was my History copy, she said.

Is it? said Edel.

Let me tell you something about your father. He… Oh, this is horrible actually, you really don't want to hear this.

254

But Edel did want to hear it. And it seemed like her mum wanted her to know too. It wasn't as if she thought Edel didn't want to hear it because it was too personal or embarrassing. It was just cheeky teenage love. It was always hard to imagine her mum being the rebellious teen she said she was because she was generally quite strict when it came to stuff like curse words and acting the clown. But now Edel could see that her mum used to be just like her once: A stupid teenager. A stupid teenager in love.

No, tell me, said Edel with an encouraging smile.

Her mum leaned forward like she was going to whisper something personal.

He used to write in my copy. That copy, she said, pointing to the dark red copybook.

Edel breathed a sigh of relief. She was expecting to hear something much worse. She thought her mum would tell her that her dad used to finger her in the middle of class or something.

Did he? said Edel. What sort of stuff did he use to write?

Oh, just little things. Trying to flirt with me or impress me. You know how your father was.

Edel looked down at the dark red copybook and opened it to the first page. She flicked through the book. There was nothing for the first couple of pages. Just notes. Edel couldn't make out any of the words though. It was written in that cursive handwriting teens were forced to use by their teachers back in her parents' time.

Then she got to a page where there was a love heart, and her mum's initials was written in pencil above it. She lifted the copybook so her Mum could see it.

Did Dad do that? Edel asked.

Oh my…

Peggy brought her hand up to her mouth and started crying. She kept her mouth covered with her hands and Edel placed a sympathetic hand on her shoulder. But then she started laughing.

That brings back so many memories, said Peggy. Oh, the things he used to write.

Edel looked back at the book. She flicked to the next page. There was another love heart, with a message below it, *missing you tons xxx.*

She flicked to the next page. There were some notes on the Great Irish Famine, but at the bottom, there was a message that was scribbled out. Edel smiled as she pictured her dad quickly scribbling out the message as the teacher walked behind them with a ruler, ready to whack the shit out of any student who misbehaved. On the next page though, there was another message: *do you love me?.* And next to it: *i do.*

Edel had to look away so her mum wouldn't see her crying. She felt so overwhelmed with emotion at that moment. She felt both the loss of her dad and the happiness her mum must have felt when he was alive. She wiped away a single tear from her eye, cleared her throat, and flicked to the next page. Some notes on the Home Rule League. There was a message written in biro in the margin: *can I come over tonight?.* There was a tick in red biro next to it.

On the next page: *i had fun last night x.*

me 2 glad daddy dident hear x.

Edel brought her hands up to her mouth. She was genuinely shocked. Like most people, she had a hard time picturing her parents in any sort of sexual situation. She found it easier to accept that she was probably adopted. She continued on. There were messages on almost every page.

i like ur skirt xx.

meet me behind the prefabs xx.

nice perfume xx.

fancy a snog at lunch xx.

Edel looked at her mum, whose attention was on the TV (The ads were on). It was really hard to imagine her dad writing any of these, let alone her mum. She supposed it was like that for everyone and their parents. It's hard to imagine them as people with emotions, needs, wants; just like everyone else. To Edel, they were always just *Mum and Dad.* But they weren't just that. They weren't just her parents. They were *Peggy and Dennis.* Husband and wife. Soul mates.

Edel was enjoying this. She was enjoying learning a little bit more about the people that gave her life. She flicked to the next page. There was some notes on Charles Stewart Parnell and the divorce crisis of 1886..

meet me in the boys bathroom xxx.

do you like when I rub ur leg xxx.

Jesus Christ, Edel whispered to herself. She turned the copybook over and placed it on her knee. She brought her hand up to her mouth so her mum wouldn't see her smiling. She didn't know if she should read on. She felt like she'd just walked in on her parent's riding or something. It felt somewhat intrusive reading these notes, but in a playful kind of way. Like she was reading her mum's diary.

Edel took a breath in and picked up the copybook again. She had to carry on with this. These messages were just too good. She couldn't wait to tell her Aunt Noreen and Uncle Rick about this. They'd get a real kick out of it.

Edel flicked the page. *im so fucking hard*, one message said. Edel's smile disappeared. She turned the page. She was at the Easter Rising now.

im gonna ride d fanny off u tonite. There was a picture of a cock drawn underneath that message. And under that picture, it said: *hows the arse this morning can you sit.*

Edel grimaced and swallowed the saliva that had accumulated in her mouth. She wasn't enjoying this anymore.

She flicked the page. The 1918 General Election and the events leading to the Anglo-Irish War. There was a crude drawing of what can only be described as a group of five men ejaculating onto a woman that was splayed across the page. Edel turned slowly to the next page. There was another cock. A bit bigger this time. On the next page, there was an even bigger cock, but exceptionally more detailed. There were pubes drawn onto the balls, shaded veins sketched into the shaft, and with the added touch of cum flying out the top and landing on the tongue of a woman drawn in the top right-hand corner

On the next page, there was no cock, but another message:

wank me off.

Edel closed the copybook. She put it back in the box, placed the lid securely back on, and slid it behind the chair. She turned and looked at her mum. At Peggy. She was chuckling over a joke Nick Hewer had made. Rachel Riley was putting numbers up for the math's problem now.

Edel sighed, jealous of the ten minutes ago her that didn't know that copybook existed.

The Waiter

So there was this guy called Craig once (I say once because I don't know if he's still alive anymore. He might have killed himself. I would explain why, but if I did, this story would end up becoming a fucking novel and I don't care that much about Craig's pointless existence to type thousands of words about the circumstances of his supposed suicide) and once he was sitting in a restaurant with two very good pals of his. They were called Clyde and Jeremy. It seemed like weeks since they'd met up. Actually, it had been weeks, because they'd all been busy with stuff like girlfriends (except for Clyde, who likes cock) and their jobs. Though it was probably because they didn't like each other enough to get off their arse to make plans. But recently, they all agreed to make a conscious effort to find time to hang out. So they decided that tonight, the three of them would have a meal at a nice restaurant and catch up on all that was going on in their lives.

Right now, Clyde was complaining about the fact that the three of them had been waiting twenty minutes for their main courses to arrive. Jeremy was just folding a napkin. It was quite awkward actually. So Craig thought it would be a good idea to buy a round of drinks for the guys. You know, just to get them to relax a little and have a bit more fun. They didn't want to pay for drinks themselves as they were both annoyingly frugal with money. They were the type of guys anyway that had to be forced into having fun. So the only way Craig could get them to drink was if he paid for them, which would cost a lot, but if it got them to chill the fuck out, he didn't mind.

Anyway, the waiter came over eventually and apologised for the long wait. He said it was a busy night in the restaurant and there was a miscommunication in the kitchen. And he seemed quite sincere about it, Craig thought. He didn't seem like a bad guy, just circumstances out of his control. And after all, he was right about it being a busy night. The place was jammed. Clyde however, replied with a very loud and noticeable scoff. A scoff that was clearly meant to show the waiter just how annoyed he was with the wait. This was a very Clyde thing to do. He's the type of guy that sighs as loud as he can when he's in a bad mood and wants to let you know. He's that type of cunt. Anyway, the waiter said he would have their meals out to them as soon as possible.

So twenty minutes turned into half an hour and Clyde was going fucking mental. He was becoming increasingly agitated and became impossible to talk to without him jumping down someone's throat. His leg was twitching violently and was hitting the roof of the table, which was causing all the cutlery and plates on the surface to rattle like the warning sign of a mild earthquake, which was very fucking annoying. Craig and Jeremy didn't mind the wait too much. They'd had a few shots now, and they were chatting away to each other. And with Clyde being Clyde, he can't go five minutes without reminding you how annoyed he is, so eventually, not only was he tapping his foot like a madman and causing everything on the table to clatter, he'd picked up a bread knife and started tapping it lightly against the plate in front of him. Craig couldn't understand why Clyde let himself get so annoyed with such stupid shit. The food would get here when it gets here. Tapping his foot or scratching his plates with the cutlery wouldn't make it get here any faster. And besides, this wasn't about the food. They were here to catch up. If they just wanted something to eat, they would have gone to McDonalds or something.

So when the waiter finally came out with their food, the three of them had been waiting for forty minutes. Thank God, Craig thought. Clyde had been threatening to leave and even Jeremy, a normally relaxed guy, was starting to get impatient with the situation. The only way Craig could get them to shut up and relax, and for Clyde not to act on his threats, was to pump them with as much alcohol as he could purchase. So by the time the waiter came out, they were all fucking polluted. At this point, the meal would only be a fraction of what Craig would have to pay for alcohol. But you know what, thought Craig, fuck it. Himself and Jeremy were now having a great time because of how drunk they were and that's what tonight was really about. Having a bit of craic.

So the waiter came over with their meals and set them down in front of the very drunk men. He apologised profusely for the long wait and told them that he'd knock a tenner off the bill. Craig and Jeremy immediately tucked into their meals, but not in an "evening dinner" sort of way. Due to their level of intoxication, they devoured their meals in a manner remarkably similar to how someone would scarf down a doner kebab at three in the morning after a very messy night out. But Clyde just had to be Clyde. He was still angry about how long they'd been forced to wait and didn't want the waiter to forget that fact. So he took one bite of his food (Which was duck with some mixed vegetables and mashed potatoes), spat it back into his plate, and loudly called the waiter back over. The waiter strolled over and politely asked if everything was adequate with their meals.

It's cold, said Craig bluntly.

I'm very sorry, sir. I'll have the chef heat that up and I'll have back out to you in a jiffy.

So, the waiter picked up the plate and walked towards the kitchen. And as his hand pushed open the door, Clyde shouted: And try and have it back to me before the fucking morning, will ya? He shouted it so loud that everyone in the restaurant turned their heads towards him.

Certainly sir, said the waiter without turning. And with that, he disappeared behind the door.

Clyde turned to his two friends and laughed loudly as if what he just said didn't make him look like a total cunt. Jeremy laughed awkwardly as he stuffed a handful of fries into his mouth. But Craig was still looking at the kitchen door. And that was because something was bothering him.

Craig was very intrigued by the way the waiter had said, *"Certainly sir"*. He didn't just say it in the traditional and professional manner a waiter would. He said it with a slight tang of sarcastic enthusiasm in his voice. And perhaps Craig was just drunk and overthinking it, but he began to think there was going to be more than duck, veg, and mashed potatoes on that plate when he emerged with it from the kitchen.

The Waiter

Craig was now watching the kitchen door like a hawk. He was intrigued by what that waiter would be carrying out once that door swung open. He had to know. He'd never wanted to know anything more in his life. He wasn't even eating anymore. His concentration was so fixed on the door. It's not like the other two noticed anyway. Jeremy was now dozing off in a drunken stupor and Clyde was talking to himself, no doubt rehearsing what he'd say when the waiter returned with his food.

When the kitchen doors swung open and the waiter emerged, he had an ear to ear smile on his face pointed directly at Clyde. Craig was examining his face intensely. That fucker did something, he thought. He must have. No one smiles like that. The waiter arrived at the table, waking Jeremy up, and setting the plate before Clyde in the most professional manner Craig had ever witnessed. If this was an exam and Craig had to score him out of ten just for the way he put that fucking plate down, he'd get a straight fucking ten.

There you go. I hope you enjoy that, sir. Nice and toasty.

And he walked away.

Aye, that fucker did something for sure, Craig thought. He didn't even have to look at Clyde's plate to know. The waiter's face told him everything. Again, he couldn't know for sure, but Craig was willing to put money on it that something out of that waiter's mouth and/or arse was now on Clyde's succulent crispy duck.

Craig turned his attention towards the plate and examined it for any traces of phlegm, snot, shite, or cum. Maybe he hid a niblet of shite among the mixed veg. Craig couldn't remember if there had been white sauce on those potatoes the first time around.

263

Clyde seemed to have the same level of curiosity with his meal that Craig had. He was probably just looking over his plate for the slightest indiscretion he could find to once again convey his annoyance to the waiter over what Clyde referred to as, *"appalling service"*. He grabbed his knife and fork and looked over his plate for a good spot to begin. He started with the mash. He scooped up a small amount with his fork and brought it up to his mouth.

He paused for a moment, eying the potentially semen-saturated mashed potatoes on the fork, before sticking it in his mouth. He chewed the food thoroughly and quickly. Craig scanned his face for any facial twitch or contortion of the mouth that signalled that the food was tainted with some type of bodily fluid. But he didn't. Clyde seemed to enjoy the mash. He swallowed the food and tucked into the rest of his meal.

Craig felt a bit disappointed. He didn't know if he wanted his friend to have ingested the waiter's future kids, but part of him felt as if he'd built up the situation so much in his head, that he was expecting Clyde to flip the table or spit out the tainted food onto his plate in a Shakespearean fashion. Maybe he just wanted Clyde to get a bit of comeuppance for the way he'd treated the waiter earlier. Or maybe he just liked the surreal idea of a waiter actually tainting someone's food. Craig shrugged and ordered another round of Sambucas.

After they finished their dinners, Craig thought it was probably time to go home, as Clyde looked to be slipping in and out of consciousness and Jeremy's head lay face down in his empty plate, a puddle of drool oozing from his mouth onto the silky tablecloth. But he thought a nice ice-cream or apple pie would be nice before closing out the evening and going home to prepare themselves for the soul-crushing hangovers that awaited them in the morning.

Craig was very confused and oddly infuriated when a different waiter came over and took their dessert orders. He turned and looked over the entire restaurant, hoping to find their original waiter, but he couldn't see him. Maybe he went home. Suddenly Craig felt like he needed a piss. He got up quickly from the table and staggered towards the men's toilet (he would have told the other two, but frankly he wasn't sure they even knew who he was at this stage, they were so fucking rotten).

As he emptied the contents of his bladder into the urinal, Craig could smell the faint aroma of nicotine nearby. He looked around and could see through the small rectangular window above the sinks that there was someone having a fag outside. When he went to wash his hands, he could see it was the waiter. In a sudden burst of excitement, Craig abandoned washing his hands and stormed out of the bathroom. He walked across the restaurant, not getting any line of enquiry from Jeremy, who seemed to have stopped breathing, or Clyde, who was chatting up a fake plant next to him.

Out in the smoking area, Craig could see the shadow of the waiter stretched across the smoking area. He was just around the corner. It was only then that Craig wondered why he'd actually come out here in the first place. He didn't know what he was going to say to the waiter or why he was even bothering with this at all, but his intoxication made it seem perfectly logical. Craig slicked back his hair and straightened himself up. He walked around the corner. The waiter gave him a weak smile and Craig returned one back. He nonchalantly asked him for a fag, which the waiter graciously gave him. Craig usually doesn't smoke, but he didn't want to just stand there like some fucking weirdo.

So how's the evening going, said Craig. He thought he'd start out with some light small talk.

Not too bad now. Almost done for the evening.

Oh, very good. Craig took a puff of the fag and summoned all the willpower he could muster to keep himself from coughing.

Hey, sorry about my mate in there and the way he was talking to you earlier, said Craig. That was bang out of order.

Ah, don't worry about it, said the waiter. I've had worse people.

Oh, right.

Suddenly the waiter dropped his fag on the ground and flattened it underneath his shiny black shoe. Craig started to panic. He ran through his mind for anything to say that would keep him here. Just something to talk about. The waiter gave Craig a smile and began to walk away.

Did you do it? Craig blurted out.

The waiter stopped and turned. Pardon me? he said.

Did you do it?

The waiter turned and looked at Craig with confusion. I'm sorry, sir. I don't understand. Do what exactly?

Umm…

At that point, Craig thought he might as well just ask him now. He had his attention and if he let it go, he had a feeling he wasn't going to get another opportunity.

Did you do something to my mates' food? Like did you spit in it or something?

I'm sorry sir, I don't –

I'm not trying to get you in trouble or anything. To be honest, I wouldn't really blame you if you did do it. I know I would if someone talked to me like that. But it's been kind of nagging at me for most of the night, to be honest.

The waiter didn't say anything. He just looked at Craig.

Like you know, continued Craig, it would be nice if I knew and he didn't, and next time he's a nob to me, I could say it to him. You know it's not often you get something on your mate they don't know about.

The waiter stared at him. Craig thought his eyes were like a nebula floating around the universe, so full of mystery. The waiter's expression suddenly switched from confused to completely calm in the blink of an eye. Like a double agent letting down his guard, or a person whose second personality just took over. He took a step towards Craig and now they were very close together. Within kissing distance. The waiter stared deep into his eyes, like he had him in a trance. Craig was afraid to move.

Do you want to know what I did? he whispered erotically. I mean, do you really want to know?

Craig gulped down hard. I…I do.

Very well, said the waiter, I'll tell you, but you must promise to keep it to yourself. Our little secret.

I promise.

The waiter looked around and stepped even closer. Craig had never been this close to another man in his life.

Most waiters would do the normal stuff to customers if they were acting the bollox, wouldn't they? said the waiter. Taint their food with some bodily liquids. Well, I didn't do any of that. None of it. I don't waste my time with that stuff. You want to know what I put on his food.

Craig couldn't hold his breath any longer. What?

A spell.

A spell?

That's right. A spell.

I don't understand.

I put a spell on your mate's food. An ancient spell. One many would call an illusion nowadays, but this was something different.

Craig didn't realise how loud he was breathing. And what did the spell do to my mate? he said.

Your mate ordered a duck with vegetables and mashed potatoes, yeah? A big meal. You want to know what I actually gave him? Nothing. Absolutely nothing. His plate was empty. That's what the spell does. It made your friend think he was eating something, but in reality, he was eating absolutely nothing. The only thing that touched his mouth all night was the cold steel of his fork. And now he's going to pay twenty-two euro for a meal he didn't even have. And he's going to be wondering all night why he feels so hungry when he just had a full meal. But he just thinks he had a full meal. The waiter shook his head. He didn't. He didn't have a single thing. And then he won't want to come back to this restaurant anymore and I won't have to deal with him ever again.

Craig didn't know what to say. He was astonished. Flabbergasted. So simple, yet so brilliant. He stood, mouth open, staring into the eyes of this ninja genius, masquerading as a simple waiter. But then something occurred to him.

But wait, he said. I get that my mate didn't notice anything, but how come I didn't notice? I was watching him the whole time.

The waiter raised his hand and gently rubbed Craig's cheek. Your brain sees what the heart wants it to feel, he said.

And then the waiter leaned in and kissed Craig. He pressed his lips firmly against his and bewitchingly caressed his cheek. Craig didn't know how long the two of them had been kissing for when they parted, but it felt infinite. It was like time had ceased and now it was just the two of them, locked together forever like that. A lifetime had been shared in that kiss. It was the most erotic experience of his life. He had one of those erections that went straight up instead of across.

When the kiss ended and the waiter pulled back, Craig didn't open his eyes immediately. He didn't want to. He thought that by keeping his eyes closed, he could stay in that kiss forever, Nothing would ever come close to that kiss again. Ever. When Craig finally opened his eyes, the waiter was gone. He looked around the smoking area, but he wasn't anywhere to be seen. Had he ever existed? thought Craig, as he touched his lips softly. Was he an angel?

When Craig got back to the table, the two lads seemed to have sobered up a little bit in the time he was gone, as they were now chatting away to each other, digging into a plate of apple pie. Jeremy asked where he was, but Craig didn't know what he said back. His mind was in another universe. He didn't touch his dessert. He just sat there, seemingly mesmerized. He didn't even know what he was thinking, or if he was thinking. The only thing he did know was he could still feel the touch of the waiter's warm lips on his.

They paid for their meals separately. First Craig, then Jeremy, and then Clyde. Craig was staring at Clyde as he inputted his four-digit code into the card machine.

Nothing. That's what Clyde just bought. Absolutely nothing. Craig was truly blown away. He turned his head towards the kitchen door. It was open slightly. It looked like there was someone there. He squinted his eyes and looked closer. It was the waiter. There was a smile on his face. Craig smiled back. The waiter winked. And then the door closed. That night, Craig had the most furious wank he'd ever had in his life.

Anyway, as it turned out, the waiter *had* poisoned Clyde's food, because he spent the entire next day on the toilet with explosive diarrhoea. The waiter was just having a laugh with Craig because he was drunk.

Craig thought it would be best if they never went back to that restaurant again.

Pinned Tweet

John sat with his laptop open in front of him, his Twitter open. He was angrily staring at the profile picture of this girl John knew from school called Sarah. A girl who over the last week, had accidentally gone viral. I say accidentally because she didn't actually mean to go viral. It just happened as a direct result of a tweet she made. Which is the way viral content works I suppose. There's not some generic formula or deliberate action that causes something to go viral. It's just pure luck. Anyway, John was staring at her profile picture because he was fucking furious. He'd couldn't handle it anymore. He tried to tell himself that he didn't care about shit like this. He didn't want something like this to bother him as much as it did. But he did care. This shit infuriated him more than anything. And he didn't think he was being unreasonably angry.

I'll take you back to the tweet itself. Basically, what happened was this girl, Sarah, posted a tweet in response to a picture that this celebrity model, Samantha McPotato put up on her Twitter. I might add that she's not really a celebrity. She was one of these reality TV contestants that just happened to have a massive following on social media. I'm pretty sure that doesn't make a person as famous. That sounds more like she's popular. I don't know. Perhaps your definition of what makes someone famous differs from mine. But anyway, that doesn't matter. The picture was a selfie of Samantha McPotato with one of those stupid fucking Snapchat filters. The one that makes you look like a fucking Barbie doll or something. The one that girls use to cover up imperfections or spots on their face. But that wasn't what caused the picture to arouse the amount of controversy that it did. Behind Samantha McPotato, in the background on a table was, what looked to be, a human vagina with bite marks on it.

And this girl Sarah, retweeted the picture, with a comment that read: *"Oh caught out eating yourself again Samantha McPotato"*, and there was one of those stupid fucking winky faces after it.

Now, Sarah said *again* because apparently Samantha McPotato's had some problems before with self-cannibalism. It was revealed by a few articles during the height of her fame that she even went to rehab a few times because of it. But she addressed these allegations when these articles first came out by saying that it was years ago and that she doesn't do that anymore.

And so it was Sarah's response to this picture that caused it to go viral. Ms. McPotato responded immediately, claiming that it wasn't her vagina, but just some food leftover from her dinner. She also said she wanted to clarify this because she knows how fast rumors can spread from the smallest of accusations.

She was clearly fucking lying though. It was so obviously a vagina. Anyone with even an ounce of intelligence could tell her excuse was complete horseshit. And about a week later, after a mountain of abuse she received from media outlets and people online, Samantha McPotato was forced to admit in an interview that it was her vagina in the selfie and that she would be seeking professional help to address the issue.

But back to Sarah's fucking tweet. Every news article that ran a story about Samantha McPotato's self-cannibalism relapse brought up that Sarah was the first Twitter user to shed light on the issue (if you can call it an issue).

"On Sunday night, the Twitter user SarahOM24 replied to a picture that McPotato tweeted, which showed what appeared to be a half-eaten human vagina on the table in the background"

The tweet got thousands of retweets and favorites. It got all kinds of responses from people, some on Sarah's side, saying it did indeed look like Samantha McPotato's vagina, and then others against Sarah, criticizing and mocking her for accusing someone of a self-cannibalism relapse based on very little evidence.

If John was being honest though, it wasn't the tweet that fucking angered him. He actually understood why someone, in this case Sarah, might think it was Samantha McPotato's vagina in the picture. It was very visible in the background and John had seen enough vagina's in his lifetime to know one when he saw one. Plus, given her previous problems with auto-cannibalism, it was easy enough to put two and two together and realize this bitch was back to eating herself.

No. What fucking infuriated John more than anything, was the way Sarah responded to the whole situation. She fucking loved every bit of attention she got. You swear, she thought the tabloids were hailing her as a hero for pointing out the vagina in the picture. Like the internet should be hailing her as a hero and the town should throw a parade in her honor.

See, Sarah is one of these Twitter users that tweets almost hourly, telling her uncaring following of 212 followers every mundane detail of her boring fucking life. This was a girl that posted frequent updates of her opinions of last nights' Home and Away episode and what foods she was unable to digest due to Irritable Bowel Syndrome. You can't get duller than that.

It genuinely baffled John. He wondered if Sarah actually thought people cared about her tweets. She never got any responses or likes or retweets or any indication that anyone was in any way interested in what kinds of curries made her shit her pants. John didn't know why she did it. No one gave a shit. You could understand if she was famous or if she had a following of people that were in the thousands, but this girl had a little more than two-hundred and not one of them cared in the least about what she had to say about a dream she had last night. But now, all of a sudden, people did give a shit (at least in her mind anyway) because she just so happened to be the first person to tweet about this random celebrity eating her own pussy.

There wasn't a reply to her tweet Sarah didn't respond to. She responded to every single one of them. Even with the messages that took the absolute piss out of her, she replied with some witty and sardonic reply that just came off as forced and artificial. She took a screenshot of her Twitter feed and posted it on her Instagram and Facebook, with the caption *"whoops, look what I've done"*. The level of cringe made John's toes curl. He saw her out in the pub that Saturday and could hear her talking about it with her friends. He felt like chucking his pint at her. It fucking made him sick. She was fucking loving it.

274

It made John furious. He didn't want to admit it to anyone though. He didn't even want to talk about it. His friends would bring it up the odd time, or when John was having a coffee with his girlfriend and she said: God, that thing that Sarah tweeted is really blowing up, isn't it? John just shrugged it off. He didn't say anything to her because he knew once he did, he'd go off on a rant about Sarah and never shut the fuck up. But he *was* angry. Probably more than anyone. He just thought she was pathetic. Just some attention-hungry girl eating up her ten minutes of fame.

And as predicted, that fame only lasted about a week and a half. Like all these fruitless celebrity scandals that some people mistake for actual news, it all died down and people moved on with their lives. John was delighted. No longer did he have to hear or even think about Sarah and her stupid fucking Twitter profile.

But just when John thought Sarah couldn't get any more deplorable, she goes ahead and does this. On her Twitter profile, she changed her biography to this:

"I'm the girl that took the internet by storm for a while by accusing Samantha McPotato of eating her own vagina".

Not only that, but she'd *pinned* the tweet, so now it was the first thing that people saw when they went to her profile.

What an absolute cunt, John thought.

Why would Sarah do such a thing? Why would you want people to identify you by something you did accidentally and that ultimately, has about as much impact on the world as a pensioners fart? How can her life be so fucking boring and hollow that this is how she wants people to view her? As this girl who got famous, but not really, for a week because of a random tweet, that by complete and utter chance, just happened to go viral. He couldn't comprehend it. It made John want to scream. He wanted to storm to her house and grab her and ask her why the fuck she would do something so pitiful. He really wanted to know because John just couldn't wrap his head around it.

This time, John knew he had to do something. He was filled with such rage. He needed some way to fucking vent his frustration. He couldn't stop staring at that fucking tweet pinned to her Twitter profile. It shocked him that people like this existed. He wanted to say something to her. He desperately wanted to. Like an itch you want to scratch more than anything but that your doctor insists you leave alone. But at the same time, John didn't want to be like the cretinous and superficial scum of the earth that he hated more than anything. He didn't want to stoop to Sarah's level.

But he really did at the same time. He wanted Sarah to know he was vehemently against people like her. People who crave attention because their lives are so empty and seriously need to get their priorities straight. She should know. She's probably surrounded by friends and family that don't tell her this shit isn't healthy for her. Someone should say to Sarah that she needs to cop the fuck on and grow up. That she should abandon these adolescent tendencies of posting online in the hopes that somebody somewhere cared.

Maybe John should be the one to say it. Maybe since she cares so much about what random fuckers online think about her, maybe she'll read what John writes and cop on. Maybe she'd thank him in the long run. Fuck it, he was going to. John pressed the tweet button and typed that she was a filthy fucking cunt whore who should fucking kill herself. John pressed the publish button and sat back in his chair as the message popped up on his screen, feeling satisfied in himself that Sarah would see what he wrote and maybe think twice before deciding to do something so pathetically trivial and juvenile again.

John ended up going to prison for seven months. He got arse raped a few times.

The County Minor

Declan played county minor for his local club, The Bumblebees and was considered one of the best corner-forwards in Kerry. As stressful as it was juggling football along with everything else in his life, and as unfair as he thought it was that he didn't get paid for his contribution to the club, he still loved playing football more than anything else in the world. At twenty-four years of age, Declan had been playing football for most of his life. In fact, he couldn't remember a day in his life that wasn't at some point occupied with football. He played other sports of course, went to the gym five or six times a week, and held down a job as a swimming instructor for primary schools. But nothing could take the sweet place that football held in his heart. It was his dream to play for the Kerry seniors one day. To be representing his county in the All-Ireland final was something he wanted more than anything.

It was a dream that only he and no one else seemed to have. His other teammates loved playing football just as much as he did, but they all had careers and ambitions. Some even had families. If Declan was to guess, they'd probably stop playing county in a couple of years or drop down to the B-team. Declan understood why. It can be stressful being a county minor, which is difficult enough when they're also not being compensated like the managers are. But for Declan, he was in it for the long haul. His sights were set on the beautiful green field of Croke Park.

Declan's best mates weren't really that sporty. In fact, most of them actively avoided any type of physical exercise. They were all into culture and arts and shit, stuff that Declan had no interest in. His mates often berated him for his lack of interest in such things, but he didn't know what to say to them. He really had no interest in stuff like that. Unless it had to do with sports. He could watch that movie, "Goal" a bunch of times. And he'd seen a few of the Rocky movies. If it was anything else, he really wasn't that interested. Declan did give some things a chance though. He attended the occasional movie here and there if his mates really wanted to go. He didn't want to be someone who didn't give things a chance just because he wasn't interested in them. He didn't want others to think of him as close-minded, which is what he guessed his friends thought he was. He saw a movie with them there the last night. He couldn't remember the name of it. Like *Star War Revengers* or something. He thought it was alright. His mates said he didn't give it a proper chance. But the thing was he did like it. He just didn't appreciate it on the emotional level that they viewed it on. To them, it was something to be experienced and dissected. To him, it was nothing more than mindless entertainment to pass the time on the weekends. Nor did he seek to appreciate movies and other shit like that on the same level as they did.

To be fair though, Declan's friends didn't give football much of a chance either. In fact, they seemed to relish at the opportunity to slag him over his love for football. They never came to any of his matches, despite him inviting them constantly on the Facebook group chat. Not that Declan was complaining or anything. It wasn't like he was putting a gun to their head. He just thought it'd be nice for them to come and show their support, seeing as they call themselves his friends, and seeing as he's always doing the shit they want to do. He always went to his friends plays, musicals, and photography exhibitions. They never even had to ask him. He just went. But his friends said that a football match wasn't the same thing. That a play or musical or photography exhibition takes months of effort and much more planning than a silly game of football. Declan didn't think that was a fair argument. He put in the same amount of effort, if not more, into his football that they put into their stuff. He trained every day and played matches every week, all the while holding down a full-time job. And all for free. Declan played only for his love of the game. If that wasn't *passion and dedication*, as his friends put it, he didn't know what was.

Their thing was the arts. His thing was sports. He didn't see a difference, despite their argument to the contrary. Declan loved football. He always did and he always would. He didn't see what the problem was. He always told them they'd enjoy his football if they just gave it a chance.

A great case in point of Declan trying to get his friends to come to his matches was his mate, Ian.

Ian was a close friend of Declan's, but he never came to any of his matches. In fact, Ian gave him more abuse than anyone else in his group of friends for his love of football. That's primarily because Ian was so far from any sportsperson you could imagine. For one, Ian was a fat fuck. Always has been, ever since secondary school. Declan had never seen him in an even remotely healthy physical condition. But besides all that, Ian was studying acting up in Cork. He wanted to be in movies and TV shows and all that bullshit.

Frankly, Declan thought he was a bit pretentious and full of himself. He was very hipster. He was one of these people that just had to be different, not because he *was* different, but just to be different. He wore very flashy and colourful clothing, which seemed more of a vehicle to show off rather than a fashion statement. Sometimes he wore these pyjama pants that were brightly chequered or had interesting designs on them. But they were pyjama bottoms. And he wore them during the day, like walking about in public like it was fucking normal. Declan would be fucking embarrassed walking around with him sometimes. What if some of the lads on the team saw him with Ian? They'd think he was a fucking queer. Ian said they weren't pyjama bottoms, they were just really loose pants. But Declan knew what they were. He didn't care what he said. They are what they are, and what they are is fucking pyjama bottoms.

What's more, Ian dyed his hair all kinds of colours. Every couple of weeks, he be walking around with blond hair, looking like some fucking albino. Then the next week, he'd have pink hair like some fucking faggot. Declan was just like, "why don't you fucking let your hair be brown the way it's supposed to?". In the last couple of weeks, he was sporting red hair. Not ginger. Like the colour red. Which Declan didn't mind as much, but he'd still be dead embarrassed if any of the lads from the team saw him with Ian.

Anyway, Declan stopped inviting Ian to his matches years ago just because of the mountain of abuse he got from him. And not like banter. Like properly insulting him. Saying football is for old men and plebs, and that no one cared about it. That his passion for the sport was stupid. It was the one time he could be a proper prick. Declan didn't know where it came from. He said he didn't want to spend ten euro just to watch some stupid game of football. Declan would say he could get in for free if he hopped the fence behind the pitch, yet he still refused. The fucker wouldn't even go to a free match.

Declan always went up to see Ian's college plays, and that was all the way up in Cork, so he'd have to travel two hours and spend twenty euro in petrol, as well as a tenner to get into the play, and then travel another two hours back down. It was a fucking hassle, but Declan did it anyway because Ian was his mate and he wanted to be supportive. He thought the least he could do was return that support by coming to a few of his games, or at least stop making out like his love of football is something to be ashamed of. He didn't make Ian feel bad for wanting to pursue acting. He thought it was stupid, but if acting was what Ian wanted to do, then that was fine. He would never put someone down for being passionate about something. He didn't care what his friends did as long as they were happy. Why couldn't Ian act the same way with him and his football?

Anyway, Ian dropped out of college there a few months ago because he couldn't afford the fees anymore, and has since moved back to Kerry until he figures out what he's going to do next. Declan thought it was annoying that seeing as he's not in college anymore, he hasn't got a job, and he's not really doing much else to occupy his time except going to the pub every second day, Ian still didn't want to go to any of his games.

But Declan knew better than to start pestering him over it every week, so he decided to just stop asking, and accept that Ian's never going to want to come to one of his games. However, recently, just after the New Year, they were cruising around and Ian said to Declan that he made a New Year's Resolution to lose a bit of weight.

Why don't you join the gym with me? said Declan. I'll train you.

Ian laughed it off. Declan said he was serious.

Seriously, I'll make a gym plan for you. We'll go four or five times a week. I'll collect you. We'll have you fit within three months.

Ian laughed again.

Seriously, man, I'll give you a hand.

How much is it?

I think it's a hundred and eighty for three months.

Ian looked out the window like he was considering it. Maybe, he said.

Declan switched to another radio station. He was quite certain he'd never see this fat fuck inside the walls of a gym in his life.

But low and fucking behold, Declan was shocked to find Ian wandering around his gym a couple of days later in a pair of tight shorts and a vest.

What are you doing here? said Declan.

Thought I'd give the gym a chance

Did you get a monthly membership?

No, three months.

Jesus, fair play. I never thought I'd see the day when I'd find you in a fucking gym, said Declan and he burst out laughing.

Yeah, well, here I am. What do you think I should do? I haven't a clue what I'm doing here, to be honest?

Okay, well why don't you do say fifteen minutes on the treadmill and then I'll show you some weights after.

Okay.

So, Declan showed Ian over to the treadmills and showed him the basic controls. Ian seemed more fascinated by the fact that you could watch YouTube and Netflix while on the treadmill, but Declan focused his attention and got him running. About ten minutes in, Declan had to stop him because he looked like he was fit to collapse. He had a feeling that Ian was trying to act more fit then he actually was, just so he didn't embarrass himself in front of Declan. But Declan understood. He knew from his time doing Health and Leisure in college how difficult it was for those new to working out.

After the treadmills, Declan showed him a few weight exercises. He started light just to get a sense of what Ian could handle. But it was fairly obvious once he tried to lift a fairly easy pair of 6kg dumbbells that this fat fuck wouldn't be able to lift a bowl of fruit above his head.

The whole time Ian was working out, Declan resisted the temptation to slag the shit out of him. It was seriously tempting considering the amount of abuse he's gotten from him in the past. He couldn't deny that it was hilarious to watch his man tit's bounce up and down while he hopped around on the treadmill, or assume the wrong position on the bench as he was about to lift weights. But still, he resisted the temptation. In fact, he was happy for Ian that he finally joined the gym. He was almost proud of him. He said this to Ian in the car afterwards. Ian was being really quiet. Declan could tell he was a bit embarrassed by the sweaty and admittedly hilarious showcase of his athletic skills.

You going to keep going? said Declan.

Maybe.

Ah, do. It's always fucking difficult for new members to get used to. If you keep at it, eventually you'll be a fucking tank.

That's hard to imagine.

I know. Hard to imagine you lifting 20kg over your head without a sweat. Ah, but in all seriousness though. Keep at it. You've already paid the hundred and eighty for the three months anyway. You might as well use it, you know. Be a waste.

I suppose you're right there.

So will I pick you up tomorrow?

Fucking hell, said Ian chuckling. I have a feeling you're going to be the biggest fucking plague over this.

Declan shrugged.

Alright, tomorrow morning, I suppose.

Lovely. I'll text you when I'm leaving the house.

And Ian did keep at it. He persisted, and despite some tough days when Declan would literally have to drag his fat arse out of the bed, he persevered and kept with the gym. Fast forward three months later and Ian had lost almost all of his body fat, losing up to five stone. His arms got fairly big as well. He didn't have the six-pack Declan was hoping for, but sure, you can't have everything. It was honestly like looking at another person. Declan was so used to seeing an Ian with bigger tits than his own mother. And it wasn't just the physical change that Declan noticed in Ian's life. All of sudden, Ian's self-confidence went up drastically. He was able to look himself up and down in the mirror and not hate himself. And he was getting laid constantly. Their weekly nights out seemed to always end with Ian going home with nine's and ten's. Declan and the lads couldn't believe it. It was honestly like something you'd see on Operation Transformation or some show like that. It really was remarkable. Declan was fucking proud of Ian. He really was. His friend had taken it upon himself to make an important change in his life and it paid off for him big time. But that wasn't the only reason Declan was delighted for Ian and his newfound body.

Over the course of the three months that Declan had been taking Ian to the gym, he'd gotten him to understand why he was so passionate about fitness.. Ian wasn't just going to the gym because he had a membership he didn't want to waste. He was passionate about it. The two of them actually bonded over it. Before, they used to just bond over Eminem songs and laughing at the expense of other people. Now, they talked about fitness regimes and different diets. Ian sometimes sent him links on Facebook of different types of warmups and bodybuilding plans. Declan couldn't believe it. If you'd told him at the start of the year that he'd be slurping on protein shakes with Mr. *I'm-going-to-be-a-famous-actor* Ian before going out to lift ten sets of 20kg dumbbells, he would have told you to go fuck your mother.

And more importantly than getting him to understand his passion for fitness, Ian started coming to Declan's football games. All of them. Declan couldn't believe it the first time he saw him on the sidelines. He thought he was seeing a fucking mirage. But no, it was Ian, cheering Declan on. Ian was even able to convince their other friends to tag along and sometimes afterwards, they'd go out for a few drinks and have a fucking great time. After a while, his friends actually enjoyed coming to his matches. Declan found he even played better when they were there. Like a good luck charm. And it was all because he pushed Ian into joining the gym. That simple little act caused a ripple effect that made Ian and all their friends finally understand his vigorous obsession with football. It made him so happy.

When Ian's three-month membership ran out, he got another one: A one-year membership. He seemed more motivated than ever to get back to the gym. After another couple of months, Ian became the biggest and most enthusiastic bodybuilder that Declan knew. He was running 5k and 10k runs weekly. He was even considering abandoning his aspirations of acting and going to college to study Health and Leisure. Declan couldn't believe it when he heard the words come out of Ian's mouth. This guy had been a creative person for so long, someone who considered himself a "*sensitive artist*". But as far as Declan was aware, he'd now abandoned his acting ambitions and had now dedicated himself to a life of fitness. He was a completely different person now. The old Ian seemed like a ghost to who he was now.

After another couple of months, Ian was almost as fit as Declan. He started a Health and Leisure PLC course at the local training college that September, and was talking about opening his own gym after he finished the subsequent four year college course. Declan had a hard time keeping up with him. The fucker couldn't be stopped. He was amazed at the turnaround Ian had made in just under a year, both in terms of his fitness and his long-term goals. He was no longer that chubby little boy that Declan had known and loved since secondary school.

Ian got so fit, that Declan suggested he start playing football. Ian would occasionally accompany him to the local football pitch where they'd kick a ball around for an hour or two. Ian said that was a stupid idea and he wouldn't be good at it. Declan immediately recognised the old, fat, negative Ian in the way he said this and told him to cop on. He suggested that he join the B-team, just to give him a taste of what playing football is `like. Declan, being a county minor, said he'd help train him, in the same way he did when Ian first joined the gym.

And Ian did. He joined the Bumblebees B-team. He found it hard at first as he'd never played a game of football in his life. But as time went on, he grew to love it the same way that Declan did. Declan tried to help him out any way he could. He'd take him to the Bumblebees pitch whenever he had free time and they'd practice drills and do laps of the pitch until they were both knackered. Or sometimes, they spend what seemed like hours kicking balls over the bar while they watched the sunset go down. It was quite beautiful. Declan was so happy for Ian. If you'd told him that he'd one day be kicking a ball around with Ian in preparation for a game on Sunday, he would have told you to go fuck your father.

Ian didn't start immediately. Most newcomers to the game usually ride the bench for a while, just until they learn the ropes. They'd bring him on as a half-back sometimes for the last ten minutes of the game, which Declan found disappointing. He knew how hard Ian was working. He'd seen the incredible improvement he'd made over the past few weeks and knew how hard he was working to make the starting team. If only the manager was willing to give him a chance, he wouldn't be sorry. Declan didn't understand why though. Ian was one of the oldest lads on the team. He'd clearly destroy anyone he was marking. Plus, the B-team was fucking useless and Ian was definitely superior to any of his teammates. Most of them turned up to training in tracksuit bottoms and still hungover from the night before.

One Saturday in a match against a west Kerry team, Ian finally made the starting fifteen. Not only that, but he started as a corner-forward: Declan's position. Declan couldn't believe his eyes when he ran out of the dressing rooms and took his place on the pitch. A year ago, something like this would only happen in a dream. This was a guy who once said he'd never watch a game of football in his life. Now here he was, starting as a corner-forward for the Bumblebees B-team. Declan felt like a proud parent. He felt like he'd raised this person. That he'd forged the person blazing up the field right now. It brought a little tear to his eye.

Ian scored a goal and four points. The goal was in the last fifteen minutes of the match and Declan knew it was what clinched the game for them. He couldn't have been prouder of Ian when that full-time whistle went. Outside the dressing rooms after the game, he gave him a huge hug and told him he was proud of him. Usually, Declan wouldn't be that sentimental with another guy, especially a close friend. But this was different. This was Ian. Although they'd been friends since second year Spanish, he hugged him like he was his son. After that, Ian made the starting line-up for every match as the Bumblebees B-team corner-forward

Ian eventually became so good on the Bumblebees B-team, that most cornerbacks would get conniptions at the thoughts of trying to stop him from fucking demolishing their team. It wouldn't be abnormal for Ian to score five or six goals in a single game. He was better than every single one of his teammates combined. It didn't take very long for Declan to see that Ian clearly didn't belong on a team where the goalkeeper stuffed his phone in his sock, and the full-forward would light up a cigarette during the game. Ian was county minor material. He said this to Ian and suggested he should show up to one of their training sessions, just to see how he'd get on. Ian said he would.

Declan was dead fucking excited when Ian said he'd come to a training session. The thought of playing on the same team as Ian was like a dream come true. He could already picture the two of them blazing the field of Croke Park together. *"Ireland's Greatest Corner-Forwards"*. It put a smile on his face just thinking about it.

Declan was a little worried that some of the other lads on the team might take the piss out of him over the red hair. He asked Ian if he wouldn't just change it back to its original colour, but he insisted the red hair was here to stay. Declan didn't press the matter any further. He couldn't stop any of the lads from taking the utter piss out of him if he kept it like that. He just hoped his performance would make up for the fact that he looked like a bit of a ponce.

Declan warned Ian beforehand that the training sessions would be very hard and would demand a lot of him. Ian seemed to take this in his stride. In fact, he didn't seem too bothered about it. He even welcomed the challenge. And as it soon turned out, Ian found the training sessions to be no harder than training at the gym. Declan was shocked. He was almost annoyed. Declan found the training sessions to be extremely difficult, especially this year as they had a new manager called Billy, that had been brought in from another team, and was a lot stricter than their previous manager, who had been a cakewalk in retrospect. He made them do the same drills over and over and run until they got sick.

290

Dear God, the fucking running. So much running. So much that sometimes Declan felt like his legs were going to stop working if he was forced to run another inch. He was very strict as well. If he caught you eating anything unhealthy or drinking any alcohol, he'd threaten to kick you off the team. And he was such a fucking plague for timekeeping. Declan had once called Billy and said he wouldn't be able to make the training session that evening as his mother had been taken into hospital. Well, wouldn't you know it, the bollox rang Declan up the next day and fucked him out of it. It was fucking bullshit. What was Declan supposed to do? Not go into hospital to visit his mother who'd just fainted at work? This was the side of playing football that Declan personally hated. It was easy for Billy, who was getting paid an attractive twelve grand a year to manage the team, to give out to the players that weren't earning a fucking cent for their contribution.

Billy wasn't a bad guy, by no means. He was just a fucking intense manager. So intense that it proved to be too much for Declan occasionally. Sometimes he'd catch himself thinking about hanging it all up and focusing on his career, which is what his parents incessantly advised him to do. So you could imagine how annoying it was for Declan that the training sessions had no considerable mental or physical impact on Ian. After Ian got fit, he swore off alcohol and began a strict vegetarian diet. So as you can imagine, he got on fucking brilliantly with Billy. He still wasn't starting, mind you, but you could see by the semi-homoerotic sparkle in Billy's eyes that it wouldn't be too long until he did.

As the season went on, Declan would be so fucking knackered twenty minutes into the second half of a match, that he'd be fucking praying Billy would take him off and let Ian play. And most of the time he did. He'd come on and score a point or two. Nothing major. As happy as he was for Ian that he was finally playing, it really depressed Declan that he wasn't able to play the full seventy minutes. To be fair, he was just back from a groin injury, but it still left him disheartened. How was he meant to play for the senior team one day, let alone start for them, if he couldn't even play a full match? Some of the lads joked around that he was losing his touch or wasn't as good as he used to be. Declan would laugh along with them, but the truth was he was very concerned these jokes were becoming a possibility.

Ian helped him out as best he could. He'd come over to his house before a game and cook him up this chicken and pasta recipe he found online, while Declan did leg exercises on the kitchen table. But no matter what he did, nothing ever seemed to work. He still couldn't play a full match. Having Ian around to motivate him helped a bit, but it also kind of annoyed him. He wouldn't be nearly as enthusiastic and motivated if he knew what it was like to play a full game of football.

During one particularly tough league game against a team from up north, Declan didn't know how much longer he could keep going for as he tore through the second half. He'd scored two goals and three points during the first half, but early in the second, he felt a sudden sharp pain in his calf muscle. It wasn't too painful, but it slowed him down considerably. He was hoping that Billy would notice and take him off, but he seemed more concerned with what was happening down at the other end of the field. In the last twenty minutes, Ian had come on in place of one of the half-forwards who got injured. He wasn't playing too bad, but he was mostly

292

brought back to defend as the other team was making a very concerning comeback. Still, Declan couldn't help but feel thankful as he watched the ball fly around at the other end of the pitch. At least he could rest his leg for a moment.

The game went into its final five minutes, and both teams were tied. It was a real nail-biter of a match. Declan pushed himself harder in those final ten minutes then he did during the entire game, despite the growing pain in his leg. For a minute after a few successive points, it seemed like the Bumblebees had secured the win, but then the other team came back to level with them again. The Bumblebees scored. Then the other team scored. Then they scored another point and it looked like they might win. Then Ian got the ball, and from the half-way line, turned and booted the ball as hard as he could. It just managed to make it over the bar and the two teams were level again.

Then in the final minute, the Bumblebees got a free kick and Declan stepped up to take it. He was their main free kick taker. This was it. All he had to do was pop this over and they'd win the game. The referee would blow the whistle after this. His leg was aching, but he tried to ignore the pain and concentrate on the free. It didn't look difficult at all. Twenty-five yards at least. This was simple. Declan had put thousands of these over before and this was no different. It was just the pressure of putting it over that flustered him. He approached the ball, trying to control his breathing.

No pressure, said the guy who was marking him.

Declan ignored him. He picked up the ball and looked up at the goals. He took a deep breath. Then another. And another. He held the ball firmly in the palm of his hands. The place was silent. He ran up and took the shot.

He missed. Declan stood and watched in horror as the ball sailed to the left, past the goals, and away from victory. He heard his teammates screaming abuse at him, but it was just a cacophony of noise. He didn't just miss that. He couldn't have. Anyone could have made that shot. He should have put that away, no bother at all. When the full-time whistle blew, the guy he was marking, came up to shake his hand. Every instinct in Declan's body told him to put the cunt in a coma. But he didn't. He kept his cool and shook his hand without looking at him.

He got some bollocking from the lads in the dressing room afterwards. Billy said a retard could have made that kick. Declan didn't respond to any of it. He just quietly got dressed. He wanted to get in his car, drive to an off-licence, and get fucking pissed. As he was walking out of the dressing room, Ian was waiting for him by his car.

I'm not in the mood, Ian, said Declan

I'm not going to give out to you.

Good, cause I'm not in the mood.

Look, man, it could have happened to any of us. You made a mistake, that's all.

Anyone could have made that free.

That's not true.

It is.

Look, just don't let it get you down. You'll come back next week and play harder.

Yeah.

Declan tossed his bag in the boot and got into the car. Ian started walking away. Declan rolled down the window.

Where you going?

Oh, yeah, I forgot to tell you. Wayne's dropping me home.

Wayne said he'd drop you home?

Yeah.

Okay.

Is that alright?

Yeah, that's fine, said Declan. He didn't know why that bothered him, but it did.

Chin up, bud. It's only a silly game of football. I'll see you at the gym tomorrow.

Declan stared at Ian as he walked away.

Only a silly game of football? This wasn't a fucking game to Declan. This was his life, his passion, his art. He put 100% of himself into this every single day, and for Ian to flippantly make out like it's some arbitrary thing that should be shrugged off is damn near fucking insulting and disrespectful. The fact that he even sees it that way just goes to show how little Ian's actually changed since he's got fit. Declan put his keys in the ignition, his hands still shaking, and drove off. *Only a football game.* That played on his mind for a while. How dare that fucker, who's been playing football for less than a year, try and tell Declan, who's been playing football his whole life, that it's all just *a silly game of football*. The fucking cheek of him.

Declan got his leg checked that week and it turned out his injury was more serious than he originally thought. His physio suspected it was because he'd thrown himself back into football without giving his groin a proper chance to heal. He ended up being out for two weeks.

Two weeks later, against his physio's wishes, Declan went back to training. He was sick of sitting on his arse at home, not doing anything. He tried not to push himself too hard, which was tough by Billy's standards, but he needed to get his head back in the game. Declan had convinced himself that he was ready to train again, but he didn't know. Everyone was still a bit sore with him for missing that free, except for Ian. Ian welcomed Declan back with open arms.

Training wasn't the same without you, he said.

Declan smiled. It was nice to hear that from Ian, even if he still felt sour at him for his arbitrary juxtaposition of football and an insignificant game.

Training wasn't as bad as Declan thought it would be. He found that the running wasn't too hard and, if anything, the drills actually seemed to help his leg. He'd kept his leg relatively immobile for the past two weeks. It was nice to get it moving again.

Over the next few days, Declan's leg started to feel much better. He was still nervous about how he'd play on Sunday against Beaufort. But Declan was more determined than ever to throw everything he had at it. He was going to play a full game and half-ass nothing. He wasn't about to let what happened during the last game happen again.

When it came to game day, Declan was fucking pumped. He'd gotten up early and did twenty-five minutes of meditation to put his mind at rest. He went for a morning run on the beach, had a healthy breakfast at the local pub, followed by more leg exercises. He was ready. The game started at two. At half one, Declan was already in the dressing rooms, kitted out and ready to kick ass. By ten to, everyone was in the dressing room and ready to go. Ian came up to him and wished him the best of luck. Declan thanked him. He was feeling good about today's game. There was a shared feeling of nervousness as they were going up against a team that, time and time again, gave the Bumblebees a run for their money, but it was nothing they haven't faced before. As everyone was getting ready, someone tapped Declan on the shoulder and made him jump.

Jesus, roared Declan.

Sorry, said Billy chuckling.

You scared the shit out of me.

Sorry about that. Listen, Declan, I want to talk to you about something real quick.

What's up?

Look, I was thinking for today, I might start Ian at corner-forward.

What?

Yeah, I'm going to start Ian first and then I might bring you on in the second half depending on how he fares.

Billy, I can start.

I know you can, but with your leg and all…

No, I can fucking start. I always start. Put me on first and bring Ian on if you think my leg is bad. I'll let you know…

Look, I'm starting Ian for now. My decisions final.

And Billy walked away.

Declan clenched his fists and almost punched the wall. This was not fucking happening.

For the first time ever, Declan walked out of the dressing room, and instead of taking his place at corner-forward, put his hands in his pocket, lowered his head, and made his way over to the subs bench. It was fucking embarrassing. What would the other lads think? The game started and Declan sat on the bench sulking with his arms folded. He wasn't even trying to hide his disappointment. He was fucking fuming. Declan had always started. Always. Who the fuck did Billy think he was? He had no right to do something like this.

By half-time, they were in the lead, not because Beaufort were playing shite or anything. They were playing just as good as they always did. The Bumblebees were winning because of Ian. He'd scored four goals and nine points. And that was just in the first half. He was fucking phenomenal. Even Declan, who was still raging at Billy's decision not to place him in the starting fifteen, couldn't deny that he'd never seen another player give the committed and beautiful performance that Ian was giving. Everyone in the crowd was fucking roaring. Even supporters on the Beaufort side started cheering for Ian. He came up to Declan during the half-time break and asked him if he had any tips. Declan smiled and told him he was playing great and to keep doing what he was doing. He didn't really care. Ian patted him on the shoulder, took a mouthful of water from one of the bottles, and ran back onto the pitch. Declan looked at Billy with gritted teeth. He better fucking bring him on soon or he'll be getting a brick through his window.

It got down to the final ten minutes of the game and Declan still hadn't been brought on. He was seething with rage. Ian had scored another five goals and an additional twelve points, putting them forty-seven points in the lead. Why the fuck wasn't Billy bringing him on? They were fucking annihilating them. It was certain. There was no way they could lose this. What did Billy have to lose by bringing him on? As the clock signalled the final five minutes, Declan finally couldn't take it anymore and approached Billy.

Billy, will you put me on? We're fucking destroying them.

Fuck sake, Cathal, roared Billy down the pitch.

Billy?

What? said Billy turning to Declan.

Will you put me on? We have it.

Billy cocked his eyes. Alright, I suppose.

The ball went out for a free kick and Billy signalled to the referee that Declan was coming on as a substitute for Ian. As Ian ran off the pitch, all his team members clapped and everyone on the sidelines chanted his name. Some people were even crying. Billy approached him and gave him a huge pat on the back. Well fucking done, man, he said. Great game.

Ian high fived Declan and slumped down onto the bench. Declan sprinted onto the field. Now was his fucking moment. To steal the show. When the whistle blew, someone kicked the ball towards the other end of the pitch. The ball bounced around there for a bit. Then there was a free kick. Beaufort took it and scored a point. The ball was kicked out and Finbarr caught it. It was getting closer to him, Declan just had to call it. He ran nearer to him and roared for the ball. Finbarr spotted him and kicked it. Declan caught it with ease and was about to boot it over the bar, but before he could do anything, the referee blew the full-time whistle.

Everyone started cheering. All except Declan. Declan felt a vein pop in his head. He could feel his face getting red. He kicked the ball as hard as he could and it disappeared over the fence. The guy next to him tried to shake his hand, but he slapped it and walked away, ignoring every hand

299

that was offered to him. He needed something to destroy right now. His eyes felt like they were boiling around the edges. This was another level of anger. As he walked into the dressing room and hopped a water bottle off the wall, Ian came up behind him.

Declan, I saw you slap your man's hand away. What the hell was all that about?

Declan stopped and looked at Ian.

I fucking made you, said Declan.

What? said Ian.

Declan laced Ian across the face and he collapsed to the ground.

Fuck off back to Cork and do your fucking acting, you pretentious, ginger-haired cunt.

His teammates rushed towards Declan and pulled him away as he started stomping on Ian with the sole of his boots. He shoved them off, grabbed his gear bag and got out of there. He could hear Billy roaring behind him as he jumped into his car and drove off. Declan screamed so loud as he drove away that he was certain he'd fractured his larynx.

Declan called Ian later that night and apologised. He said he was just a little pissed off because he didn't get to play. Ian said he understood and told him not to think about it. Declan hung up, downed the rest of his Guinness, and ordered a shot of tequila from the bartender.

Things only got worse from there on in. Declan made the starting team sometimes, mainly if Ian was a little injured or if he needed to rest for a bigger game that was coming up, but for the most part, Ian replaced Declan as the Bumblebees left corner-forward. He became their best player. He was so good that this one time at training, he went up to Billy and said:

300

Billy, I'm a little wrecked from running.

Ah, no bother, man, Billy said. You just sit down there now and have a rest for yourself.

Now let's get something clear. If anyone ever said to Billy that they didn't want to run, you can bet you weeks wages that a water bottle would be shoved so fucking far up their arse sideways, that they'd need a team of surgeons to remove it. But no, Ian got a free pass from the arse-licking Billy because he knew how valuable he was to the team.

Declan really started to resent Ian. Ah, fuck it, he hated the cunt. He ceased going to the gym with him and no longer interacted with him in any social or physical way, except for training. He didn't even drive him around anymore. Ian would ask him sometimes if everything was alright between them, and Declan would always say it was. But it wasn't. He was only saying that because he knew Billy would crush his balls in a vice if he found out that Ian was off his game even a little or was involved in another tiff with Declan. He had to beg Billy not to kick him off the team when he beat the shit out of Ian after the Beaufort game

After another while, Declan spent more time on the bench than he did on the field. He had visions of choking the life out of both Ian and Billy in their sleep. He found himself browsing the Dark Web most nights, looking for a hitman to take out the two of them. Eight months later, most of his teammates and Billy had forgotten that Declan was even playing for the Bumblebees. He'd show up to games without his gear on and he'd just sit on the bench in his tracksuit bottoms and hoodie. Billy gave him the odd job sometimes, like running onto the pitch to give players water bottles or if they needed an extra umpire. Declan and Ian's mates now came to every single game. They sat on the sidelines with face paint and posters, cheering like fucking madmen. They were all so happy and proud of Ian for how far he'd come. He was far from the fat fuck all of them once knew. They asked Declan sometimes if he wanted to join them in their antics, but he said he shouldn't in case he was asked to come on. They would chuckle. Like that was ever gonna fucking happen.

This one time. Declan was sitting on the grass during a game and his mate Danny sat down next to him.

They ever going to bring you on, Declan?

Yeah, maybe in the second half.

Danny looked out onto the pitch. Ian just sent a ball flying over the bar from the other end of the field. That was his 57th point of the game.

Man, look at him out there.

Yeah.

I'm so proud of him, you know, said Danny.

Yeah.

None of this would have happened if you hadn't pushed him to go to the gym, you know that? He'd still be sitting at home on his arse. You should be proud of yourself too, Declan.

I know, said Declan, emptying a naggin of vodka into one of the water bottles.

***

That year, the Bumblebees won the county final for the first time in decades. Before the match, Declan went up to the guy on the opposing team who was going to be marking Ian, and paid him five hundred euros in cash to break his leg. To be fair, the guy did try his best, but he just

302

couldn't. Ian was too fast for him. It was an extremely tight match, but they just managed to win thanks to a last minute goal from Ian.

They all went out on a huge piss up that night. Ian walked up to Declan, who was standing at the bar, and slid a shot in front of him.

What's that for? said Declan.

None of this would have been possible if not for you. I wouldn't be here if you hadn't pushed me. Thank you.

Okay.

I love you, Declan.

Okay.

You coming over? he said. We're going to fill the cup with beer and pass it around.

Be with you in a sec.

Alright, said Ian, and he re-joined the lads, who were all singing away in the corner of the bar.

Declan downed the shot that Ian bought him, then turned to the bartender. Two double whiskeys, he said.

He downed the two of them quickly, turned to the girl next to him and said, with piss streaming down his leg:

I play county.

Following their county final win, Ian won an award for Minor Footballer of the year. No one was surprised by that. The following year, Ian was approached by somebody asking if he wanted to play with the Kerry Senior team. Everyone was fucking ecstatic. It would be the first time that a Bumblebees player would play for the Kerry team. Declan was found passed out in a drainage ditch the next morning with alcohol poisoning. A few weeks later, Ian came on as a sub for Kerry in the last fifteen minutes of a league game. He scored two points. Everyone was so proud of him. Months later, he was starting and scoring points regularly.

***

The September after that, Kerry made it to the All-Ireland final against the title holders, Dublin, and Ian was starting corner-forward. He didn't play very well during the first half, due to an unrelenting performance from Dublin. But five minutes into the second, Ian surprised everyone by scoring two goals. These were two very important goals as they were a major confidence booster for Kerry. He went on to give the man-of-the-match performance, scoring an additional nine goals and eight points, as well as assisting in a bunch of others.

When the full-time whistle went, the stadium erupted into a noise louder then Croke Park had ever witnessed in the one hundred and thirty-six years it's been open. Kerry had won the All-Ireland! Back in Kerry, Ian's family and friends were all huddled around the television in the sitting room, and everyone started screaming when the full-time whistle went. Ian's mum started balling crying. His dad ran around the sitting room, shouting,

"THAT'S MY SON! THAT'S MY BOY!".

Moments later, the Kerry team lifted the cup and there wasn't a dry eye in the entire County. Ian gave a huge speech to the stadium.

I want to thank my family and friends for believing in me and always pushing me in the right direction. A few individuals in particular back home, you know who you are. I wouldn't be here on the most historic day of my life if it weren't for them. But most of all, I want to thank my nan, who's sick at home in bed right now and who's always supported me. Nan, this one's for you.

Ian's mum was weeping. She blew a kiss at the television. His dad had her arms around her and he was crying as well. No one had ever seen Ian's dad cry before.

After all that was done, Ian's mum brought some food out and everyone started drinking. Ian's mum asked Declan if he'd go check on her mum to see if she was sleeping alright. Declan said he would. He walked down the hall and peered into her bedroom. The old woman was lying in bed with her eyes open, her hands shaking. Ian's mum said she didn't think she had long left. Maybe a week or two. Declan walked into the room and looked around at the pictures of her family and friends organised neatly on the dresser. He walked up and picked up a picture. It was of Ian when he was a boy. He was sitting on his nan's lap. He was very fat. Just then, Ian's nan made a noise. Declan put the picture down and walked up beside her. She stared up at him, her eyes old and brittle.

Hi there, said Declan.

She made a gurgling noise.

You okay? Do you want me to get you some water?

She made another noise Declan couldn't make out.

Sorry, I don't understand.

Ian's nan struggled to lick her dry lips. She tried to say something else but it was nothing more than a whisper.

I don't care what you have to say, said Declan. But do you want to know something?

Declan leaned in real close to the old woman's face.

I hate your grandson. I hate him so much. I hate him more than anything in this fucking world.

She gasped for air. The match? she said.

Oh, you want to know the result of the match, do you?

She nodded.

Your grandson lost. He said he hates you and wishes you were dead.

She stared up at him, her pale eyes wide open. Her mouth opened but the words seemed lodged in her throat. Declan picked up a pillow that was resting on the chair next to her bed.

I wish he was dead, he said.

Declan pressed the pillow hard over Ian's nan's face. She didn't put up much of a fight. She squirmed around a bit and her decrepit curved fingers brushed against the pillow, but it was nothing Declan couldn't handle. When it was over and she stopped moving, Declan dropped the pillow on the floor and went running into the living room to get Ian's mum.

Ian came home three days later and brought the cup with him. It raised everyone's spirits somewhat, given the circumstances. After the funeral, they went to a pub afterwards for refreshments and Ian gave a moving speech. He concluded it by lifting the cup in the air, saying it belonged to her. Everyone cheered and raised a glass to Ian's nan. That evening, they went back to Ian's parents house and the cup was left in Ian's bedroom after he was done showing it off to everyone. Declan walked in, took out his car keys and scraped all along the front of it. Everyone was outraged when it was noticed, but Ian said he must have dropped it or something. He said it wasn't important. Two of his friends had to drag Declan out of the house that night after he threw up in the sink.

***

Ten years later, Ian had won an additional four All-Ireland titles. He is now frequently listed among the greatest GAA Footballers of all time. He developed the nickname, *"The Flaming Amarant"*, on account of his red hair. His entire life changed. People would queue up behind him to buy him a drink in the pub. Kids would huddle around him in the street to get a selfie with him. He travelled around to schools in Kerry, talking about sports and mental health awareness.

But tragically at thirty-seven, Ian suffered a severe heart attack and tragically passed away. It was really sudden. It just happened while he was out walking his dog. Just dropped dead. It was a real day of mourning in Kerry. God knows how many people went to the funeral. There was a parade in town and the whole Kerry team and Ian's family were there. A huge statue of him was erected in the town centre. The hair was designed to be flowing in the air, like he was some Irish legend. There was a documentary on television shortly after his death, talking about his legacy and impact on the GAA. Declan watched it in his local pub. One of the old alky's across the way from him started crying.

He just had a baby, said the old alky.

I know, it's awful, said the old alky next to him.

He was a fat fuck, Declan muttered.

The two old alky's turned to him. What? they both said together.

I fucking made him. Look at the red hair on him, the faggot.

The two old alky's ignored him and turned back to the TV. Later that night, the owner of the bar had to throw Declan out after he started shouting abuse about Ian, and was afraid the locals would beat the shit out of him.

***

Another five years later, at the age of thirty-nine, Declan was still a county minor for the Bumblebees. He didn't start of course. He never even played. Some of the younger players questioned whether he was even a player, seeing as all he did was show up for training and matches, and get absolutely pissed.

Declan's wife, Ariadne, couldn't hack him either. All he fucking talked about was football. It did her fucking head in. They'd sit at the dinner table and Declan would be rambling on as usual about his glory days playing for the Bumblebees.

I remember this one game against Ballyduff, he said. I can't even remember how many points I sent sailing over that bar. That was definitely the best game I ever played. PJ will tell you the same. I swear when that full-time whistle went, I could have kept going for…

I swear to God, said Ariadne. If you don't shut the fuck up and stop talking out your fucking arse about what a great footballer you used to be, I'm going to light you on fire in your fucking sleep.

She didn't get it. How could she?

After a few years though, she couldn't take it anymore. All Declan seemed to care about was the club. He barely even looked at his two boys anymore. They were mere accessories in his life to make him look normal to society. As they grew up, he tried to get them to play with the Bumblebees, with not much success. The boys weren't the least bit interested in playing football, but he still made them train, nonetheless. It wasn't even that they were too lazy. They tried it and simply didn't like it. He'd slap them if they complained or said they didn't want to play anymore. They were fucking petrified of him. After one of the boys came out as gay at thirteen, Declan pinned him to the floor and started beating the shit out of him.

The Under 14's aren't faggots! he roared as Ariadne and their other son wrapped their arms around him and tried to pin him to the floor.

That was the final straw for Ariadne. She wasn't going to allow her children to be raised around this sociopath anymore. She was the only one looking after the boys at this point anyway. So one day, she asked Declan to quit playing football.

I can't abandon the team like that, he said. They need me.

They don't need you, Declan. I need you. The boys need you.

We have a league game next weekend and…

Declan, you haven't started a game in fourteen years! It's time to stop kidding yourself and come back to reality.

Don't talk to me like that. The club is my life.

We're your life now. The boys. Me.

And what about the boys? You going to take them away from the club too? The club is who they are, it's their whole life.

The boys don't give a fuck about football, Declan! You're the one who wants them to play.

That's not true.

It's time to choose. The club or your family?

You're not going to rob the future Kerry team of their two best players. I'm not going to let you.

Seeing no way out of the situation, Ariadne contacted the Guards and managed to get herself and the boys away from Declan. There was months of court proceedings after that. Ariadne was easily able to get full custody of the kids. The judge didn't see Declan's argument of, *"She'd be robbing the future Kerry team of an All-Ireland"* as a valid argument for full custody. Ariadne moved away with the boys to Australia that November and Declan never saw them again.

***

Ten years later, Declan became like every other old person at a football game. He shouted mountains of abuse at everyone, got into fights, and gave bullshit advice to the players. He became that guy at his local pub that talked non-stop about his glory days playing for the Bumblebees. Everyone just ignored him. No one believed him when he said he still played with them. But he technically did. On paper, anyway. He showed up to every training session and every match, despite the fact that he hasn't played a single game in twenty-five years.

The manager, Pat, begged Declan constantly to consider quitting. Declan said he would never abandon his club like that. Pat said there were more and more young people coming onto the team every year, and there was a very small chance he would ever get to play. Declan said he'd always be around if the Bumblebees needed him. Pat would just sigh, turn, and walk away. There was no arguing with him. To all the younger guys on the team, Declan was just a wee alky that hung around all the time. The only reason they put up with him was because he claimed to have played football with the great Ian *"The Flaming Amarant"* Culloty. They all thought it was bullshit when they first heard it, but Patrick's dad said it was true.

What's Declan's story? said Stephen, the half-back, one day.

What about him? said Pat.

Stephen would point behind him and Pat would turn around and see Declan asleep on the grass, snoring loudly, a half-empty naggin of Captain Morgan in his hand. Sometimes, a few of the lads would play a game to see how many wet tissues they could throw into his mouth before he woke up or choked.

He keeps saying he's a player, said Stephen. But I've never once seen him play a game or wear any gear. What's his story?

He's an old man, Stephen.

I know, but he's around all the time.

So?

He comes to every training session and every match. The fucker's in his fifties and he still plays with the county minors.

I know.

Doesn't that bother you.

Just ignore him, okay? Don't focus on him.

Is it true he played football with Ian Culloty or is that all bollox?

Don't think about it. Here, grab the lads, I'm going to get you doing some passing drills.

Right, whatever, said Stephen.

Pat would shake his head, angry at himself that he still sticks up for Declan after all this time.

***

On Declan's sixtieth birthday, it was one in the morning, and he was walking around The Bumblebees pitch, waving around a shoulder of Jack Daniels, singing the clubs anthem. His zipper was wide open and his shirt

311

was hanging off his shoulders. He walked up to the goals and stood with his arms outstretched, like he was a goalkeeper.

Liam, get back on him, he shouted at nobody, drool stumbling from his mouth.

Declan turned to the right.

Matt, he roared. Stop fighting with your man and cop on. Get your head back in the game.

Declan moved around the goal. The imaginary ball was coming. The imaginary player had managed to weave his way around the imaginary defenders and now it was one on one. Declan didn't know if he could block it. But he did. He soared through the air and caught the imaginary ball on the tip of his glove.

Declan fell on his back. He looked at the stars. Soon, it started lashing. The rain fell on his face and mixed in with his tears. He got up and downed the rest of his Jack Daniels. He picked up the imaginary ball and kicked it down the field.

It's nearly full-time, lads, he said quietly. It's time to wrap this up.

***

At their next match, Declan showed up fully kitted out. Everyone was shocked. No one had ever seen Declan in club gear before. Pat was equally shocked but ignored him. He was amazed the old alky still thought he could play a game after all this time.

In the final ten minutes of the game, Declan approached Pat.

Pat, can I talk to you for a second?

What do you want, Declan?

I want to go on.

312

You know I can't do that.

Just let me go on. We're well in the lead. What's the harm?

I have a row of young guys here that take more of a priority then you.

Put me on and I'll never bother you again.

Pat turned to Declan.

I'll never come to another training session or another match. Put me on and you'll never hear from me again.

Pat looked out onto the field, then at his watch. He sighed.

I'll put you on full-back for the final five minutes. But that's it, Declan. I don't want you around anymore after this.

Thank you, Pat.

Five minutes later, Pat called for a substitution and the full-back came running off. He never looked more confused in his life by who was replacing him. Declan patted him on the shoulder and ran onto the pitch. It'd been a while since moved this fast. The full-forward he was marking looked equally confused at the sight of a sixty year old man running towards him. Declan ignored the bewildered faces he was getting and focused on the match. The whistle blew and the game continued. Declan looked up the pitch. The ball was bouncing around at the other end. They just got a point. Declan clapped wildly. The goalkeeper kicked the ball out. Someone on the opposing team caught it and was running in his direction. The ball was kicked to the right and then to the left. A player on the opposing team caught it and ran towards the goal. Declan ran towards him as fast as his legs could carry him. He ran straight into the player and he went flying through the air. The ball flew out of his hands and Declan caught it in mid-air. The referee blew the whistle for a foul.

Declan stood with the ball in the palm of his hands. A player on the opposing team came forward and tried to slap the ball off him.

It's a fucking foul, old man. Give us the fucking ball.

NOOOO! roared Declan, throwing his fist into your man's face. Two teeth flew out of his mouth as his head went straight back. Declan clutched the ball under his arm and started sprinting forward.

Declan sprinted as fast as he could down the middle of the pitch. What the fucks he doing? someone yelled. Players tried to chase him and tackle him to the ground, even players from his own team, but Declan punched them away with ease. When he got past the half-way line, two of his own players were standing in front of him, blocking his way. He held the ball tightly under his arm and kept running. He swung his arm up at the first guy and cracked his jaw. The second player came lunging at him but Declan shot his leg out towards his ankle. A bone popped out the back of his leg and he collapsed to the ground.

Declan continued forward. Tears were falling from his face. He was almost there. He was almost at the goals. He could hear the crowd cheering him on. Then Declan felt a sudden sharp pain in his heart. He clutched at his chest and felt weak, but kept going. He had to keep going.

He was almost there. He was almost at the goals.

Just a bit closer…

Acknowledgments

Thanks to all my family and friends for supporting me and putting up with me while writing this. I love you all.

I'd like to thank Michael "Mixer" O'Brien. The amount of shite we've talked and unbelievable situations we've concocted while cruising around has always given me, and continues to give me, an endless stream of great writing material.

And a special thanks to Kelby Guilfoyle. Your constant encouragement and ability to listen and be yourself has helped me more then you know. More than I give you credit for. And not just with the writing of this book. With just living in this fucked up world and in my own skin.

And thank *you* for reading this book. Hope you enjoyed it.

xxx

Printed in Poland
by Amazon Fulfillment
Poland Sp. z o.o., Wrocław

57304310R00188